CW00732310

cocktails, wedding bells and summer madness

JULIA SUTTON

For Jill, always my bestie

acknowledgments

I would like to extend my thanks and gratitude to my publisher, Next Chapter Publishing, for their fabulous cover art and their assistance in the publication of this novel.

Thank you to my wonderful editor, Lorna Read, who worked so hard and did a fantastic job.

Thank you to my family, friends and all the kind people on social media, who support me with my writing.

This novel was inspired while on a holiday to Majorca and I loved writing it. I hope that you enjoy reading it.

So relax, put your feet up and lose yourself in my fictitious world...

one

"Hello, Fulham Banking, how may I help you?" Rose Archer stifled a yawn and listened to a man complaining loudly about the cost of his house insurance.

"It's gone up three times in five years," he grumbled. "If you don't give me some discount, I'm switching to Redrock Bank, and I mean it this time."

"Just let me transfer you to our insurance department." Rose's finger hovered over the switchboard.

"Eh? Why can't you deal with it?"

"I'm the receptionist, sir. Just a moment..."

"I beg your pardon?" The customer's tone had changed from mild annoyance to affronted outrage in under ten seconds.

Rose's spine stiffened as she wondered what she had said wrong. She had been cheerful, she had been polite. Yes, Rose admitted she was bored and tired, but that was nothing new and especially at the end of a hectic Monday when she had felt like crawling back into bed the whole day.

Rose reached for a tissue to wipe her red, streaming nose. There was silence on the other end of the line.

"Sir, are you still there?"

"I'm a she," came the hissed reply.

Oops! Roses' eyes widened. "Sorry, madam," she gabbled, "would you like a staff member to call you back?"

From the corner of her eye she could see her manager Liliana loitering with a group of the sales girls. Rose affixed a beaming smile to her face and picked up her pen in preparation.

"What was your name, sir ... I mean madam?"

"Never mind what my name is. Have you heard of gender fluidity? You can keep your effing insurance. I'm paying my money to a company where the receptionists aren't gender bigoted." Buzz, the line went dead.

Rose blinked, Liliana was watching her, pursing her mouth into a tight line of disapproval.

"Yes, of course you can call back. Thank you, madam. Goodbye." She pressed a button and the red light disappeared. Just in time for Liliana to come stalking over in her patent high heels.

"A touch of hay fever, Rose?" She fluffed out her long, raven black hair.

"A nasty cold," Rose smiled sweetly, "my ears and nose are blocked, and my throat feels as if I've swallowed a packet of razor blades."

"So you won't be coming to the after-work drinks then?" Liliana tapped her fingers on Rose's computer screen. "Marjorie from accounts is leaving. Did you not get the email?"

"No." Rose sipped from her bottle of water.

"It was sent to everyone," Liliana's eyes slanted suspiciously, "although you and Marjorie have never been friendly, have you?"

No thought Rose, mainly because she's loud and vulgar and has always been mean to me.

"We're very different," Rose said diplomatically.

Liliana sighed. "Oh Rose, you really should make more effort to be sociable with your work colleagues. Why don't you come? Let your hair down and live a little."

Rose busied herself stapling sheets of paper together. "I can't tonight. Sorry. I have folk choir on a Monday. I play the organ and we sing and chat and have tea and cake afterwards. It's very enjoyable..." She trailed off as she noticed her manager's eyes had glazed over.

"Sounds thrilling." Liliana yawned. "Meanwhile, in the real world we'll all be getting sloshed. Here," she scribbled down a mobile number on a scrap of paper, "if you change your mind, text me ,yeah? I'll let you know what pub we're in."

Rose took the slip of paper and watched Liliana totter back to her friends. Surreptitiously, she stuffed it down the side of a bulging wastepaper bin and then reached under the table for her bag. It was five o'clock and time to leave.

"Finished for the day have you, love?" Ron, the twilight security guard, ambled towards her, twirling a set of keys in his hand.

"I have." Rose smiled his way. "Another day over."

"And mine's just starting." He leant on the counter, and winked at her with watery blue eyes. "Like my new truncheon?"

"Pardon?" Rose pushed her spectacles up her nose.

"This!" He wielded what looked like a metal stick at her.

"Are you sure you need that, Ron?" She watched him warily as he jabbed it in the air.

"Of course I do. You never know who's lurking around these parts." He made a thumbing gesture towards the back of the building. "Those fields attract all sorts of low life. Druggies and crazies being some of them, and now the teenagers have taken to hanging around there, too."

"Oh, it's probably kids just being kids." Rose packed her lunchbox inside her rucksack and smiled. "You do a great job, though."

"I do." Ron puffed out his chest with pride. "Maybe I should get a guard dog? A big nasty Rottweiler or Alsatian."

Rose smirked at the thought of Ron strutting around the offices with a growling companion in tow. "How about a Bichon Frise?"

"A what?" His lips flapped with laughter. "One of them silly cuddly things. Hardly a guard dog, Rose."

"Cute though." Rose closed down her computer. "How is your wife?"

"Not too good. Her nerves are playing up again. Knitting's about the only thing she enjoys nowadays – that and Murder She Wrote.'

Rose clacked her tongue in sympathy.

"I don't suppose..." He paused. "No, I couldn't ask you."

"Ask away."

"Well, the thing is, Rose, there's a knitting club started up at the community centre, but my Betsy hasn't the confidence to go alone." He looked at her with pleading eyes. "I wondered if you fancied keeping her company? It's only one night a week, Tuesdays I think."

"I have absolutely no idea how to knit," Rose replied.

"It's for absolute beginners. Here," Ron pulled a scrap of paper out of his pocket, "these are the details and I've written Betsy's number on the back for you."

She took the paper from him, a warm smile on her face. "Can I have a think and let her know?"

Ron's grin was wide. "You're a kind girl, Rose. Betsy would be made up if you went with her."

Rose sighed. "Okay, you've convinced me – I'll go."

"Fantastic! Thanks, love." He leaned towards her and pulled her into a rough embrace. "Now, you get off home and relax."

"Goodnight, Ron."

He walked with her to the door, watching her from behind the pane of glass as she unlocked her car and started up the engine. As she was preparing to reverse, a large group of women clattered behind her, shouting and whooping with laughter. Rose watched them leave, thankful that she wasn't attending Marjorie's leaving do and she could go home to her family and her safe, warm abode.

· · ·

Rose lived on the Upper Belmont Estate. Her street was long and wound upwards to the crest of a hill. On a clear day you could see the whole of Twineham Village laid out: houses and shops surrounded by fields of luscious green. Rose took a moment to enjoy the view, drawing the fresh spring air into her lungs. The houses behind her were linked in terraces, each one painted a different colour. It looked like a seaside scene, but they were nowhere near water. Twineham didn't even possess a lake. It was farming countryside: patchwork fields, old gnarled trees and wild flowers slap bang in the middle of England. Rose had lived here all her life and she loved it.

"Evening, our Rose." Mrs Bowler was on her front step, watering her hanging baskets. "Looks like it's going to be a nice day tomorrow." She nodded at the blazing red sky.

Rose shielded her eyes from the glare of the sun and smiled at her neighbour. "Red sky at night – shepherd's delight?"

"That's right. How are you, Rose?" The friendly octogenarian limped up her broken path, stopping to admire the colourful butterflies along the way.

"Tired." Rose swung her bag onto her shoulder. "Another Monday over."

"It will soon be the weekend." Mrs Bowler tipped the last dregs from her watering can over a tub of petunias. "You haven't forgotten the fete is Saturday?"

"No," squeaked Rose. She had.

"And will you still be organising and manning the cake stall?"

Rose nodded and mentally added it to her to-do list.

"I'm overseeing the tombola myself. Your mother's given me a whole box of knick-knacks for the raffle. If you have anything you want to donate, Rose, it would be very much appreciated."

"I'll have a look." Rose pushed open the gate. "'Bye, Mrs Bowler."

"'Bye, dear. Enjoy your evening."

. . .

Number 35 had a lilac, weatherbeaten door, surrounded by climbing ivy and two rose trellises. It attracted the wasps and other flying midges and often Rose had snagged her clothes on the inconspicuous thorns, but it was pretty and was her grandmother's pride and joy. Rose slotted her key in the lock and pressed on the door until it opened. Warmth rushed towards her and Rose jumped as her hand brushed against the hot hall radiator.

"For heaven's sake," she mumbled, slipping off her shoes, "it's almost May and isn't even cold."

"What was that?" Her mother, Fran, stood in the kitchen doorway, a bowl balancing on her hip.

"Hello, Mum," Rose shrugged off her jacket, "what are you baking now?"

"Just a banana loaf and you know your Granny feels the cold."

"I know." Rose smiled apologetically as she walked past her into the kitchen.

Granny Faith was sitting at the kitchen table staring down at the crossword section of her weekly puzzle magazine.

"What's a tooth for chewing?" she enquired without looking up.

"Incisor?" Fran gave the mixture a last beat before tipping it slowly into a prepared baking tin.

"Too many letters," sniffed Faith.

"Molar?" Rose suggested.

Faith counted the squares. "Perfect."

"What's the prize then, Gran?"

Faith glanced up. "A spa weekend for two. Fancy coming with me if I win, Rose?"

"Would it involve books?" Rose reached down to rub her aching feet.

Faith snorted. "You and your books! It would involve being pampered. Having your nails and make-up done, having a massage and maybe a full body wrap and then spending the evening quaffing champagne and dining on grotesquely expensive food like caviar."

Rose looked at her with disdain. "I can't think of anything worse."

"Are you sure she wasn't switched at birth?" Faith said to Fran. "My only granddaughter is a tomboy."

Faith laughed, a lovely tinkling sound.

"I'm not a tomboy!" Rose insisted. "I'm just not into all that girly stuff. Hair and beauty does not interest me in the slightest."

"We can tell," Faith smirked. "When was the last time you visited a hairdresser?"

"Leave her alone," Fran chuckled. "Rose, be a dear and lay the table. Your father and brother will be home soon."

Rose went to fetch the cutlery out of the drawer. "Anyway, what's wrong with my hair?"

"Technically nothing," Faith lisped in her thick Scottish brogue, "it's just been like that forever. Couldn't you have it coloured pink, for example? That seems to be all the rage nowadays."

"Will you listen to yourself, Mother!" Fran jumped to her daughter's defence. "Rose has beautiful hair; thick and curly and the redness must be her Scottish roots, eh?"

"At least she's inherited something from me," Faith sniffed. "You on the other hand are fair, like your poor, deceased Daddy."

"It must have skipped a generation." Fran bumped Rose playfully with her hip. "Lucky me, eh?"

"So anyway, Granny, let me know if you win any book vouchers or any day trips to museums." Rose ducked her head into the pantry after the salt and pepper pots. "I'll be happy to come with you then."

"Me in a museum?" Faith chortled. "They're likely to keep me! Have me embalmed in a Victorian kitchen."

The three of them were still laughing when Rose's father, Rod and her elder brother, Marty, burst into the kitchen.

"What's all this frivolity?" Rod dumped down his tool bag, kissed his wife and went to wash his hands.

"Female matters," Faith said waspishly.

"Oh, erm ..." Rod ducked his head, "what's for tea then?"

After a hearty meal of stew and dumplings, Rose helped her mother clear away.

"I have choir practise tonight," Rose yawned, "but to be honest, I'm not feeling up to it. My nose has been dribbling all day long."

"Then don't go, love." Fran wiped over the drainer with a damp dishcloth. "You devote far too much time to that church. Have a night off."

Rose contemplated calling the vicar, but then said with resolution, "No I'll go. The summer concert isn't far away, we need to practise."

Fran nodded. "Take a paracetamol before you go then."

Rose tugged the medicine box off the high shelf and popped two in her mouth. "Another thing, Mum," she washed the tablets down with a gulp of water, "I've let myself be talked into attending a knitting club. Do you fancy coming along?"

"A knitting club!" Fran rolled her eyes. "For goodness' sake, don't tell your granny. Haven't you enough to do with working full time, the church, your book club and now knitting? You'll be worn out, Rose."

"It's only a couple of hours on a Tuesday evening." Rose put on her most pleading expression.

"No can do," Fran replied, with stalwart firmness. "That's the best night for my soaps. Coronation Street is exciting at the moment, I refuse to miss it."

"Oh, okay." Rose attempted to shake off the disappointment. It looked like it would be just her and Mrs Ron then.

"You should learn to say no, Rose." Fran's words were softly spoken. "You're far too kind." She chucked her daughter underneath the chin. "Please tell me you're not helping at the fete this weekend?"

Rose nodded. "Sort of. I'm in charge of the cake stall." She winced at the look on her mum's face. "It's for charity, Mum. That charity that helps the poor children in Africa gain an education."

"Okay, but maybe I'll just check and make sure the money raised won't be lining any of the villager's pockets." Faith gave her daughter a warm smile. "Who knew I'd given birth to an angel? Maybe I should have called you Gabriel."

"My name is lovely enough," Rose called as she hurried up the stairs, "and Gabriel was a man, Mum."

"Mary then," her mum shouted, with a resigned sigh.

two

The bathroom was occupied. Rose could hear her brother Marty singing above the noise of the shower.

"Are you going to be long?" She rapped on the door.

"What?" He carried on singing – or screeching may have been the correct verb.

"Don't be long!" she shouted. Rose went into her bedroom and flopped on the bed. It was soft and comfortable and smelt fresh like an ocean breeze. She plumped up the pillows and sank back to stare up at the lemon-coloured ceiling, where shadows danced and the light off her lamp created a soft silhouette. She wiggled her toes and emitted a sleepy sigh. If she didn't have choir practise, she could curl under the duvet with her latest novel and a bumper bar of chocolate, put on her pyjamas and her fleece bed socks and relax. The thought of power napping crossed her mind. Granny Faith swore by it. Just ten minutes, she decided, turning onto her side and wrapping the edge of the duvet across her frame. The sound of the rain pattering on the windowsill was like a gentle lullaby, soothing away the Monday blues. Five minutes later, Rose was fast asleep.

From far away came the sound of ringing. It sounded like the fire alarm at work, only this was quieter and softer. Rose stretched one arm, blew a curl off her nose and slowly opened one eye. She could hear muffled voices. It was her mum firmly telling someone that she wasn't well. Rose shot up, glanced at her wristwatch and emitted a squeak. Seven o'clock in the evening meant one thing: the choir was about to start. They would be waiting for her, preparing their voices to sing, wondering where she was. Rose bounced off the bed, tripped over her shoes and fell flat on her face, squashing her nose into the carpet. Could this Monday get any worse? Her head was thumping, her nose was streaming and she was late. Rose Archer was never late. Punctuality was one of her strongest traits.

"Mum," she yelled, "I'm up!" Well, not literally but ... Rose heaved herself to her feet and pulled open her bedroom door.

Fran was standing at the bottom of the stairs, phone pressed to her ear. "She's coming." She handed the phone over, shaking her head as she did so.

"Hello." Rose's head felt fuzzy, a combination of cold symptoms and napping. She never napped in the day. What was happening to her? she thought, as she plonked down on the bottom step.

"Ah, Rose," the dulcet tones of Mr French, the parish vicar, wafted into her ear, "we were just wondering where you were. Are you okay?"

"Just a cold." She sneezed into the cuff of her blouse. "I'm coming now, give me ten minutes."

"Be careful how you drive now. Goodbye." Buzz, the line went dead.

Rose went into the lounge where her mum, dad and gran were watching T.V.

"You off to that church again?" Rod was bent over, clipping ferociously at his toenails.

"I've been going every week for the past ten years, Dad."

"Well maybe," he waved the clippers at her, "you should do something else with your life?"

Granny Faith harrumphed with agreement. "Why not start with that new wine bar in town?"

Rose sighed. "I'm happy at my folk choir. Why does everyone have such a problem with me attending church?"

Fran put down her magazine. "There's no problem, love, apart from the fact that life seems to be passing you by. You should be out there seeing the wider world."

Faith pulled at her whiskery chin. "Maybe if she got herself a fella, that would be a start. You're twenty-eight and I bet you're still a virgin."

"Mum!" Fran scolded Faith. "That's none of your business."

Rose's cheeks flamed as red as her hair. "I have a... friend. Jeremy, remember?"

"A friend who wears tank tops and speaks like he's got a plum stuck in his mouth," Faith snorted. "What you need is a lover. Someone hot like... Daniel Craig."

"Who?" Rose was perplexed. "I have no idea who you mean."

Faith clicked her fingers. "You know, the guy who plays James Bond. Very nice body, especially in those swimming trunks..."

Rose picked up her keys and bag. "I'm leaving now," she said firmly, "I won't be late."

She could hear the three of them tittering as she banged the door shut behind her.

When Rose arrived at the church, Brenda the clarinet player was waiting for her on the car park.

"Rose, you're here!"

"Of course." Rose slid out of the car with a smile on her face. "Have you started without me?"

"No, Rose, we were just having tea and cake," said Brenda. "The vicar's wife has made the most delicious fruitcake and Jeremy's back."

"He is?" Together, they walked through the arched doorway,

past the pews and the font and towards the partitioned-off meeting room.

"He's been regaling us of tales about Africa, where he met the most wonderful people and magnificent beasts." Brenda sighed. "It all sounds so exciting." She propped her umbrella in the stand with the others and Rose followed her into the room.

The folk choir consisted of ten people: six singers, Brenda the clarinet player, Rose on the organ, Mr French the conductor and Jeremy who played the guitar. They were sitting at an old oak table scratched by years of use, eating cake and drinking tea from delicate china cups.

"Oh Rose, you came." Mrs French stood to kiss her cheek. "Are you feeling okay? Your mother said you were unwell."

"I'm fine," she replied, shaking the raindrops from her hair. "Hello, Jeremy."

He was holding out one hand, pushing his spectacles up with the other. "Rose, how lovely to see you. It's been a while..."

"It's been two months." She smiled widely. "It's good to have you back. And how was Africa?"

"It was amazing." Jeremy's gaze flickered away from hers and there ensued a moment of awkward silence.

Mr French clapped his hands. "Shall we commence with the music and then we can chat afterwards?"

The others murmured in agreement. Rose frowned but made her way to the organ. Her fingers tinkled softly over the keys as, next to her, Brenda blew on her clarinet and Jeremy strummed his guitar. They ran through a list of hymns which began with Rose's favourite, All Things Bright and Beautiful. By the fifth song, Rose was sneezing profusely and a halt was called by Mr French.

"I think we should stop for tonight," like many vicars, his tone was deep and melodious, "poor Rose is obviously not well. You should be at home in the warmth, dear. Come back to us next week, fighting fit."

"Okay." Rose nodded his way with gratitude. "Would you like a lift, Jeremy?" She was eager to speak to him about his adventures. During his time away, she had missed him. Her mind cast back to the last time she had seen him. The way he had held her hand when no one was looking and his declaration of love for her on the church car park. At the time, Rose had been confused and not sure how to react. She liked him a great deal but was that enough? Yet over the last two months, she had thought about him constantly and realised she did like him as more than just friends. So tonight, she decided, was the night she would reciprocate his feelings. Jeremy was nice, and handsome in a bookish kind of way. He was gentle and kind and his eyes were an attractive blue. She didn't know if he resembled Daniel Craig, but he definitely reminded her of Clark Kent from Superman. And she wanted to kiss him: tonight.

"Just let me pop to the loo," Rose said, "and I'm all yours." She skirted around Brenda who was struggling into a navy blue raincoat.

"See you at the fete, dear." Rose waved and hurried to the ladies.

The bright white walls and chrome furnishings of the tiny toilet added to the chilly ambience of the room, but Rose was hot. She looked in the cracked mirror as she washed her hands. Her cheeks were bright red and her hair was gravitating upwards from the damp and humidity. She scooped cold water over her face and smoothed down her hair. Should she apply lipstick, she wondered? A thorough search of her handbag revealed the only make-up available was a squashed eyeliner pencil. She tossed it back in and popped a peppermint in her mouth instead.

Jeremy was waiting for her at the entrance, fiddling with the What's On In Twineham leaflets.

"There's a food-tasting festival in August." He raised his head to peer at her. "Have you got a temperature, Rose? I can catch the bus home if it's out of your way."

"Of course it isn't," she replied hastily, "really I'm all right, I just need a good night's sleep. We can go... to the food-tasting festival... together, if you want to?" She was aware she was gabbling and inwardly flinched.

"Oh, erm, maybe?" Jeremy looked down at his feet.

"Come on then," Rose said, with a forced brightness she didn't feel, "you can tell me all about Africa."

Rose wound down the windows to allow the fresh evening air to filter into the car. "Did you go on a safari?"

"Oh yes." Jeremy's face took on a dreamy sheen. "We saw them all, Rose. Lions, elephants, giraffes, wildebeest..." He trailed off to look down at his lap and she wondered who the 'we' meant.

"I thought about you." She patted his hand. "I thought about what you said to me the last time we spoke."

There was no reply, just the rumble of the engine as she manoeuvred it around a corner. "Jeremy," Rose took a deep breath, "I feel the same way."

"Ah." Jeremy slunk down in his seat. "About that..."

"Yes?" She glanced at his face which had paled to an off-white colour. "It's okay. What you said to me was beautiful, poetic even. No one has ever said my hair resembled fire before and... and that my eyes were like beautiful blue whirlpools." She sniffed, paused as her mind searched for a suitable compliment to say about him, and went on, "You're kind, Jeremy, noble and decent. Handsome, too. I would like very much to be your girlfr..."

"Rose!" He cut her off abruptly. "Things have changed."

"Wh-what?" Her hand slipped off the gear stick.

"I've met someone else. While I was in Africa."

Rose felt her heart sink like a lead balloon. "Oh," was all she could manage.

"Please don't make this difficult," Jeremy beseeched, "I hate doing this to you, Rose, but I think you and I are destined to be just good friends."

"But... but the things you said to me!" Rose pressed her foot on the accelerator a little too firmly and they shot forward. "You said that you... "

"Please!" He held up his hand. "Don't get emotional. I can't bear hysterics."

"I'm hardly hysterical, Jeremy," she felt suddenly cross, "just confused."

He emitted a shuddering breath. "My feelings have changed. The first time I met Sabrina, well, she took my breath away."

"Sabrina?" Rose tutted. "Does she have hair like fire, too?"

"No, her hair is golden like the most beautiful sunset ..." He trailed off as he noticed her mouth set into a firm line. "Sorry." He played with the cuff on his jacket which Rose noticed was dirty and frayed. "We didn't mean to fall in love..."

"It just happened," Rose finished for him. "Is she British?"

A quick nod confirmed she was correct. "She resides in Berkshire. Sabrina is on a gap year from university where she studies environmental science."

Rose swallowed. "That must be interesting. But wait, how old is she?"

"Twenty, but she is very mature and wise for her age. You would like her, Rose. She plays the piano like you."

"I play the organ," she corrected. "How old are you now, Jeremy?"

"Only thirty-two!" His tone became defensive. "Age is no barrier to true love."

Rose flicked the indicator on and turned left into his street. "Well, I wish you luck, Jeremy and ..." she searched for a suitable term, "happiness."

"Thank you." Jeremy patted her hand. "There's someone out there for you, too, Rose. You'll find true love when you least expect it, like Sabrina and I."

"Will I?" Rose stopped the car outside his flat and glanced in the mirror. "Maybe I'm destined to be a spinster."

"A spinster?" Jeremy chuckled. "How old are you?"

"Twenty-eight."

"Well then, you're still a babe. Plenty of time for you to find Mister Right."

Rose gave him a tight smile. "I should get home now. Work tomorrow."

Jeremy unclipped his seatbelt. "Thank you for the lift, Rose and ..." his tone turned contrite, "I'm sorry."

"It's okay." Rose searched in her glove compartment for a tissue. "Will you still be coming to the folk choir?"

"I will. Good night, Rose," he leant across and brushed her cheek with his lips. A gentle kiss, but not the type of kiss she had been anticipating. Rose watched him walk up the path and, with one last wave, he had disappeared from view. With a sigh, Rose pulled up the handbrake and drove away up the darkened street, back towards home and her empty bed.

three

The following morning, Rose was thoroughly 'under the weather'. She had tossed and turned for most of the night, sneezing and coughing. Finally, at five o'clock she had given up on sleep and was shuffling about the kitchen with a mug of hot Lemsip and a wet cold flannel pressed to her perspiring forehead.

"I'll ring in for you," her mother decided, "and on my way home from work I'll bring you some cough medicine."

"I should go to work," Rose bit her lip, "it's really busy; new clients continually signing up, trying to stop the old, disgruntled clients from leaving. And I'm supposed to be taking the security guard's wife to the knitting club."

"Never mind the knitting club," Fran fussed around her, "your health comes first. Now go on back to bed. The house will be quiet today, your dad and Marty are working late and Gran is off to the daycentre."

"Did someone mention me?" Granny Faith hobbled into the kitchen.

"I was just telling Rose she should stay off work," Fran explained, clicking on the kettle.

Faith glanced at her granddaughter. "You do look peaky. How did it go last night between you and Jeremy, by the way?"

"There is no me and Jeremy." Rose slumped in the chair. "He's no longer interested."

"The sly bugger." Faith prodded her stick in the air. "Wait until I catch hold of him!"

Fran frowned at her mother. "We thought you were stepping out together," Faith continued. "Didn't he tell you he loved you a couple of months ago?"

Rose shook her head. "He's had a change of heart and I really don't want to discuss it anymore."

"Plenty more fish in the sea." Faith settled herself in her rocking chair. "I never liked him much, anyway. Always thought he had sly eyes. You can do better, our Rose."

"You are beautiful," Fran agreed. "Jeremy must be crazy."

Rose stared down at the powdery drink. "Maybe I'll finish this upstairs."

Fran patted her shoulder. "Don't worry about work. You never have time off. They'll just have to cope without you for a day or two. Go on back to bed and try to sleep."

Rose stood up and kissed her mum on the cheek. "Thank you."

As she climbed the stairs, she could hear Fran chastising her gran: "Stop poking your nose in Rose's business."

"I'm worried about her," Granny Faith bit back. "That girl needs someone to take care of her. A real man. An alpha male."

If only, thought Rose as she pulled back the duvet and wearily snuggled back into dreamland.

By lunchtime and after more sleep and paracetamol, Rose was feeling slightly better. She showered and then padded downstairs to watch mundane afternoon T.V with chocolate and crisps as an unhealthy accompaniment. Her dad came home for lunch, banging down the hall with his toolbox and with her brother Marty in tow.

"How are you, our Rose?" Rod stood in the doorway. His hair and face were flecked with splatters of paint.

"Not too bad," she replied, breaking off a piece of Galaxy and offering it to him.

"You'd say that if you were on your deathbed!" He flopped down on the sofa next to her, munching on the chocolate.

Marty sat down on the other side of her and all three of them stared at the panel of women on the afternoon debating show.

"Feminists everywhere." Marty shook his head at the television screen. "No wonder Janey's given up on me."

"Have you had another fall-out?" Rose slid a sympathetic glance at her brother, who had helped himself to her bumper bag of Doritos.

"Yep. This time it's for good." He waved a crisp in the air. "She wants time out to find herself."

"Oh." Rose noticed her brother's face growing redder by the second.

"You haven't heard the best of it," he continued. "Now she's not sure she even likes men anymore!"

Rose hid her gasp with a cough.

"She's given up her job. Said she's enrolling at university with her new best friend, Lola. They're going to do art." He spat the last word out, his face twisting into a sneer. "She thinks going out with a painter and decorator is beneath her now."

"You're brilliant at your job," Rose soothed, looking at her dad for confirmation, "isn't that right, Dad?"

"Course it is, love." Rod shoved more chocolate in his mouth. "Me and your brother own the best painting business in the Midlands, I reckon. He's my protégé and will be carrying on the family's decorating business when my knees finally pack up."

"I need to have kids," Marty gabbled, "then I can pass on my expertise to my son and carry on the family name."

"You might have girls," Rose pointed out.

"Then they can pick up the paint brushes, too." He pointed

at the screen. "What is it these feminists say? There should be no gender bias in employment anymore."

"You need to settle down with a woman first," Rod argued, shaking his head at his son. "How many girls have come and gone over the past few years?"

"Maybe he hasn't met the right one," Rose cut in, wanting to defend her brother.

"He's had enough blooming experience!" Rod shot up just as the phone began ringing shrilly.

"Where the heck is it?" Marty and Rose got up to look underneath the cushions and down the side of the armchairs.

"I miss the static telephones," Rod complained, scratching his head. "There it is – underneath your granny's crossword magazines."

The three of them dived for it but it was Rod who reached it first.

"Hello, Archer residence."

Rose rolled her eyes and suppressed a titter as her dad strutted regally around the room.

"Yes, she's here. But she ain't well. Who is it?"

Rose held out her hand, but her dad was craning his neck, concentrating on listening to the voice on the other end of the line.

"Shelly?"

Rose's eyes widened with surprise. "Shelly?" she echoed.

"Hot Shelly from school?" Marty was making googly eyes. "You sure she doesn't want me, Dad?"

"Yes, she's here. Hang on, love." Rod pressed his hand over the mouthpiece and mouthed the obvious. "It's Shelly from school."

Rose took the phone off her dad. "Hello, Shelly?"

"Rose!" came the screech from the end of the line. "Yes, it's me, Shelly."

An image of her oldest school friend popped into Rose's

mind. A voluptuous blonde teenager who had been popular with everyone; especially the boys.

"How are you?" Rose fumbled with the TV remote, searching for the mute button.

"I'm good. No, I'm great, still living it large in Australia."

Shelly had left Britain ten years ago to travel around the world. Hopping from country to country until finally settling in Australia. It had been years since Rose had heard from her.

"It's been so long," Rose said. "What are you doing with yourself now? Are you still hairdressing?"

Shelly snorted. "I gave that up years ago. Now I'm doing something far more exciting. I work for a radio station in Sydney, as a researcher. It's my dream job Rose, I love it."

Rose could hear the excitement in her friend's voice and smiled. "That's wonderful."

"How about you? What are you up to now?"

Rose swallowed. "I'm... still working in the call centre."

"You're still there?" Shelly's tone had turned incredulous. "And you're obviously still living in Twineham. But are you married? Do you have kids?"

"No and no." Rose glanced at her dad and brother. "I'm still living with Mum and Dad and Gran lives with us now, too."

"Granny Faith," Shelly laughed, "love her." Rose could hear the sound of thumping music in the background. "Look, I have to go, I'm on my lunch break. I just wanted to ring and tell you that I'm coming home, Rose. Back to Britain."

"You are?" Rose stared at the phone.

Shelly chuckled. "You could sound happier. Your oldest school friend is returning from her travels!"

"That's fantastic!" Rose bit her lip. "When are you coming home, Shelly?"

"In a week or so. That's if I can get organised in time. I have to go now but I'll see you real soon, Rosie." The line crackled then went dead.

"Shelly's coming home?" her dad queried.

"Sexy Shelly's coming back here?" Marty thumped the arm of the sofa. "Yes!"

"She's coming back." Rose's head was spinning. "My best friend is coming home."

Rose and Shelly had first met in infants' school. Rose could still remember her first day. Standing in the playground clutching onto her mum's hand, looking nervously down at the floor while hundreds of other children whooped and raced around her. The bell had rung and the children had begun lining up. Rose had clutched onto her mother's hand even tighter. Pure dread had coursed through her five-year-old veins. The thought of spending an entire day away from home had her stomach in knots. Tears had escaped from her eyes when her mother had tried to prise her hand away. They had escalated to loud sobs, which had intensified when she noticed some of the other children sniggering her way. Eventually, a teacher had come over and had taken a wailing Rose inside. The doors had closed and her mum had gone. School had officially begun.

Rose was a quiet, shy child, who didn't make friends easily. Her teachers often described her as reserved. In Rose's young mind, the boys were far too boisterous for her liking and the girls were far too giggly. While her peers were expounding their energy on scooters and balls, Rose would prefer to sit and read a book. Then, halfway through her first year of school, Shelly had started.

The new girl had been buddied up with Rose. "Look after her," Mrs Price had asked, and Rose had taken Shelly under her wing. They had been best friends all the way through primary and secondary school. At sixteen, Shelly had secured a job as an apprentice hairdresser and Rose had started working at the call centre. Two years later, Shelly announced she wanted to see the world and was going travelling. Her late father had left her a substantial amount of money in his will, which paid for an around-the-world ticket. Of course Shelly had invited Rose to go with her, cajoling, pleading, even resorting to begging. But Rose was adamant; her home was Twineham and she was happy here. She was progressing well at work; the money was good, and they were sending her on business courses. And Rose couldn't bear the thought of leaving her family, her mum and dad. She was a home bird; always had been.

On a wet February morning, Rose had hugged her friend for the final time. Shelly had left with one suitcase and a promise to write every month. For a while, she did write, telling Rose about her adventures in America, Europe, Asia and then, when she decided to stay on in Australia, the letters and postcards slowly dwindled away. The last correspondence she had received was an envelope full of photographs of Shelly at the Great Barrier Reef. There had been other friends since Shelly; people from church and the book club, but no one could make her laugh like her nomadic friend; no one sparkled like Shelly. And she was coming home, her best friend was coming back to Twineham and Rose Archer couldn't be happier.

four

"You're going to organise a party?" Fran's cerulean blue eyes were sceptical as they looked at her daughter.

"I think it's a great idea." Rose pulled another tray of cakes out of the oven.

"A surprise party sounds fab to me." Faith was sitting at the kitchen table, smearing the cool cakes with pink icing and jelly tots.

"But love, Shelly's coming home next week. How are you going to organise everything for then? You need a room, for a start." Fran shook flour off her skirt.

"That was a problem," Rose conceded. "I thought I might be able to hire the hall, but Mrs French told me they're fully booked for the next two months."

"There you go then," Fran shook her head, "it's too short notice."

"Then I thought of asking at one of the local pubs."

"The new wine bar?" Faith's eyes lit up at the thought of the recently opened trendy establishment.

"No, Gran." Rose shook her head with amusement. "All super busy, too."

The smile slid from Faith's face. "What will you do then, our Rose?"

"I have a suggestion." Fran placed her hands on her hips. "Why don't you and her just go for a meal, love? Have a real catch-up."

"Boring," came Faith's verdict.

"For once, I agree with Gran." Rose carried the dirty kitchen utensils to the sink. "You know how bubbly and outgoing Shelly is. She does not do quiet."

The two other women nodded with agreement.

"So... I thought we could have a soiree here."

Fran's eyes widened. "You mean a house party?"

"A jovial get-together. Please, Mum?"

"Well, what does your father say?" Fran blustered.

"He said it's fine with him and that I needed to clear it with you."

Rose and Faith stared at Fran, waiting for her answer.

"That's typical of Rod, that is, putting the pressure on me. What about her own family?"

Rose sighed. "What family, Mum? Her dad has passed away. Her mum is in a care home sick with Alzheimer's, and her only sibling lives miles away in London. I need to do this for her. No, correction – I want to do this for her. It's been ten years since I saw her and she was my best friend. My only true friend. She deserves to be made a fuss of."

Fran sat down next to Faith. "I always liked Shelly. She was like a bottle of fizz, all bubbly and full of life."

"Aye," agreed Faith, "she was a canny lass."

"But people change, Rose." Fran frowned. "Shelly might not be the same person. You might have grown apart, for a start."

"Well, if we have, that's okay." Rose smiled. "I still want to do this for her, though, if it's okay with you."

"My daughter the angel." Fran chucked her underneath the chin. "Of course it's okay, love. Let's just hope that Shelly doesn't turn it into a rave."

The three of them chuckled and carried on organising the cakes for tomorrow's spring fete.

Later on, Rose decided to contact Shelly's older sister and tell her about the party plans. Marian was a city high-flyer who worked in advertising. Rose vaguely remembered her before she left to live in London. A tall, domineering woman who hated village life. She had purchased a one-way ticket to the capital and left on a stormy New Year's Day. Shelly had disclosed it had been her sister's resolution to never come back to Twineham. Therefore Rose didn't hold out much hope of her returning, not even for her own sister.

Rose searched through her contacts, hoping that the number she had been given a decade ago was still current. There it was, a work number but a contact nonetheless. Rose cleared her throat and tapped the screen. After a few moments, the line connected and it began to ring.

"Yes?" The person that answered was a cross-sounding woman.

"H-hello," Rose began, "may I speak to Marian, please?"

"You mean Ms Regan?"

"Erm, yes. Is she available?"

"Meeting," came the curt response, "call back at lunchtime."

"Can I leave a message?" Rose persisted.

She heard a distinct tut. "Name and number?"

Rose relayed her details.

"Reason for call?"

"It's a personal matter. I'm a family friend and need to speak to her about her sister Shelly."

"Okay. Goodbye." The line went dead.

How rude, thought Rose as she stuffed her phone back in her handbag. Then her mum was calling to her that tea was ready. Rose clattered downstairs to eat shepherd's pie with the rest of her family, thoughts of Shelly swirling through her mind.

~

On Saturday morning, Rose was up early. She made herself toast and marmalade and sat in the conservatory, watching the tropical fish swimming around their heated tank.

"How are you feeling?" Fran poked her head around the door, smiling brightly.

"A lot better thanks, Mum, those lemon drinks seem to have done the trick."

"Good." Fran went to open the window blinds. "It looks like it's going to be a nice day. I think I'll tidy up the garden."

"You mean you're not coming to the fete?" Rose smirked.

"I promised your father I'd take him out for lunch." Fran rolled her eyes. "This is the first Saturday he's had off for months."

"Dad works hard," said Rose, "he deserves some down time."

"Yes, well we all do, but some of us just get on with it without complaining."

Rose raised an eyebrow. It was unlike her mum to complain about her dad, they were usually so loving towards each other.

"How's your job going?" Rose swallowed a crust of bread and watched her mum's face turn into a scowl.

"Busy as always." Fran had been working in the same supermarket for the past twenty-five years as a till operator. "It pays the bills, I suppose," she said with a sigh. "Sorry I'm being grouchy."

"What's up?" Rose asked, patting the empty seat next to her.

"Nothing really. Okay, your dad forgot our wedding anniversary. No biggie."

Rose gasped. "That is a biggie, Mum. How many years is it?"

"Thirty-four. Not a special one." Fran sniffed. "It would have been nice to receive a card, though."

"I'm sorry. I forgot, too." Rose was contrite.

"It doesn't matter." Rose heard the creak in Fran's knees as she stood up. "Hark at me – ancient, falling to bits, as well as forgotten."

"You are not!" Rose scoffed. "Mum, you're brilliant for your age and Dad might not have forgotten after all. He's still in bed, isn't he?" Rose's mind was racing.

"Yep. Still snoring away."

"Well then. Don't be so impatient. Anyway, I need to get ready for the fete." Rose jumped to her feet and kissed her mum on the cheek. "Happy anniversary and thank you for letting me have Shelly's party here." She dashed out of the room and up the stairs.

After lecturing her dad on the importance of remembering his wedding anniversary, she watched Rod sneak out of the house in search of flowers and chocolate. Marty was in the bathroom again, getting all spruced up for a hot date with the 'woman of his dreams'.

"Who's the lucky girl?" Rose asked, as he passed her on the landing with only a towel wrapped across his hips.

"Eh? If I tell you, Rose, promise you won't let on to Mum and Dad?" He leant casually over the banister and lowered his voice. "I'm taking Marjorie Mason out for the day."

"Mrs Mason the butcher's wife?" Rose was shocked.

"Ex-wife," Marty corrected, "they separated last year. Keep up, love."

"But... but she's..." Rose searched her vocabulary for a polite term, "mature."

"Yep." Marty rubbed his hands together. "Isn't it great?"

"I suppose." Rose looked at him with dubious eyes. "So why haven't you told Mum and Dad?"

"Oh, you know how they fuss." Marty flicked back his wet hair. "Are you ageist, Rose? Because I certainly aren't."

"Of course I'm not," Rose sighed. "Just have fun, Marty, but be careful, that's all I'm saying."

"I gotcha." Marty flashed a smile before disappearing into his bedroom and Rose went to turn on the shower and brush her teeth.

Rose's cakes were a success with both adults and children. By the end of the afternoon most of them had gone, apart from some plain fairy cakes that had been overlooked. She popped them back in an empty tin and went over to Mrs Bowler on the tombola store.

"How have you done, Rose?" the little lady asked.

"Very well. I've made fifty pounds."

"Excellent," Mrs Bowler nodded, "the vicar will be pleased and very thankful I should say, being as all the proceeds go to charity."

"Would you like to take these home for yourself and Mr Bowler?" Rose offered the remaining cakes over.

"Are you sure, dear?" Mrs Bowler's eyes lit up. "I won't say no to cake and I'm sure my Frank won't, either."

Rose slipped them beside Mrs Bowler's handbag. "Do you need help packing up?"

Mrs Bowler regarded Rose over her steel-framed spectacles. "No, but thank you, dear. You're such a kind-hearted girl. Why don't you get off home? Put your feet up."

"I will," Rose looked round at the debris covering the floor, "but first I'll just sweep up this mess." She went in search of a broom and as she was rounding a corner, she bumped into Jeremy.

"Rose!" he cried. "It's so lovely to see you here. I was just introducing Sabrina to some of our friends."

Rose looked at the young woman on Jeremy's arm. She had long fair hair and big, sky-blue eyes, teamed with a tiny frame, Rose could understand the attraction.

"Hello, Sabrina." Rose stretched out her hand.

"You must be Rose," Sabrina smirked, "Jeremy has mentioned you."

"I was telling my love what a fine organ player you are."

"Thank you," Rose smiled, "it's a pleasurable pastime." There ensued an awkward silence.

"Jeremy mentioned you play piano?" Rose said politely.

"God no," scoffed Sabrina, "I was just forced to take lessons as a child by my parents. I hate all that church music. Give me dance and hip-hop any day."

Jeremy laughed, a deep rumbling sound. "Sabrina entertained us all in Africa with her snazzy dance moves."

"That's because I am a dancer," Sabrina hissed through gritted teeth, "and I'm going to make it big one day."

"Oh." Rose noticed Jeremy blushing. "Is that as well as gaining a degree in environmental science?"

"That's just a back-up to keep the olds happy," Sabrina guffawed. "Imagine me as a proper scientist. No, thank you! What I really want is to be on the stage, you know, the West End, doing the splits and pirouettes. Getting famous."

"Is everything all right here?" Mrs French the vicar's wife bustled over, carrying a pot of geraniums. "Rose, these are for you. A thank-you for all your hard work." She thrust the flowers at Rose and turned to Jeremy. "The tables need packing and putting away, would you mind?"

Jeremy inclined his head and strode off, with Sabrina trailing after him.

"And he's given up on you for her?" Mrs French shook her head with dismay. "I apologise if this sounds unchristian, but he really must have come down with some kind of fever while he was in Africa."

"It's fine," Rose protested, "I'm over it."

Mrs French swiped the cake crumbs off the tablecloth. "Jeremy Payne has always been a fool. You can do better, Rose, much better."

"Thank you," Rose grinned, "but I've given up on finding Mr Right."

"Your time will come." Mrs French winked. "Did I ever tell

you I was engaged to another man when I met the vicar? Viran, his name was. We were totally unsuitable for each other, of course. I heard he's a gangster now, been in and out of prison."

Rose gasped at the thought of Mrs French being unfaithful. "But what happened?"

"Mr French swept me off my feet, that's what happened. I just couldn't refuse him. Oh Rose, he was enigmatic even back then thirty years ago. He captured my heart, body and soul."

"That's so romantic," Rose sighed.

"It will happen to you, too," Mrs French patted her hand, "when you least expect it. But until then you just carry on being your unique, beautiful self."

Rose nodded distractedly, watching Jeremy across the room with melancholy eyes.

"And forget Jeremy Payne!"

five

During her lunch break the following Friday, Rose had arranged to meet her mum at the local shopping precinct. She parked her car next to a Warburton's truck and watched people rushing back and forth with trolleys full of groceries. Rain was falling steadily from a slate grey sky and the air smelt fresh; full of flowery scents and recently cut grass. Rose flicked on the windscreen wipers and then the heating to demist the car. As the window cleared, she peered upwards. It was too cloudy today to see any planes, but she knew Shelly was up there somewhere, winging her way back to Britain. She had received a message with news that airplane tickets had been purchased and she would be home Friday evening. They had arranged to meet on Saturday, after Shelly had slept off some of the debilitating jet lag. Hence Rose had compiled a to-buy list and was now awaiting Fran, to assist her with her purchases.

It had been a better week for Rose. Her cold had almost gone; vanquished with shop-bought medicine and plenty of sleep, apart from a dry cough which was annoyingly lingering. Work had been uneventful; quieter and drama-free and thankfully there had been no more invitations to staff nights-out. She had attended the knit and natter club with the security guard's wife. Betsy was sweet and chatty. She had been good company and Rose had enjoyed the two hours spent with her and the dozen women who were knitting scarves and baby clothes. Rose pulled out her diary and was just checking what birthdays were coming up in May when there was a sharp rap on the side window. Fran's face was half covered by the hood of a red coat. Her hair was twirling in the strong wind and she was mouthing to Rose to hurry.

"Let's get inside," she said, as Rose opened the door and unfolded herself from the vehicle. They scurried across the car park, dodging around the slowly moving vehicles.

"Can you believe it's May!" Once under cover, Fran wiped raindrops from her nose and smoothed back her matted hair.

"The hanging baskets will be ruined." Rose passed her mum a tissue.

"I did tell you it was too early to put them out. They'll be withered to bits."

Rose's bottom lip turned down.

"Never mind now." Fran's gaze softened. "We can soon make some more up. So, shall we go shop?"

A little while later, Rose and Fran were running through puddles back to the car park. Their arms were full of shopping bags and bobbing helium balloons.

"Thanks for today." Rose put her purchases in the boot and slammed the door. "I should get back to work."

"And I should get back home."

Rose turned to face her mum. "What are you doing for the rest of the day?"

"Housework," Fran grimaced, "and then I'm taking your granny to have her nails done."

"Gran's having nail extensions?" Rose grinned.

"Yes. She's so excited about Shelly's party, she wants to look pretty." Fran dug in her bag for her own car keys. "How many people have you invited, by the way?"

"There should be about twenty. That's if they all turn up, of course."

"Of course they'll come. Free food, drink and music? I just hope that Shelly appreciates the trouble you're going to."

"It's no trouble," Rose replied, "she's my best friend and I'm looking forward to seeing her."

Rose patted her hand. "You girls can have a right royal catch-up. See you later, love."

"Bye, Mum." Rose clambered back into her car, started the engine and drove carefully back to Fulham Banking.

The phones were quiet for the rest of the afternoon, leaving Rose a chance to catch up with some filing. It was almost home time when Liliana clattered into reception with an armful of papers.

"Would you be a darling and photocopy these before you leave, Rose? Graham needs them straight away." Graham was one of the senior managers. A suave, ambitious man who had ruthlessly worked his way up the ranks of the banking structure.

Rose hovered uncertainly over her phone. She had been told on numerous occasions not to leave her desk. The reception desk must always be manned.

"I'll watch reception." Liliana plonked down on the swivel seat and began filing her nails. As Rose was sorting the messy photocopying into a neat pile, Liliana asked what her plans were for the weekend.

"I've organised a party for my friend. A homecoming party." Rose unpicked the staples from the edge of the papers.

"Wait – you've organised a party?" Liliana guffawed. "Is it a tea party, by any chance?"

Irritation welled up inside Rose. "Nope. We've got food and alcohol and even a DJ. They'll be lots there."

"Sounds thrilling." Liliana's eyebrows shot up. "Have a guess what I'm doing."

"A pub crawl?" Rose saw with satisfaction that she had irked her boss.

"Actually, I'm going abseiling."

"Oh?"

"You know, sliding down a wall with only a rope?"

"I know what abseiling is," Rose replied. "I didn't think you were the sporty type."

Rose was pleased she had managed to get a little dig in.

"Absolutely I am." Liliana tossed her hair. "The instructor is hot. In fact, I'm pretty sure he likes me."

"Be careful of your nails." Rose glanced at Liliana's long scarlet talons.

"Never mind them. It'll be worth it if I bag myself a date."

There was a silent pause

"Of course you prefer the more sedentary pastimes, don't you, Rose?" Liliana's lip curled up. "I heard you've joined the knit and natter club."

"How do you ..."

Liliana raised her hand. "My nan goes. She told me there was a new member there who worked at Fulham Banking. I knew it could only be you."

Rose felt herself blushing and looked away.

"Just be careful getting too friendly with that security guard. What's his name?"

"His name is Ron and I go with his wife."

"But still, you shouldn't fraternise with the lower staff. I've heard he's an odd sort. Remember, confidentiality is paramount at Fulham Banking."

"Ron is lovely," Rose protested, "and I like to treat everybody here with equal respect. Whether they're managers or lower-paid employees. And obviously I wouldn't discuss business matters while outside work."

"That's good then," Liliana sniffed and looked down at the flashing board. "I suppose I should answer that, then."

"And I should photocopy these." Rose picked up the papers and pressed the button for the lift to take her up to the fourth floor.

Rose's brother Marty had volunteered to oversee the music for Shelly's homecoming party. He lugged down two speakers from his bedroom and spent most of the morning messing with his i-Pod. While Rose, Fran and Faith rushed around, he sat with Rod on the couch, eating peanuts and discussing music choices.

"What kind of music does Shelly actually like?" He wanted to make a good impression on the girl of his teenage desires.

"Erm... party music?" Rose was balancing on a stepladder pinning a glittery banner above the fireplace.

"Well, that narrows it down." Marty shook his head and pointed a salted nut at his sister. "From what I can remember, Shelly was quite the dancer. Good at arm waving and hip rotation... reminded me of J-Lo, whereas you, Rose... erm..." He trailed off as Rose gave him a death stare.

"I can dance!"

"Sure you can, love," Rod winked, "as long as it's to cheesy Eighties music or hymns."

Marty thought that was hilarious and threw his head back with laughter.

"Maybe I'll take lessons," Rose replied curtly.

"Another club you're planning on joining?" Granny Faith bustled in, slapping the men's feet off the coffee table. "Dancing's an art form. You've either got natural rhythm or you ain't." To the surprise of the others, she lifted her arms and swivelled her hips. "Can you make sure there's some Tom Jones on that music list of yours?"

Marty snorted. "Oh yes, Granny, tell us again how you threw your knickers at him while he was on stage."

Faith nodded. "I did and let me tell you, I wasn't the only one who did it, either. There he was, sweating away and singing his little Welsh heart out, surrounded by all these knickers. At least mine were clean, mind you."

"You're going to behave, aren't you, Granny?" Rose swallowed as possible scenarios ran through her mind. Granny Faith had always been unpredictable, fun-loving, wild at times. She remembered one New Year's Eve when Faith had consumed too much Prosecco. She had stumbled past the vicar's house singing a rude version of O Come All Ye Faithful and then she had been sick in Mrs Bowler's privet hedge. Rose hadn't been able to look either of them in the eye for a few weeks afterwards.

"Probably not," came Faith's light-hearted reply. "Don't you worry about me. You just concentrate on having a great time. It's been a long time since we had a house party, in fact I think the last one was when Marty was ten. Can you remember it, Rose?"

"Oh yes!" Rose chuckled as she backed down the steps. "Was that when Mum hired a clown and Marty was so scared, he ran and hid in the pantry?"

"I don't remember that," scowled Marty.

"Surely you do, little brother. You wouldn't come out until the clown had gone and then you were miffed because all the lime jelly had been eaten."

Marty cast her a withering look. "I was a child."

"So you won't be wanting any of Mum's lime jelly then?"

Marty's eyes lit up. "I suppose I could fit some in."

"You two, pack it in," grumbled Rod, "I'm trying to watch the telly."

"Rose, go and help your mum with the food, I'll finish up with the decorating." Faith nudged her gently towards the door. As Rose left the room, she pulled a face at her brother, happy that for once she had gained the upper hand.

"How can I help?" Rose went to place the Sellotape and scissors back in the drawer and turned to look at her frazzled-looking mum.

"You can start by washing up!" Fran swiped a lock of hair

behind her ears before emptying a pot of cress into a mixing bowl. "Pass me the mayonnaise, please."

She squirted a big blob on top of a dozen mashed eggs and gave it a good stir.

"Everything under control in here?" Rose rolled up her sleeves and twisted the hot water tap.

"I think so." Fran sounded decisive. "The cooking's all done. Just the sandwiches to make and then we can lay the table. What's the time?" They both glanced at the chrome wall clock. "Gah, only a couple of hours left till the guests start arriving!"

"Plenty of time." Rose sounded calm but inside her stomach was churning. Please let this be a success, she fretted silently, please let everything be okay between me and Shelly. Outwardly, she smiled brightly and began tackling the mountain of washing-up.

An hour later, the food was laid out on the table: sausage rolls, pizza, vol-au-vents, cheese and pineapple, quiche and chicken drumsticks. An assortment of different types of sandwiches, salads and sinful-looking desserts. Rose sprinkled star confetti around the plates and positioned the helium balloons around the table edge.

"It looks good," Fran commented as she rubbed her tired feet.

"But is it enough?" Rose wondered aloud.

"This house looks like it's Christmas. It's enough!" Fran bobbed her head at the lights strung all around, the balloons and banners. "Shouldn't you be getting ready?"

"Yes! Thanks again, Mum, you're a star." Rose gave her a quick hug and then bounded out of the kitchen and up the stairs. Quickly, she showered, brushed her teeth, dried her hair, applied a light layer of make-up and stood in front of her open wardrobe wondering what she could wear. Her fingers ran across her clothes: black jeans, black trousers, black skirts. Most of her wardrobe consisted of work wear; plain, simple, practical and not suitable attire for a party. Squashed right at the back hung a few summer dresses. Rose held up a red, flowing, cotton number, with a sweetheart neckline and thin straps; it was perfect. She teamed it with flat cream ballet pumps and a pretty pearl necklace and earrings. A squirt of perfume and she was ready.

Rose's dad did a double-take when he saw her coming down the stairs. "Don't you look lovely?" He smiled up at her. "Shelly won't recognise you."

Rose had to agree. The last time Shelly had seen her, she was wearing braces, was covered in acne and her hair was a frizzy ginger mess. Thankfully, the years had been kind and Rose had matured into a pretty young lady.

She followed her dad into the lounge.

"Can I start up the music then?" Marty looked at her expectantly.

"Sure." Rose grinned at the sight of her brother in his best jeans and shirt, with a baseball cap squashed backwards on his head. "Is this your DJ look?"

"It's my weekend 'here for the ladies' look," Marty winked. "I'm just hoping your mate is still single."

"What about Mrs Mason?" Rose whispered, glancing furtively at her dad who had his back to them, bent over the Bombay Mix.

Marty grimaced. "Back with the hubby, unfortunately. Good news is I'm still available. Right then, let's get this party started." He fiddled with the buttons on his i-Pod and hooked it into the deck. Moments later, Eighties pop music filled the air. Rose nodded with approval and tapped her feet in time with the beat.

"Looks like your first guest is arriving," Rod was peering through the netted window, "and it's someone I don't recognise."

"Oh, right." Rose smoothed down her dress and hurried to open the front door. An annoyed-looking woman was struggling up the path, pulling a suitcase.

Wow, thought Rose, Shelly has really changed. She squinted through the dim light and realised it wasn't Shelly at all. Shelly was, had been, blonde and petite. This woman was tall, with an athletic build and jet-black cropped hair falling just below her jawline.

"Hello," Rose said warmly, "are you here for Shelly's party?"

"Well yes, duh." The woman pulled her case a little too hard, causing the handle to slip down and snag on her expensive looking tights. "Shit!" the woman screeched, "can this day get any worse?"

"Can I help you?" Rose stepped towards her, but the woman held up her hand.

"Please. I can manage." She tugged her case through the doorway and appraised Rose with her hands on her hips. "Don't you recognise me?"

Rose blinked. "Are you a school friend?"

The woman snorted. "I'm her sister, Rose Archer."

"Marian? You came!" Rose beamed at Shelly's older sister.

"Yes, I came back... here." Marian glanced over her shoulder. "This place hasn't changed, still as dead and lifeless as ever! I almost hopped straight onto the next train back to London."

"So you managed to get the time off work, after all?" Rose took Marian's coat, draping it over the stair rail.

"I told them it was a family emergency." Marian looked Rose up and down. "You look different... a good kind of different."

"Thank you." Rose touched her hair. "I guess we've all grown up."

"Ain't that the truth?" Marian replied. "But why are you still here? Haven't you ever wanted to live somewhere different?"

"I love it here," Rose replied simply, "I've never wanted to live anywhere else."

Marian stared at her, aghast.

"Come into the kitchen." Rose led her down the hall. "What would you like to drink?"

"G and T?" Marian asked hopefully.

"Sorry, it's wine, beer or soft drinks."

"I suppose I can cope with wine, but tell me you have rosé?"

"We have." With a happy smile, Rose splashed some into a glass. Marian gulped it down and passed it back for a refill.

"It's so weird being back here." Marian took a handful of Doritos out of a bowl and began nibbling. "Who exactly is coming tonight?"

"School friends and neighbours, mainly. There's even a few teachers coming."

"Christ," Marian rolled her eyes, "this is going to be like a school reunion!" She narrowed her eyes. "Michael Kent isn't coming, is he?"

Slowly, Rose nodded. "Yes. He actually stopped me in the street the other day to ask me if he could. Is that a problem?"

Marian threw herself onto a chair. "Yes, it's a problem. He's one of the reasons I left here, Rose. He broke my heart. Chose Victoria Clemens over me."

Rose frowned. "They split up years ago. I think he's single now. Marty's friends with him, shall I go and ask him for you?"

"No!" screeched Marian. "That would be so embarrassing." She shook her head, "I'm a successful businesswoman, Rose and I am totally over Michael Kent. I just wondered if he was still here, that's all."

"As you do," Rose grinned, just as the doorbell rang. "That's probably more guests. Will you be okay on your own?"

"Of course I will," Marian said flippantly. "Your personality hasn't changed, has it? Still kind Rose. Now, what time is my sister arriving?"

Rose consulted her watch. "In about an hour's time. Make yourself at home, help yourself to... erm... more wine and feel free to mingle."

"Will do," Marian called as Rose hurried down the hallway, ready to welcome more guests.

Six

Rose spent the next hour opening the front door and giving people a quick tour of the house. As the evening was warm, Fran had opened the French windows and the guests were spilling out onto the patio. The music was thumping, the guests were chatting and the atmosphere was laid back and happy.

"No one's dancing," her brother complained, "and why is everybody outside?"

"Because it's a nice evening," Rose nudged him, "and they'll probably dance later."

"Yeah," he grinned, "when they're all sloshed."

Granny Faith appeared in the doorway, a plate of buffet food in her hand.

"Gran, the food's not open until after Shelly arrives." Rose looked at her with dismay.

Faith picked up a cheese and pineapple with a shrug. "There sure seems to be a lot of people here. I thought you'd only invited twenty?"

"I did," Rose mumbled, "word must have got around. I'd forgotten how popular Shelly was."

Marty cracked his fingers, an annoying habit which had

progressed from childhood through to adulthood. "But when she sees me, no one else will matter."

"That's funny," Rose said with a chuckle. "How much younger than her are you?"

He looked affronted. "Hey! Toy-boys are in fashion, aren't they?" He looked to his gran for confirmation.

"How the hell should I know?" Faith retorted. "Nowadays, I'd be happy with any man, young, old, rich, poor, as long as he's dish..." She trailed off as Rose gave her a friendly push.

"Go and supervise the buffet and stop daydreaming about men!"

Faith turned on her heel and limped off, chuntering.

"I'm sure she puts that limp on." Rose watched her go with suspicious eyes.

"Course she does," Marty agreed, "she's after some sympathy, that's all. Leave her be, Rose. In another hour's time, she'll be bopping away with no cares in the world." He paused for a breath. "Is Jeremy coming this evening?"

"No." Rose plumped up a cushion. "He didn't go to our school and he doesn't know Shelly."

"Oh, I forgot. He went to the grammar school, didn't he?" Marty adjusted his cap slightly. "Maybe it's a good job he's not coming, Dad's well miffed over the way he treated you. Want me to scare him, Rose, break an arm or leg? Me and my mates could have a quiet word with him."

"Don't be ridiculous!" Rose regarded him with amused eyes. "I'm well and truly over Jeremy Payne. Sabrina is welcome to him."

"That's the spirit." Marty nodded his head in part approval and part tempo to the song that was currently playing. "So what do you want me to play when Shelly finally arrives?"

"Dancing Queen," Rose replied without hesitation. "That was our tune when we were growing up."

Marty flicked through his playlist. "Yep. Got that one. So, shouldn't Shelly be here by now?"

"She should have been here half an hour ago." Rose pulled the velvet curtains back and peered out at the lit-up street, "Maybe I'll text her – see where she is."

Her fingers flew nimbly over the phone screen. A few minutes later, a reply beeped in her inbox.

On my way, honey. Won't be long.

"Aargh!" Rose felt a sense of panic well inside her. "Cut the music, Marty, she's almost here." She dashed into the kitchen and explained to the guests that Shelly was arriving very soon, and they had to make their way into the lounge to surprise her. Then she repeated the words for the people in the garden.

After squashing everyone in, the lounge was packed full of people. Rose put her finger to her lips to denote that everyone should be quiet and then Marty clambered over the sofa to switch off the lights. Darkness fell like a shroud. Rose could hear the sounds of people breathing and one woman complaining that somebody was treading on her toes. Then the squeak of a door and a female's voice calling Rose. That's her, thought Rose, her heart racing, that's Shelly.

"Why is the front door open?" The sound of the words wafted down the hallway. Rose could hear other muffled voices. It sounded like a man's. Rose cursed whoever was out there, spoiling the surprise.

"Mr and Mrs Archer... Rose?"

Slowly, the door to the lounge opened and as it did, Marty flicked on the lights and there was a chorus of mismatched shouts of "Surprise!"

Shelly stood bathed in the light, surrounded by three of the handsomest men Rose had ever laid her eyes on.

Rose was vaguely aware of people clapping and surging forward. They jostled behind her, pushing her towards the open arms of her best friend.

"Rose!" Shelly cried. "Is it really you?"

"Yes," squeaked Rose, then emotion overcame her and tears glistened in her eyes. She was pulled into a tight embrace that smelt of hair lacquer and strong perfume.

"It's so good to see you," she mouthed against her friend's ear, "it's so great to have you home."

"Let me look at you." Shelly moved back and looked Rose up and down. "You look so pretty."

"And you look stunning!" Rose grinned at the sight of Shelly in her clinging cream dress which accentuated a glowing tan. "How was your flight?"

"Never mind her flight," Marty yelled, "let's get this party started!"

The first beats of Dancing Queen swooned around the room and Shelly was carried off to be plied with exuberant hugs and warm kisses. Rose watched her friend being picked up and twirled around by Billy Baxter. Head thrown back, laughing uproariously, this was how Rose remembered her. Like a sparkly star shooting beams of gorgeousness all around her. The guests vied for her attention and Rose dithered nervously on the edge, waiting for some time alone with her best friend.

"I think it's time to open the buffet." Rose motioned for her mum to help her with the unravelling. They went into the empty kitchen and began pulling foil and clingfilm off the plates of food. Rose was vaguely aware of a ginger-haired man standing in the doorway watching them. She turned to smile at him and offered him a drink.

"Can I get a beer?" His deep Australian accent resounded in the kitchen.

"Of course. Is lager okay?"

"Perfect."

Rose snapped a can off a four-pack and handed it over to the broad-shouldered man.

"You came with Shelly?" Rose asked, busying herself with arranging celery sticks in a tumbler.

"I sure did." His grin revealed a set of even teeth which were so white, they almost seemed sparkly. "So you're the legendary Rose? I've heard a great deal about you. Finally I get to meet you."

Rose blushed. "All good, I hope."

The man crossed the room and pulled her into an embrace that lifted her from her feet, saying, "Any friend of Shelly's is a friend of mine."

"Th... thank you." Rose wriggled out of his grasp. "This is my mum, Fran."

"Now I know where you get your looks from." The man picked a surprised Fran up, too, depositing a kiss on her cheek.

"Oh, that's kind of you to say," Fran patted her hair, "and you are?"

"Harry," he replied, grinning, "but I'll let Shelly explain who I am."

It was at that moment that Rose's dad came into the kitchen. "What's going on here, then?" he said good naturedly. "I turn my back for five minutes and another man's got hold of my Fran."

Harry guffawed. "Apologies, mate. That's the way we greet a pretty woman in Australia."

Rose noticed her mum was red-faced and at a loss for words.

"Have you known Shelly long?" Rose snagged a black bin liner off the roll and began emptying the rubbish into it.

"A couple of years," he drawled, "we were friends before..." He trailed off as the door opened and a blond-haired man bounded into the kitchen. "This is my brother, Boyd."

Rose looked across at the muscular, tanned man.

"Call me Fin." He grinned and sat astride one of the kitchen stools.

"He had a close encounter with a shark a long time ago," Harry explained. "Fin's his nickname."

"A shark?" gasped Rose. "What happened?"

Fin picked up a celery stick and took a big bite. "I was twelve. Surfing with friends on Bondi when this great white appeared from nowhere. Took a chunk out of my board, missed my leg by a couple of inches."

"That must have been terrifying," Rose said. "What happened next?"

"I swam as fast as I could, didn't look back," Fin shrugged. "I'm a fast swimmer and I guess I just got lucky. The shark had swum away. Cleared the sea for a couple of hours, though."

"You mean people went back in, knowing there could've been a shark lurking?" Rose was scared just hearing about it.

"Australians are tough." Fin grinned. "We thrive on danger."

"You mean you do," interjected Harry. "We're not all adrenaline junkies."

Rose smiled. "So you like surfing. Any other dangerous activities?"

"Oh yeah, I regularly jump out of planes, do bungee jumps, snowboarding in the winter, white water rafting... "

"Is he for real?" A wide-eyed Rose glanced at Harry.

"Afraid so."

Fran chuckled. "Our Rose doesn't even like kiddie rollercoasters. The teacups are more her thing."

"Mum!" Rose blushed. "I'm afraid of heights."

"She's never flown," piped up her dad. "Every year we go to the same holiday caravan in Weymouth and even then she doesn't like travelling on the motorway."

Rose noticed Harry and Fin exchange a glance. Rose decided to change the subject.

"There was another man with you?"

"Oh yeah," Harry pulled a slice of pepper out of the salad bowl, "that'll be our Tom."

"Tom's the quiet one of the family," Fin explained.

"You mean he's your brother, too?" Rose was finding this intriguing and wondered how Shelly had met the enigmatic trio.

"Yep. Harry there is the brain-box eldest, Tom is the middle left out one and I'm the fun-loving younger brother. And talking of fun, will you come and dance with me, Rose?"

"Oh, I..." Rose blushed even more.

"Course she will." Fran gave her a little shove. "Go and enjoy yourself. Me and Dad can finish up here."

Fin grabbed her hand and pulled Rose out of the kitchen before she could refuse.

The hallway was full of people bopping away.

"Buffets open," she mouthed, pointing in the direction she had just left.

There was a stampede for the kitchen, Rose and Fin were pressed close together against the wall as the guests charged past.

"Come on then, English angel, show me your dance moves." Fin spun her through the doorway of the lounge and onto the makeshift dance floor. Marty grinned as she revolved in Fin's arms.

"Let's just slow it down a bit, shall we?" He abruptly switched tracks to a gentle love number.

"This is perfect, eh?" Fin grinned down at her.

"I'm a hopeless dancer." She smiled shyly up at him.

"Jeez, you English are so humble." Fin spun her gently round. "Is there anything you are good at?"

"Reading?" Rose replied lamely.

"I should have known it," Fin replied. "I, of course, can't sit still long enough to read."

He pressed his chin on the top of her head. "What kind of books do you like?"

"I love the classics. Jane Austen, the Bronte sisters?"

Fin raised a puzzled eyebrow. "Are they erotic books? Like Fifty Shades of Grey?"

"Erm... no," Rose laughed, "they're masterworks of literature. Very clever. I can't believe you've never heard of Jane Austen."

"And I can't believe you've never been on a plane." He gazed down at her. "Why are you hiding, Rose? What are you frightened of?"

Rose was saved from answering by Shelly, who pulled her away from Fin and draped her arms around her. "I can't believe you've done all this for me! Thank you so much, Rose." She planted a sloppy kiss on Rose's cheek. "It's so good to see you again. I've missed you."

"And I've missed you." Rose squeezed her friend's midriff. "How does it feel being back home?"

Shelly looked around. "It feels good, it feels safe and familiar," she lowered her tone, "and I can't believe you got Marian to come here. My sister, the high-flyer who said she would never return."

"There's a lot of people who wanted to see you again, Shelly. You were missed and you're loved very much."

Shelly's eyes filled with tears. "You're still as lovely as ever. My Rose, my best friend." They embraced again and then Rose heard Shelly sigh.

"What's wrong?" Rose asked.

"Tom is what's wrong." She motioned surreptitiously to the dark-haired brother, who was sitting on the sofa playing with his baseball cap.

"Is he okay?" Rose whispered.

"He's not exactly a party animal." She winked playfully. "Hey Tom, come and dance."

Tom held up his hand and pulled a phone out of his pocket.

"I think that's a no." Rose glanced over at him with interest. He was wearing dark jeans and a tight-fitting white shirt. His dark hair was swept back, and his chin and cheeks were lined with stubble.

Shelly let go of Rose and shimmied over to him. In a flash, she had pinched his phone and held it aloft, out of his reach.

"Come on, Shelly," he said, "give it me back."

"Not until you've had one dance."

Tom rolled his eyes. "Fine." He rose to his feet, towering over Shelly.

"Not with me," Shelly protested, "with Rose."

Tom's eyes flashed over her and Rose felt her skin prickle uncomfortably. "It's okay." She took a step back. "I don't like dancing much, either."

"Since when?" Shelly laughed. "You used to."

"Probably when I was eight," Rose mumbled. Feeling embarrassed, she turned away, but Shelly grabbed hold of her hand and pulled her towards Tom.

He gave her a lopsided smile. "She won't give up."

"I know." Rose smiled back, feeling her stomach clench with excitement. Close up, this guy was pretty handsome. As he took her in his arms, she was vaguely aware of Marty wolf-whistling.

Rose blushed. "Ignore him, he's only my little brother."

"I know all about annoying brothers." Slowly. he spun Rose around. "I'm Tom, by the way, pleased to meet you."

She looked up into the most startling green eyes she had ever seen. They were deep green, like the grass after a lengthy bout of summer rain.

"I'm Rose."

Tom cleared his throat. "So how did you meet Shelly?"

Rose was distracted by the closeness of his warm body and the heady smell of his aftershave. "Wh – what?"

He looked amused; a smile playing on his lips. "You're Shelly's best friend?"

Rose shook her dazed head. "Yes. We met at primary school and have been best friends ever since."

Tom emitted a low whistle. "That's a long time. She's been talking about you non-stop on the flight over here."

"She has?" Goosebumps appeared on Rose's arms as he hooked a hand round her waist and pulled her closer. "I mean, that's lovely. How was your flight, by the way?"

"Extremely tiring." Tom stifled a yawn. "Sorry I'm not much company. Jet lag's kicking in."

"You don't need to apologise." Rose smiled up at him. "Have you eaten? There's a table full of buffet food in the kitchen and I noticed you haven't got a drink, either."

"Are you always this concerned about your guests?"

Rose blinked. Is he mocking me? she wondered.

"I guess I like taking care of people," she replied, drawing back a little.

They stopped moving and Tom was staring down at her, his face serious. He opened his mouth to speak but was cut off by a shriek from Shelly, who had climbed up on the sofa and was waving her arms for everyone's attention. Slowly, people filtered back into the room, curious to see what was occurring. Feeling self-conscious, Rose backed out of Tom's arms and turned to face her friend.

Shelly clapped her hands. "Attention please. Firstly, I would like to say a massive thank you to everyone who has come here tonight to welcome me back home." There was a round of clapping. "And to my best friend," she pointed her flute of fizzy wine at Rose, "who organised all this, thank you, thank you, thank you. I love you, Rose!"

Rose grinned and gave her a little wave.

"As you all know, I've been travelling around the world having a blast. But finally, finally I've settled down, folks," Shelly took a long swig of her wine. "I met a man in Australia, a perfect gorgeous man and we fell madly in love and he only went and proposed six months ago. Yep, people, party animal Shelly is actually settling down and getting married!"

A series of cheers erupted and Shelly was surrounded by people vying to kiss and congratulate her.

"Lucky Shelly." Fran placed a hand on Rose's shoulder. "What lovely news. But I'm really surprised she's engaged, and to a gorgeous Australian as well."

"Yes, but Mum, which brother is she marrying?"

SEVEN

"Where is he?" Shelly stood on her tiptoes, almost tumbling off the sofa in the process. "Where's my husband-to-be?"

Rose glanced at Tom who was sitting back on the armchair. Why did she suddenly feel relieved it wasn't him? Fin! It had to be fun-loving Fin.

Then through the crowds Harry appeared, his shock of ginger hair shining like a beacon in the dim light. Harry lifted Shelly into his arms and she squealed with delight, wrapping her legs around his waist.

"I'm making her an honourable woman," he shouted. The crowd clapped and someone yelled that it was about time.

When Shelly and Harry had finished their sultry dance, they beckoned Rose over.

"Congratulations!" Rose hugged them both. "You make a lovely couple. How did you meet?"

"In Accident and Emergency." Shelly placed a hand on Harry's stomach. "He's a doctor, Rose. He treated me for a dog bite then gave me his number, along with a tetanus jab."

"You mean you prised my number from me!" Harry nibbled her ear.

"So can I see the ring?"

Shelly held out her left hand for inspection. On the third finger glistened a beautiful cluster of diamonds set on a gold plate. "He proposed in Paris, at the top of the Eiffel Tower."

Rose smiled at the happiness emanating from her friend. "That's so romantic. I'm so thrilled for you."

Shelly grasped her arm. "We need a catch-up. Just us two alone. A bestie reunion."

"Sounds a good plan." Rose's eyes slid to Tom, who was sprawled back on the chair, his eyes closed and his baseball cap wedged firmly on top of his head. She looked from him to Marty, who was also sporting a similar cap, albeit wearing it backwards. Was this a new fashion for men? she wondered.

"How about tomorrow?" Shelly's eyes were shining with excitement. "We could go for Sunday lunch. Oh, how I've missed roast beef and Yorkshire pudding!"

"Okay." Rose nodded. "I'll pick you up at twelve. Where are you staying, by the way?" Her eyes widened when she heard that Shelly, Harry, Fin and Tom were all booked in at the five-star Belmont Hotel, on the outskirts of the village.

"That's a posh hotel."

"It's okay, I suppose," Shelly rolled her eyes, "apart from a couple of pneumatic-drill-happy workmen making a whole heap of noise right outside our window."

"Your sister's giving us the eye." Harry nodded in the direction of the doorway, where Marian surveyed them with arms crossed and a disapproving glaze on her face.

"I suppose I should go spend some time with her, huh?" she whispered to Rose.

"Of course." Rose stood aside. "You should be mingling. We can catch up tomorrow."

"Thanks, honey," Shelly pulled her into another embrace, "and thanks again for organising this amazing homecoming."

〜

Rose woke early the next morning. Sunlight filtered through the window blinds, bathing the room in a golden hue and warming her exposed face and arms. She turned onto her side and peered at the alarm clock. Oh, what joy to be wide awake at seven o'clock on a Sunday morning. Rose reached for her glasses, slid them on and picked her book up off the table dresser. Her mouth was dry and her head was throbbing. She rarely drank, but last night she had consumed four large glasses of wine followed by a dubious-sounding cocktail which Shelly had made for her. The result was that Rose felt rough. Rougher than she had felt last week when she had been bedbound with influenza. It was no good, she was unable to concentrate on her latest romance, so with a sigh she flung back the covers and rose groggily to her feet. For a moment, the room spun, and Rose reached for the bedroom furniture to assist her on her travels.

The house was quiet. Rose made her way down the stairs, grimacing at the debris strewn across the floor. She had a vague recollection of people dispersing last night, and her mum insisting that the clearing-up could wait until the morning. The kitchen was the messiest room; crockery piled up in the sink and half-eaten food curling from the warmth and being left out overnight. Rose clicked on the kettle and spooned a generous amount of coffee granules into her mug. She perched on a stool and flicked through the camera roll on her phone. She smiled at a picture of her gran, arms akimbo as she danced, and one of her mum and dad in an amorous embrace as they smooched to a slow song. There were numerous selfies of her and Shelly and a lovely photograph of Shelly, Harry and Fin in a group hug. There were none of Tom; she remembered him shying away from the camera. He hadn't danced again and Rose had felt too shy to try to instigate a conversation with him. Marian had monopolised Shelly's attention for the remainder of the evening. She had a flashback of her berating her younger sister for not warning her of her engagement. It had been a great night, though, thought Rose; a resounding success.

As she was filling her mug with hot water, the door squeaked open and Fran slunk into the room, clutching her forehead.

"Want a drink?" Rose asked, with a glance in her direction. "You look as bad as I feel."

"Worse," Fran groaned. "I am never drinking again." She opened one of the overhead cupboards and swallowed two paracetamol.

"Why don't you go back to bed, Mum? I can start cleaning up down here."

Fran shook her head. "I've come down to help. It shouldn't be left to you to do it all."

"I'll cook us a bacon sandwich and then we can get started."

Five full bin bags later, the house was looking back to normal.

"I should take these down." Rose gathered up all the wall banners and squashed them into the rubbish. "Did you enjoy last night?"

"Oh Rose, it was terrific!" Fran wiped washing-up liquid off her hands. "You did good. Everyone seemed to be enjoying themselves, especially Shelly."

"We're going for lunch, so I won't need any dinner."

"Okay, love." Fran yawned, "I think it might be a chippy today. I'm in no mood for cooking."

Rose nodded. "What did you think of Shelly's guests?"

"Very handsome," Fran laughed, "and Fin is so funny. It's been a long time since a young man has made a fuss of me."

"He certainly took a shine to you." Rose nudged her mum. "I reckon Dad has some competition."

"Imagine that!" Fran's eyes were wide with merriment.

"Shelly's fiancé seems nice, quite grounded. He'll be good for her, don't you think?"

"Yes. He'll calm her down," Rose picked up a tea towel and began drying the plates and cutlery, "and what did you think of the middle brother?"

"Gorgeous," came Fran's verdict, "but painfully shy. He could barely look at me when I asked him if he wanted some cheesecake."

"Maybe it was jet lag," Rose suggested. "The flight from Australia is awfully long."

"Yes, I'd die of boredom." Fran swiped back a tendril of hair. "So the kitchen's pristine. Shall we go sort out the lounge?"

Later on in the morning, Rose left to pick Shelly up from the hotel. She pulled up in a parking bay and messaged her to tell her she was there. Shelly came bouncing out of the hotel ten minutes later, looking fresh-faced and happy, dressed in a white summer dress and immaculate make-up. Rose felt dowdy in comparison, in her faded jeans and hoody and a face bare of make-up.

"I had the best time last night." Shelly clipped her seatbelt on and beamed at Rose. "We all did."

"Even Tom?" Rose swallowed. "Mum mentioned how quiet he was."

"Oh, he's always like that." Shelly winked. "You know, the brooding, angst-ridden type. Gotta admit he's fit though, eh?"

"I suppose so." Rose cleared her throat. "I thought we could go to The White Swan for lunch?"

"Sounds good. Do Roger and Sue still run it?"

"Yep, still going strong. They refurbished it about five years ago, but they still have the quiz nights on a Monday."

"They do?" Shelly bounced on her seat with excitement. "We should go."

"I have folk choir on a Monday," Rose replied, "but I could meet you there afterwards."

"It's a date then." Shelly slid a glance at her friend. "You still go to church?"

"Yes. Although I missed it this morning. The house was in chaos, I helped clean up."

"You're still as sweet as ever," Shelly passed Rose a chewing gum, "even Tom noticed."

"He did? I mean... what did he say?"

Shelly raised a quizzical eyebrow. "He asked me about you, that's all. Said you seemed a nice girl, which is high praise indeed from our Tom."

Rose's heart sank: nice? Puppies were nice, sweet old ladies were nice, cake was nice. Couldn't he think of a more interesting adjective?

"Look out!" Shelly pointed through the window screen at a bus which had suddenly slammed on its brakes. Rose did the same, flinging them both forward.

For the rest of the journey, Rose pushed away thoughts of brooding Tom and concentrated on the road. They listened to music and chatted about the school friends who had turned up last night. Shelly told her about Billy Baxter's wandering hands and the stern telling off she had given him.

"Didn't you and Billy Baxter have a thing going on?" Rose teased.

"When I was fifteen," Shelly huffed. "Now I prefer men to boys and let's face it, Billy Baxter hasn't matured much."

Rose had to agree with that. She slowed down as the entrance to the White Swan loomed in front of them. The car park was almost full, but she managed to find a space underneath a towering oak tree.

"It's busy," Rose commented, "I hope we can get a table."

Shelly pulled her arm. "Let's sit in the beer garden. Do they still have the inflatables?"

"Yes. They still have the children's bouncy castle." Rose laughed. "Go grab a seat and I'll get us drinks."

She followed a man on a disabled scooter through the arched doorway and into the pub. As anticipated, it was busy. All of the inside tables were occupied and there was a two-deep line of people at the bar. Rose stood behind a man wearing leathers, who smelt of incense and cigarette smoke. She dug in her purse and pulled out a note, then waited to be served.

The White Swan was the oldest pub in Twineham. Before its refurbishment it had been a proper old-fashioned boozer, with a bar that housed a dart board and an oak-panelled lounge complete with a pool table and juke box. Rose's father had played for the domino team and prior to her retirement, Granny Faith had worked here for years as a cleaner. Then a big brewery had bought it and completely transformed it. The bar and lounge had been merged and it had been rebranded as a family restaurant. Nowadays, the décor was modern and fresh. The old dark wood had been replaced by white panelling and classy pictures. The juke box had been carted away and replaced by wall speakers, and the pool table was now a dining table for eight. To top it all off, dominoes and darts were cancelled, replaced by themed music nights and karaoke. Sue, the bar manager, was out collecting glasses and she stopped when she saw Rose.

"Hello, love." Sue was balancing numerous glasses in her fingers; years of experience of working in a pub. "Haven't seen you in here for a while." She asked how her dad and gran were, while battling her way through the crowds to deposit the glasses on the bar.

"They're both well, thank you." Rose smiled at the tiny Welsh woman. "Shelly's back from her travels."

"She is?" Sue placed her hands on her hips. "I better go say hello then and Rose, tell Roger your drinks are on the house."

"She's outside!" Rose called after Sue as she moved away.

A gap appeared at the bar and Rose quickly slotted in.

Roger and two young women were busy behind the pumps. Rose waited for the landlord to finish serving a middle-aged couple before asking for two cokes.

"I heard Shelly's back." Roger leaned on the pop dispenser and mopped at his perspiring brow with a handkerchief. "She's brought the heat back with her."

"And the glorious sunshine." Rose glanced out of the dusty window, where the midday sun gleamed in a cloudless sky.

He passed over the drinks. "It's good to see you back in here, Rose. Don't be a stranger now."

"I'll be in tomorrow night as well. That's if... the quiz night is still on?"

"It sure is," Roger confirmed, "and this week's prize is a full English breakfast free of charge, as well as a bottle of vinegar... I mean wine. So make sure you come, I'll be looking out for you now."

"Will do." Rose flashed him a bright smile and then turned to battle her way through the crowds and back out to Shelly.

eight

Shelly was watching the children racing around the play apparatus with a melancholy look upon her face.

"How fast has the time gone?" She smiled up at Rose as she set the drinks down. "Remember when we camped out in my garden overnight when we were eight?"

"I remember," Rose replied. "Your tent was huge, almost as big as the entire lawn."

"Dad brought us hot dogs and fries and a family-size trifle to share. Some days, I forget he's not here anymore." Shelly gave a big sniff. "I'd give anything to talk to him again."

Rose reached across to give Shelly's arm a consoling rub. "He'd be proud of you. Hadn't he wanted to live in Australia himself?"

"New Zealand," Shelly corrected, "but Mum wouldn't leave England and now she doesn't know where she is. Poor Mum..." Shelly trailed off.

"I could take you if you want to go see her," Rose offered, sipping her drink through a bent paper straw.

"I'm going later with Harry, but thanks, Rose." Shelly picked up a menu. "Shall we order food? I'm famished."

"Two Sunday lunches, with all the trimmings?" Rose grinned.

"Sounds heavenly," Shelly licked her lips, "but what shall we have for pudding?"

~

"This is as good as I remember it." Shelly was tucking into her lunch. "Mmm, can't beat great British pub grub."

Rose smeared mustard on the side of her plate. "What's it like?"

"Hmm? The beef's divine."

"I meant Australia," Rose said with a laugh.

"Hot. Vast. Beautiful."

"What about the spiders?" Rose asked, with a shudder.

"Never come across the poisonous sort. Snakes, on the other hand, yep. Bruce has caught a few."

"Bruce?"

"He's our dog, Rose. Harry bought him when we moved in together." She fished in her bag for her phone. "He's still a puppy, a bit of a handful but adorable. Here he is." She flipped her phone onto its side.

"Ah!" Rose cooed at the picture on the screen of a close-up shot of a black and white dog. "Is he a Dalmatian?"

"Yep. Staying with friends until we figure out what our next move is."

Rose swallowed. "Your next move?"

Shelly stared at her. "I mean when we've figured out where our future lies – Harry and I."

"You mean... I just presumed that you would be going back to Australia. I thought this was just a fleeting visit, Shelly."

"Well," Shelly put her fork down, "we're not absolutely sure where we're going to be living. When we're married, I mean."

"You're considering moving back to Britain permanently?" Rose's eyes were wide.

"Yeah, maybe. Truth is, I'm homesick. I want to settle down in one place. Travelling around the world has lost its appeal."

Rose nodded. "It would be fantastic if you came back here." She thought for a moment. "Harry would get a job as a doctor here with no problems. Isn't there a shortage of doctors? And imagine working for a UK radio station!"

"I could also branch out into television," Shelly agreed, "there are lots of opportunities for us both over here. But first I must organise my wedding. And that's what I wanted to discuss with you, Rose."

Rose looked up from her broccoli, suddenly envisaging Shelly in a flouncy white princess number at an old-fashioned stately home, or, even better, a castle. She would have a horse and carriage, of course, and a sumptuous five course wedding lunch, and fireworks that could be seen and heard for miles. No expense would be spared, Shelly would be toasted as the most gorgeous bride ever. A women's glossy magazine could do the photographs and Harry would organise a plane to fly overhead, chugging out their names and hearts in the brilliant blue sky. 'Romantic' would be an understatement. Rose sighed, a dreamy look on her face.

"Erm, Rose, aren't you going to ask me what I've organised?" Shelly had finished her meal and was staring at Rose with a bemused look upon her face.

"Sorry." Rose grinned. "Tell me about the wedding of the century then."

"Whoa, you need to rein your imagination in, girl," Shelly chuckled. "Actually, I can't stand the idea of a big formal affair."

"Really?" Rose was surprised. "I didn't think you'd be capable of small and quiet."

"That was the old Shelly. I've calmed down a lot since I've met Harry. He's grounded me."

"Grounded you?" Rose repeated the words. "You were lovely before, Shelly."

"I feel safe with him," Shelly twirled her hair around her finger, "content, complete. Hell, I know it sounds corny but I love him so much, Rose."

"I can see that." Rose smiled. "So tell me about the wedding then. Are you going to ask Mr French if you can have it at his church? It's so beautiful... so quaint and romantic. The folk choir could sing for you, it would be perf–"

"I'm not getting married in Mr French's church." Shelly grasped the table edge. "Not in any church, as a matter of fact." She let out a long breath. "I'm getting married abroad, Rose, on the beach and I want you as my matron of honour. Harry and I aren't getting married in England or Australia, though. We're getting married in Majorca."

~

"Majorca? On a beach?" Rose dropped her cutlery with a clatter.

"Yes, Majorca," Shelly smirked, "you know, that Balearic island in the Mediterranean."

"I've heard of it, of course." Rose dabbed her mouth with a napkin. "I didn't know you'd been there, though. You never sent me a postcard."

"Sorry, honey. I worked there for a while, in a restaurant right by the sea. I wanted to improve on my Spanish."

Rose had a vague recollection of Shelly taking Spanish lessons at night college, just before she left for her around the world trip.

"That's lovely," Rose said, picking at a loose thread of cotton on her sleeve, "but... but what about your guests?"

"They'll be going," Shelly replied brightly. "At least the important ones will."

Flying? Rose gulped. I'm terrified of flying.

"Please say you'll come." Shelly leant towards her. "I want you to be my matron of honour, Rose. That's why I came home. For you."

"For me?" Rose's eyes widened and a feeling of trepidation swirled in her stomach. "Is it just for the weekend?"

"The weekend? Of course not! It's a ten day holiday."

"But my job... I don't know if I can get the time off work."

Rose blanched at the look of disappointment in Shelly's eyes. "When exactly are you getting married?" she added hastily.

"The middle of June."

Rose did a quick calculation. "That's three weeks away!"

"Yes. It was all very last minute. I know I haven't given you much notice, but Harry and I… we don't want to wait any longer. You are going to come, aren't you, Rose?"

Images of her and Shelly flashed through Rose's mind. Playing dress-up as children. Experimenting with make-up as teenagers. Laughing at school together. Sharing secret crushes with one another. Of course she would go. Of course she would be there for Shelly. She was her best friend, after all and there was no way she was going to miss out on the happiest day of her life.

"Yes, I'm coming." Rose squashed the nerves and reservations. "Now tell me all about it."

On Monday morning, Rose arrived at work almost thirty minutes early. Fulham Banking was still in darkness as she keyed in the entry code.

"Morning." Ron ambled towards her. "You're keen, lass."

"I need a chat with management." Rose stuffed her bag underneath her desk. "Holiday entitlement."

"Good for you." Ron leaned on the desk. "Betsy and I are going to Cornwall again. St Ives. We love it down there. Where are you off to?"

"Abroad, Ron, for the first time ever."

"You mean you've never flown?"

"Nope." Rose bit her lip. "Is it… have you?"

"Oh yes." Ron pulled the end of his moustache. "We've been to Thailand…" he held up seven digits to denote how many times.

"I'm going to Majorca, which is only a two hour flight, thank goodness."

"Last time we went, the turbulence was dreadful." Ron shook his head.

Rose shuddered at the thought of it, but put on a brave face. "I'm thinking positive."

"You'll have a great time." He leant one arm on the desk. "The management team are already in. Some kind of power meeting. They sent out for a McDonalds breakfast delivery – can you believe that, the lazy buggers!"

Rose took a gulp of water before straightening her skirt. "Well, wish me luck."

"Go tell them!" Ron walked with her to the lift. The doors slid open and Rose gave him a little wave before pressing the button for the fourth floor. It shuddered and bumped upwards and Rose was reminded why she usually took the stairs.

Finally, it groaned to a halt at the top of Fulham Banking and she shot through the opening doors onto the open plan office. She followed a path past the photocopiers, heading in the direction of the noises which were emanating from the kitchen. The acrid smell of coffee hung in the air. Rose hung back to let the cleaning ladies pass. They looked relieved that their shifts were almost over and gave her friendly smiles as they pulled their hoovers and buckets by.

The door to the kitchen suddenly opened and Graham, the senior manager, strode out, nodding at Rose as he passed her. Others began filtering out, boosting up their computers and chattering amongst themselves. The kitchen was now almost empty, apart from Liliana and the accounts manager. They were collecting up empty food wrappers, chuntering as they did so.

"Ah, Rose!" cried Liliana. "Could you give us a hand with the clearing-up?"

"I need to speak to you," replied Rose, eyeing the dirty crockery.

"We'll speak and work," Liliana said cheerfully.

"Okay." Rose picked up a pair of rubber gloves. "I need to put a holiday request in."

Liliana's smile froze. "When for, exactly?"

"For the middle of June. I have the dates written down in my handbag."

Liliana's mouth flapped open. "But that's only a few weeks away. I thought you were going to ask for next year, Rose."

"It's a last minute thing," Rose cleared her throat, trying to sound assertive, "a wedding and I'm matr–"

Liliana held up her hand. "Sorry, it's too short notice. There are six staff off already that month and they booked months ago."

"But it's my best friend's wedding!"

Liliana scowled. "Sorry, Rose. No-can-do."

Rose sighed heavily, her shoulders drooping with resignation. Liliana smiled triumphantly and then tied the black bin liner into a neat knot. "I'll be at my desk. Some of us are rushed off our feet." She left the kitchen, the aroma of her strong perfume wafting in the air.

"Are you just going to accept that?" The accounts manager, Amanda, placed a hand on Rose's shoulder. "Go above her. Go and see Graham."

Rose bit her lip. "He'll side with her."

"Then don't tell him you've spoken to her." Amanda gave her a friendly shove. "Sometimes in life you have to fight for the things that you want. Go on, girl, you can do it."

Rose smiled at Amanda with gratitude. "I'm terrified of flying," she confessed. "If it was anywhere in Britain, I would have been firmer."

"So you're going to let your friend down?"

"No." Rose's tone turned firm. "I'm not going to let her down. How bad can a two-hour flight really be?"

"Exactly." Amanda enveloped her in a quick hug. "Now scoot! And don't take no for an answer!"

She rapped gently on Graham's door. He called her inside and she stood awkwardly in the opening, fiddling with her fingers. Graham's secretary looked up from her notebook and smiled Rose's way.

"He's all yours," she said, sliding her pen behind her ear and rising to her feet.

"What can I do for you, Rose?" Graham asked, when his secretary had closed the door gently behind her.

Rose took a breath and stepped forwards. "I wanted to put in a last minute holiday request." She explained briefly about Shelly's plans and told him the dates.

Graham gazed at her across his table. His hands linked together to make a small steeple. He was one of the longest-standing employees and Rose had always liked him. His manners were impeccable, and he was cheerful and professional.

"I know it's short notice and I wouldn't usually ask, but ..."

"It's fine, Rose." His face creased into the warmest smile. "You're a hard-working employee, one of the best here at Fulham. Of course you can have the time off."

"Oh, thank you!" Rose felt like a huge weight had been lifted from her shoulders.

"We'll muddle through without you." Graham picked up his phone which had started to ring. Rose turned to leave.

"And Rose," he said, "go and have fun!"

nine

Later that evening, Rose was the first to arrive at The White Swan. She perched on a stool at the bar, chatting to Roger and Sue and watching the quiz man set up his apparatus.

"How's your gran?" Sue asked, as she swiped over the drip trays with a damp cloth.

"As mischievous as ever." Rose dug in her bag for her phone. "This was her at Shelly's homecoming party."

Sue and Roger chuckled over the shot. "You would never believe she's in her nineties."

"Ninety-two, to be exact. Still fit and sprightly, apart from a touch of arthritis in her knees and fingers."

"I miss Faith," Sue sighed. "the cleaning staff we have here now aren't a patch on her."

"She worked hard," Roger said, "and she added a touch of fun to the place. Always cheerful, was our Faith."

"And her granddaughter's the same." Rose gazed at Rose. "What you having to drink, love? And don't tell me pop."

Rose shifted on her seat. "Actually, I'm not driving, so what do you recommend?"

Roger passed her a drinks menu. "Here. Try one of these."

"Cocktails?" Rose scanned the list. "I have no idea which one to choose."

"How about starting with something tasty and simple?" Sue ran her forefinger down the list. "Ah yes, a Bellini. Perfect."

Sue ambled to the other end of the bar and rummaged through the various spirit bottles, leaving Rose to fire off a text informing Shelly she was here and not to be late. She swung one leg over the other knee and waited for Sue to add a slice of strawberry to the wine flute.

"Enjoy!" The drink was presented to her with a flourish and a wink.

Rose took a sip; the fizzy wine and strawberry syrup tingled on her tongue. "This is delicious." She nodded her approval.

"And you'll be having lots more of those." A voice from behind startled her. It was Shelly, looking seriously glamorous in a little black lacy number.

"You're on time!" Rose slipped off the stool and hugged her friend.

"And you're early for a change." Shelly slapped her clutch bag on the bar. "I'll have whatever Rose is drinking."

Sue nodded. "You're looking good, Shelly... and very posh for a quiz night."

"I forgot my jeans," Shelly said with an eye roll. "Luckily for me, England seems to be in a heatwave."

"We'll be acclimatised for Majorca." Rose grinned. "I've managed to get the time off work."

"Fantastic!" Shelly squealed. "Another one I can tick off my list."

They picked up their drinks and went to look for a table. Rose went to place her bag down on a two-seater but was stopped by an excited Shelly.

"The boys are coming," she disclosed.

Rose swallowed. "All three?"

"Yes." Shelly shook her glorious mane of hair. "Harry, Fin and

Tom, of course. They're looking forward to their very first British pub quiz."

"I would have made more of an effort..." Rose trailed off, embarrassed that she had voiced her inner thoughts.

"What do you mean?" Shelly appraised her. "You look as lovely as usual."

"I do?" Rose looked down at her faded jeans with disbelief.

"In fact," Shelly touched Rose's hair, "you could look even lovelier, you know."

"I like the way I look," Rose protested.

"Of course you do." Shelly flashed her a warm smile. "You were never vain, even when we were self-absorbed teenagers."

They reclined back in their seats and watched a large group enter the pub.

"I, on the other hand, have always been vain. I'm going for a makeover," Shelly announced, "ready for my wedding. Hair, fake tan, nails. I want to be perfect for Majorca."

"You're beautiful already," Rose said firmly.

"And you could be stunning." Shelly opened the internet browser on her phone. "This is where I'm going to book."

Rose glanced blankly at the image on the screen. "I have no idea where or what that is."

"It's Candleswick House." Shelly nudged her friend.

"A stately home?" Rose grabbed the phone. "I love historical places. Do you think they might have one of those archaic libraries full of first editions?"

Shelly slid a glance at her. "Er... maybe? I thought we could go together. A spot of pre-wedding pampering and there's a great shopping mall nearby."

She told Rose the finer details; where it was located and when exactly she wanted to go.

"Also," Shelly fluttered her long lashes, "we need to get our dresses."

"You mean you haven't got your wedding dress yet?" Rose coughed in surprise.

"Nope. Nor the bridesmaid dresses, obviously."

"Shelly," Rose began slowly, "exactly how many bridesmaids are you having?"

"Just the two of you." Shelly sighed. "I think Marian was a bit miffed that she's not matron of honour, so I made up this emotional spiel about her being the best sister ever, and that she could organise the hen night – or should I say hen week." She chuckled and stretched out her left hand. "I've been practising my signature. It's going to be so cool being a Sinclair."

Rose took a large gulp of her drink. "You're certainly laid back about the whole affair. Aren't brides-to-be supposed to be stress-heads?"

"This is why I'm getting married abroad. No stress. Just sun, sea, sand and cocktails. No moaning families to fret about. No awkward seating plans to organise. Just fun and relaxation. It's going to be awesome – don't you agree?"

"I suppose so." Rose was suddenly overwhelmed by fear. Fear of flying and being away from home. Fear of the unknown.

Shelly squinted at her. "Look, hun. I know it's not the kind of wedding you'd organise. But trust me, we're going to have a blast."

Rose nodded fervently to show her loyalty. "It's your choice, Shelly and whatever you organise, I'll fully support."

"Thank you." Shelly's face softened. "You been to the church?"

"Yes, I go regularly and I'm in the folk choir now..." She stopped as the door swung open and Harry, Fin and Tom entered. Tom noticed them first and held up his hand in a salute. Rose waved and flashed him a smile as her stomach began flipping with excitement and attraction. That was the word Rose was searching for. Tom Sinclair was the handsomest man Rose had ever encountered and it seemed that all of the other females in the pub had noticed that, too. Sue the landlady rushed to serve him, shoving Roger out of the way in the process.

"Harry!" Shelly whooped with excitement, sprung from her

chair and elevated herself into her husband-to-be's arms. Rose watched with a smile as they kissed, oblivious to the stares they were attracting.

"Hi, Rose." Fin squatted down on a stool next to her. "Want to kiss me?"

Rose grinned. "You joker! I hardly know you."

"Well," he drawled, leaning closer, "while we're on holiday, we can get to know each other a whole lot better. Whadd'ya reckon?"

Rose felt her cheeks flame with embarrassment, but was saved from answering by Tom enquiring what she wanted to drink.

"Try a different cocktail," Shelly urged. "I'll order and surprise you." She sashayed off to the bar, following her husband-to-be and an annoyed-looking Tom.

Rose cleared her throat and smiled at Fin. "How's your day gone?"

He pushed a section of golden hair that had flopped into his eyes away and flashed her a brilliant white smile. "We went go-kart racing. Bought us some suits for the wedding... that didn't take long, though. What have you been up to?"

Rose fidgeted in her seat. "Just working. My boss gave me the time off for the wedding."

"That's good," Fin drawled, "'cos without you there, I don't think Shelly would be going through with this wedding."

"Oh, really?" Rose glanced at her friend, whose limbs were still wrapped around Harry. "It's been years since I saw Shelly. I thought she'd forgotten me, to be honest."

"Are you kidding me?" Fin flipped his stool back on two legs. "She's been talking about you for months. Telling everyone in Australia she wants to come back home and see you. When Harry proposed, we were all anticipating a beach wedding in Oz. Thought they'd settle down there, have a couple of sprogs. Live happily ever after."

"Why Majorca?" Rose asked. "Australia must be beautiful. Why travel around the world to get married on a little Mediterranean island?"

"Because my sister is mad, that's why." A voice from behind startled Rose and she whipped round to face Marian. "Make that three cocktails!" Marian shouted in the direction of the bar and then slumped down next to Fin. She began complaining about a rude attendant in the petrol station and the lack of chocolate variety attainable in the supermarkets here.

"They don't sell Toblerone!" Her voice was indignant. "Apparently it's a seasonal confectionary, along with After Eights and Matchmakers. In London, you can get them all year round. How do you cope?" She stared at Rose with bewilderment.

Rose shrugged. "It's never bothered me."

"Course it hasn't." Fin hooked an arm across Rose's shoulders. "Rose has better things to do with her life than worry about the choice in chocolate."

Marian pursed her lips at Fin. "It's the little things that make life bearable. Luckily for me, I no longer live here."

"I think Twineham's kind of quaint," Fin grinned, "a proper English country village."

"I love it here," Rose replied, with a smile. Marian snorted her disagreement.

"Here you go." Shelly set down a tray of drinks. "So Harry's bought crisps, nuts and scratchings, help yourself."

Rose stared at the selection of snacks in front of her. Opting for a bag of plain crisps, she prised open the packet and offered them round. Fin dug his hand in, but everyone else politely declined.

"Hmm, this is heavenly." Marian sucked the cocktail through a straw.

"What is it?" Rose eyed the green cloudy drink dubiously.

"It's called a Margarita. Try it," urged Shelly.

Rose leant forward and took a tentative sip. After a moment, she smiled. "It tastes like pop."

"Nice, isn't it?" Shelly settled herself on Harry's lap, leaving the only vacant stool next to Rose. Tom hovered for a second with his pint of ale and then sank down with a quiet "Hi."

"When I worked in Majorca, I made hundreds of these." Shelly motioned to her drink. "They're really popular over there."

Marian began questioning her sister about the wedding preparations and Rose felt her attention wandering. She was acutely aware of Tom's thigh resting lightly against hers and instinctively turned to face him.

"Have you had a nice day?"

He wiped a blob of froth off his top lip. "Great, thanks."

Rose waited for him to elaborate, but as he remained silent, she began gabbling about her day at work.

"What do you do?" he asked, when she paused for a breath.

"I'm a receptionist, at a financial call centre. Fulham Banking. Have you heard of it?"

Tom looked blank. Of course he hasn't heard of it, her thoughts taunted, he's not even British.

"It's extremely boring," she carried on, "but it pays the bills, I suppose."

"Why do you do it then?" He regarded her with his unusual eyes. Rose had never seen eyes so dark green before.

"Do you wear contacts?" she blurted out.

"Nope," he replied, looking faintly amused, "they're all natural."

"Oh." Rose looked down at her lap. What had he asked her? she wondered.

"You were going to tell me why you work at a job you hate?" he reminded her.

"Hate's a bit of a strong word," she explained. "Dull would be more fitting."

"Then why do it?" He took another sip of his ale. "What did you want to do at school?"

Rose looked up and was immediately ensnared by his strangely hypnotic eyes. "I wanted to work with animals," she swallowed, "at a vet's or a zoo."

"Then why didn't you?"

"Because I ..." she tried again, "I guess I took the safe option.

Fulham Banking came to our school. Gave this inspirational speech about their firm and all the positives about working there. I needed the money and I thought, why not...?" Rose trailed off, suddenly aware that everybody else had stopped talking and was listening to her.

"And if I'd have been here, I would have stopped you." Shelly gave her a hard look. "You gave up on your dream, Rose."

"That's all it was – a dream." Rose emitted a high-pitched laugh. "I'm earning good money. My job is... secure and I'm... happy."

Shelly pursed her lips and shot her a look of disbelief, but was then distracted by Fin, enquiring if she would like another cocktail.

"What do you do?" Rose looked at Tom, eager to take the spotlight off herself.

He opened his mouth and then closed it again. Looked away and fiddled with his cap.

"Tom's an electrician," Harry said firmly, "and a damn good one."

"That's fab." Rose gave him an encouraging smile.

Tom wedged his baseball cap onto his head and stared moodily down at the table. Rose waited for him to elaborate on his career, but when there was no information forthcoming she edged slightly away and smiled brightly at Marian.

"How is life in London?"

"Manic," snapped Marian, "non-stop work, work, work." She flicked her hair back. "I'm a manager at last and proud to say I am living the dream."

"But what about personally, sis?" Shelly fiddled with her hair clip. "Is there a Mister Marian we should know about?"

"No and that's just the way I like it." Marian stood up abruptly. "Where's the ladies?"

Rose pointed in the direction of the lavatories. When she had gone, Shelly rolled her eyes. "She never changes. Still as uptight as ever."

"It's kinda hard to believe you're sisters," Harry said and Rose had to agree with him. She remembered Marian as a person who had always been serious and ambitious, even as a teenager. Shelly in comparison was the opposite; fun-loving, with a great sense of humour and an excitable, laid back nature.

"This holiday will do her the world of good, we are going to have such a good time. My dear sister will have no choice but to go wild and enjoy herself." Shelly lifted her glass. "Here's to cocktails, wedding bells and summer madness."

The liquid sloshed out of her glass as she chinked it against the others. Rose felt a surge of nerves well up inside her. It was too late now, there was no going back. This holiday was happening whether she liked it or not. She felt compelled to add her own hopes for the holiday. "Here's to friendship and relaxation." Underneath the table, her fingers crossed in a 'please let it be okay' plea.

ten

"First stop is the hairdresser's." Shelly was perched on Rose's bed, painting her toenails a romantic pink hue.

Rose regarded her friend over the top of her latest chick-lit novel. "What were you planning?"

"For me, a cut and highlights," Shelly grinned, "and for you, I thought a complete colour change would be good."

"Hang on a minute!" Rose inserted a bookmark and closed her novel. "My hair's always been this colour and I happen to like it."

"Really!" Shelly's tone was derisory. "You always told me you hated your hair."

"It's naturally curly," Rose pulled out a ringlet, "there's not much I can do with it. I tried straightening it once, remember? It was a disaster."

"I'm not criticising your glorious curls. I meant the colour and the length. You really could do with a good cut, honey, I mean it just hangs there, looking like it always has. There's a great hairdresser at the spa. The head stylist is award-winning, apparently. Let him take a look."

There was a knock on the door, then Fran stuck her head round. "I brought you food and beverages." She laid a tray of sandwiches and squash down on Rose's dressing table. "You girls okay?"

"We're great, thanks, Mrs Archer."

"Call me Fran," came the reply. "Mrs Archer makes me sound like a geriatric."

"Fran," Shelly bounced off the bed, "what do you think about Rose having a hair transformation? I'm thinking a completely new colour, a trendy cut. It's about time she had a change. Don't you agree?"

Fran placed her hands on her hips and surveyed her head-shaking daughter.

"Yes. I think that would be a great idea. Her gran and I have been nagging her for years to get a change. Go for it, Rose."

"Have I any choice in the matter?" Rose grumbled.

"Nope." Shelly flashed her a happy smile. "You are going to be absolutely gorgeous when I've finished with you. What do you think of these dresses, Mrs... er, Fran?" She slapped a glossy magazine down and Rose escaped to the bathroom while they ummed and ahhed over bridal gowns. When she returned, her mum and best friend were reminiscing.

"Remember that time when we made rock cakes in your kitchen and almost set fire to the whole house?"

"How could I forget?" Fran tutted. "The neighbour called the fire brigade after seeing clouds of smoke in the garden and you pair were upstairs, playing with my make-up."

Shelly threw back her head and laughed. "I was grounded for weeks because of that."

Rose sat gingerly on the bed. "I've never cooked a rock cake since," she said, with a smile.

Fran folded her arms across her chest. "I saw Jeremy Payne at the supermarket yesterday. He was as sycophantic as usual." She put on a posh accent. "Mrs Archer, how wonderful to see you! And I must say you're looking beautiful today."

"He said that?" Rose queried.

"Oh Rose, stop being so kind. You've had a lucky escape there. Jeremy Payne is a prize creep!"

Shelly glanced from Rose to her mother. "And who is this guy? An old boyfriend, Rose?"

"No!" Rose cast a furtive glance at the photograph of her and Jeremy with their arms round each other after the Christmas folk concert. "He's just a friend."

"Is this him?" Shelly padded across the floor and picked up the frame. "Nice tank top."

Rose followed her, taking the photograph off her friend and placing it face down in her sock drawer. "There, he's gone."

"Good." Fran nodded her approval. "Well, I'll let you girls carry on with your evening." She turned and walked towards the door, "Oh Rose, your friend who you go to the knit and natter club with rang earlier when you were in the shower. Just to remind you that they're starting an hour earlier tomorrow night." Fran paused. "Maybe you could take Shelly?"

"A knit and natter club?" Shelly's mouth twitched with suppressed mirth. "That's one I've never been to. Count me in, honey."

Rose picked up Betsy after tea on Tuesday evening. Shelly stared curiously at her from the back of the car and waited for Rose to introduce them. Today, Betsy was wearing a multi-coloured bobble hat – an item which she had started last week at the knitting class.

"You've finished it!" Rose commented.

"Do you like it?" Betsy pulled down her mirror and inspected her reflection. "Ron called it psychedelic."

"It's very colourful," Rose said kindly, "and it looks warm. Perfect for the winter."

"Er... isn't it almost summer?" Shelly voiced from the back.

Betsy's head snapped round. "I feel the cold, and I suffer from migraines. I'm hoping this will keep my head warm all year round."

Rose glanced in her mirror and winced at the look of incredulity on Shelly's face. She clicked on the radio and the three of them sang along to Queen's Bohemian Rhapsody as they headed towards the community centre.

"Did I tell you about the karaoke bars in Majorca, Rose?" Shelly's face broke into an enormous grin. "The bar I worked in used to have them. Hordes of drunken tourists screeching their way through Madonna and Whitney Houston. And when we closed, the staff would have a lock-in and carry on until the early hours."

"Did you ever sleep?" Rose asked. She could just picture Shelly up on stage with a microphone and the mental image made her smile.

Shelly chuckled. "Yes, usually until lunchtime and then I'd spend the afternoons on the beach, topping up my tan. Oh, I loved it there." She emitted a sigh and pressed a button to open her window. Fresh air wafted into the car, ruffling Rose's hair.

"And whereabouts in Majorca did you stay?" Betsy asked, as she opened a bag of mints and passed them round.

"Sa Coma. A beautiful resort."

Betsy nodded. "Ron and I have been to Alcúdia. That was lovely. The beach there is amazing."

"It's an amazing island." Shelly nodded with enthusiasm. "So much to see and do. We're going to have so much fun." She leant forward to pat Rose's shoulder.

Rose cleared her throat and pulled onto the community centre car park. "Here we are, don't forget your knitting needles now."

"I haven't got any," Shelly protested from the back. "Am I going to get kicked out of knit and natter for not having the correct utensils?"

"Of course not!" Rose laughed. "I'm sure they'll have a spare pair. Come on, we're late."

"Is this your idea of fun?" whispered Shelly twenty minutes later. "Who knew that knitting was so complicated!"

"You're not holding them right. Here," Rose gave her a demonstration, "it's not a competition, Shelly. Just relax."

Shelly looked around at the frantically clacking needles. "Everyone else is so good. What are you making, by the way?"

"A scarf for the homeless centre." She looked at Shelly's creation with raised eyebrows. "What is that?"

"A hankie?" Shelly shrugged.

"A woollen hankie with holes in?" Rose chuckled. "So maybe knitting isn't your greatest skill at the moment, but I'm sure with time and practise you'll be good."

Shelly grimaced as Rose's laughter escalated. "Cut it, Archer, I can't be good at everything."

Mrs Edwards, who organised and ran the class, paused beside them. "Oh dear," she said, peering down at their handiwork, "well, it's all about taking part, I suppose."

Betsy had gone to get them drinks and was now returning with a tray of tea. "Here we go, girls." They took the proffered cups, sipping at the milky drink.

"So," Shelly winced as the drink burnt her bottom lip, "as well as this knitting group, what else do you get up to, Archer?"

"Folk choir on a Monday. Book club on a Thursday." Rose thought for a moment. "Oh and I go swimming two evenings as well."

"Your social life is full, so why are you still single? And don't tell me you never get a chance to meet any men, either. I bet that swimming complex is full of them – posing in their miniscule shorts."

Betsy raised an eyebrow but carried on silently working on her babies' cardigan.

"Maybe I haven't met the right person," Rose replied, clacking her needles with more vigour. "Plus, I'm happy as I am. My life is great, Shelly. Not every woman needs a man to fulfil themselves. There are other ways to gain, er... satisfaction."

Shelly guffawed with laughter. "Tell me more!"

Rose slid her a withering look. "I mean, through a career, for example."

"You hate your job," Shelly pointed out. "So what else satisfies you?"

"Erm... oh, don't pressure me," Rose snapped, feeling defensive. "So maybe I'm not living the dream. We can't all be like you, Shelly, and some of us don't want to be ..." She trailed off. "Sorry, that sounded mean. Of course I'm happy you're living this amazing life in Australia and have met the perfect man. Truly I am."

Shelly's hands stopped moving. "I know you are," she said softly, "but it wasn't always like that for me. It's been tough being on my own all these years. But I can happily say I am completely, extremely happy. All that positive bullshit – yep, that's me." She gazed at Rose. "And now it's your turn, honey."

"What do you mean?" Rose looked up from her knitting.

"I'm here to help, Rose. You're my next project. I'm your Fairy Godmother and I'm going to transform your life."

On Friday evening, after another dull day at work, Rose packed a weekender bag and bade goodbye to her family.

"Have fun now," Fran said, as she gently kissed her daughter's soft cheek.

"I can't believe you're actually going to a spa." Granny Faith watched Rose climb into her car. "What will you do without your books?"

"I've got one," Rose patted her bag, "and I intend finishing it."

"Well, goodbye then, love." Fran slipped an arm around Faith's hunched-over shoulder and waved with the other one. Rose watched them disappear in the rear view mirror and then pressed her foot on the accelerator to pick up Shelly.

Shelly bounced into the car full of joy and happiness. She smelt of wild flowers and the freshness of youth.

"We've been wedding ring shopping," she disclosed, as she clicked her seatbelt into place. "It all feels so real now."

Rose concentrated on the road in front of her. There was a long line of traffic building up on the motorway junction and a neon sign warning of long delays.

"Do you have directions to this place?" she asked.

"Even better," Shelly waved her phone, "I have the postcode, and this has a built-in sat-nav."

"Then let's get outta here and follow the 'B' roads." Rose indicated right then executed a perfect U-turn.

The countryside passed by in a blur; hedgerows and trees, wild flowers swaying in the breeze. Rose followed the twisty roads, humming along to the radio.

With the windows open, the smell of the bracing air filled the vehicle.

"So what's your wedding ring like?"

"Just a plain eighteen carat gold band," Shelly replied. "Wedding rings are pretty standard, aren't they?"

"Yes," Rose confirmed with a nod, "and who is going to be Harry's best man?"

Shelly propped her feet up on the dashboard. "He's eventually asked Tom. It's taken him ages to decide. He was worried he was going to offend the other one, but I definitely think he's made the right decision. Tom is very capable and Fin... well, he's not the most reliable of people," she bit her lip, "but he's going to be an usher, so he won't be left out."

"I'm sure everything will be fine." Rose slowed down to manoeuvre her car round a hairpin bend. "Guys don't seem to make such a fuss at weddings, do they?"

"Not my Sinclair brothers. Harry is so laid back, he's almost horizontal. Fin is preoccupied with having fun and Tom has always been the solitary, doesn't like a fuss one. This wedding has been pretty much left up to me to organise and that is just the way I like it."

A flash of white darted across the road and Rose slammed on the brakes. The car screeched to a halt. "It's just a rabbit," she said breathlessly. The wild creature paused to observe them for a second before hopping away into the undergrowth.

"Actually, is it okay if I stretch my legs? I'm feeling a bit sick. Must be the bendy roads." Shelly pointed to a ditch off the road and Rose slowly pulled over.

"Are you okay?" she asked, noting Shelly's pale countenance. "Here, have some water." She passed over the bottle for Shelly to take a long swig out of.

"That's better." Shelly wiped her mouth. "Now, according to my phone Candleswick House is close by."

"You're not going to be sick in my car?" Rose was rummaging around for spare bags. Shelly still looked queasy.

"It's passing." Shelly's feet crunched over the gravel. "I'll keep my window down."

"And I'll take it slowly." Rose restarted the engine and switched the cool air vents on.

They cruised slowly along the country lane. "This is spooky," Rose commented, peering up at the overhead trees which blocked out the sunlight.

"It's beautiful," Shelly sighed. "I missed the English countryside."

"You're not pining for Australia yet then?"

"A little." Hair flopped across Shelly's eyes. "I have a lot of friends there, a great job, an adorable dog. You would love it, Rose. Australia is…"

"Very far away," Rose interjected, "and a hell of a long plane flight."

"I was going to say amazing," Shelly shook her head, "and the flight is the start of the fun."

Rose slid her a look of disbelief. "Grandad always said that the sky was for the birds only."

Shelly chuckled. "That must be where you get your phobia from. I read somewhere that flying is the safest method of transport. Don't worry, honey, the journey to Majorca will be over real quick and you might even enjoy it."

Rose felt a knot of fear harden in her stomach. "I'll reserve judgement on that one. Where is the turning?" She shifted in her seat.

"There!" Shelly pointed to a break in the trees, giving Rose no chance to flick on her indicator. Luckily, there were no cars behind, or in front, or anywhere near for that matter. She swung her car left, bumping up over a dirt track onto a road which cut through an expanse of luscious green field. "Wow, this really is an away-from-it-all retreat."

"Fabulous, isn't it?" Shelly craned her neck. "But where's the house?"

"I presume we just carry on." Rose pressed the accelerator, stirring embedded dirt and pebbles. Soon, they reached a fork in the road and a sign half covered in trailing ivy that read Candleswick House.

"This sounds like something from a Dickens novel," Rose said with excitement. They began an ascent, the car juddering over potholes. Then, at the brow of the hill, in the distance they could make out a large, white-fronted building surrounded by paddocks and fences.

"Oh my, they have horses!" Shelly was beaming with delight.

Gah, thought Rose, another thing I'm scared of.

Rose followed the drive round in a horseshoe shape and reversed into a parking space.

"We're here," she said simply, gazing up at the towering, archaic-looking house where birds nestled in the eaves and a welcome sign flapped gently in the breeze.

"C'mon," Shelly took hold of her hand, "relax and unwind, Rosie. That's what this girly weekend is all about."

eleven

"Hello and welcome." The smart-looking receptionist flicked back her hair and smiled brightly at them across the desk. "You're on the second floor – room twenty-one. Would you like some help with your bags?"

"We'll be fine," Rose said, hoisting the strap of her holdall onto her shoulder and taking the proffered swipe key. "Thank you."

"So once you've settled in, feel free to have a look around and book any treatments you want. The pool is open until ten p.m., you can collect fresh towels to use if required. A list of all the facilities is on here." She thrust a laminated card at them. The phone behind the desk rang shrilly and the receptionist turned away, giving it her full attention.

They crossed the marble foyer and up a flight of winding stairs, pausing midway to appreciate a sparkling ceiling chandelier.

"Good morning." A lady with shining eyes and a high ponytail nodded their way politely.

"Morning," Shelly and Rose said in unison, passing her by.

"This is posh," Rose whispered. "I'm paying half towards it."

"No, you're not," Shelly's tone was firm, "this is my present to you for being my matron of honour."

"But I haven't done anything!" Rose protested. "You've already organised it all."

"Then you can just look pretty on the beach and enjoy yourself. Yes?"

"I'm happy with that." Rose grinned. "Here's us." She fumbled with the key card, waiting for the flashing light to turn green and the door to swing open.

"Oh, how lovely!" cooed Shelly as they walked into a room of pink and cream. Sunlight blazed through the open windows, highlighting two beds decorated with swan towels and rose petals.

"I feel like I'm on honeymoon." Rose turned in a circle, taking in the huge wall T.V. and the pretty bedroom furniture.

"Look at that view." Shelly was peering out of the window. Rose put her bag down and went to join her. Their room overlooked a huge garden which was ablaze with summer flowers and striking marble statues. There was a maze in the middle and a fountain that gushed a steady stream of water. Beyond that lay a forest and, in the far distance, high hills complete with grazing sheep.

"It's beautiful." Rose inhaled deeply, taking in a lungful of fresh, bracing countryside air.

"We have a mini bar." Shelly had spotted the fridge and was peering inside. "No cocktails but plenty of wine."

"And a snack selection." Rose nodded at the assorted crisps and nuts.

"So I thought we could hit the gym, go for a swim, have lunch and then have a pamper afternoon."

"Sounds like a good plan." Rose bit her lip. "I've never been to a gym before."

"What about the leisure centre you're a member of? Surely they have a gym there!"

"They do," Rose shrugged, "I've just always stuck to the swimming."

"Well, today you're going to get sweaty." Shelly pulled the zip on her bag open. "Let's do this."

"Is this your idea of fun?" A breathless Rose was on a stationary bike, climbing a vertiginous mountain in the snow-capped Andes or some other mountainous region of the world.

"Hell, yeah!" Shelly was hunched upright, pedalling fast, her face slick with sweat. "Beats knit and natter, eh?"

At this very moment, Rose vehemently disagreed. Thankfully, her screen was flashing three minutes remaining.

"Come on," urged Shelly, "put some effort in. You're hardly sweating."

Rose increased her speed; her forehead was growing clammier by the second. "My palms are sweating," she retaliated.

"You need a whole body workout." Shelly jumped off the bike energetically. "That'll do for a warm-up."

"We've been on here twenty minutes," protested Rose. "Can't we go for a swim?"

"Nope." Shelly pointed at a row of scary-looking machines. "Now we do ten minutes on them."

Rose stopped pedalling and, with shaky legs, clambered ungainly from the bike. Her thighs were sore and her buttocks were throbbing.

"These are called cross-trainers, they're great for a cardio workout." Shelly hauled her across the gym floor, passing two ladies balancing on exercise balls. Rose stepped onto the machine, letting Shelly lean across and mess with her programme pad.

"I think you could start on level five. There, away you go." Rose moved her feet and wobbled for a second, before grasping hold of the arm handles.

"Do you go to the gym much?" she asked Shelly, who was pedalling furiously next to her.

"Every lunch break," Shelly announced, "but I have the week-ends off. We usually go to the beach."

"All three of you?" gasped Rose.

"Fin's usually there with his surfing mates."

"What about Tom?" Rose said it as lightly as she could muster under the duress of an intense aerobic workout.

Shelly frowned, "Tom's usually busy... erm... working."

"Harry said he's an electrician?"

Shelly coughed. "Er... yes. So, bridesmaid dresses. What colour do you prefer?"

"I don't mind," Rose replied, longing to quiz her friend about the enigmatic Tom. "Blue would go with the sea, I suppose."

"I was thinking of putting you in orange frills to go with the sun," Shelly countered, with a grin.

"Can you imagine Marian?" Rose snorted with laughter. "Has she gone back to London?"

"Yes and left me a to-do list as long as my arm. Anybody would think it's her wedding."

"It must be nice to see her again after all these years?"

"I suppose so." Shelly mopped at her brow with a tissue. "She's just so bossy. Always has to be in charge."

"Maybe it's a work thing," Rose said sympathetically. "I'm sure when we're in Majorca she'll relax."

"And you're relaxing too much," Shelly berated her. "Move that ass, Archer."

And surprisingly, Rose did just that.

"Did you enjoy that?" They were in the changing rooms, struggling into their bathing costumes.

"It wasn't too bad." Rose emitted a happy sigh, secretly glad that the gym session was all over. "Now you get to do something which I love."

They walked past the shower cubicles and a cleaning lady who was swiping the disabled toilet with an antiseptic-smeared mop.

"You were always brilliant at swimming." Shelly spat her gum into a bin. "I swear you could have represented Great Britain in the Olympics."

Rose shook her head. "I doubt it. Remember all the eye infections and verrucas I suffered with? Not to mention the thousands of other faster, better swimmers than me. No, swimming is just a very nice hobby."

Shelly wrinkled her nose. "Mum showed me her feet when I went to visit the other day. Riddled with bunions and yeast-infected toe-nails."

"Are they looking after her?" Rose dipped her nail-varnished toes into a lukewarm pool.

"As well as can be expected, considering she hates everyone in the care home," Shelly said with weariness. "She kept calling me Aunt Teresa, asking me repeatedly to bake her a fruitcake for Christmas."

Rose touched her friend's shoulder consolingly. "Your mum is a lovely lady, I'm sorry she's not well."

"Thank you," Shelly sniffed. "At least I don't have to contend with a wedding and an interfering mother, eh?" With that, she pushed an unsuspecting Rose straight into the deep end.

Rose swam for half an hour, head tucked down, goggles strapped tightly on, powering through the water in the fast lane. After a combination of front crawl and backstroke, she stopped, pulling herself out of the water to sit on the side of the pool, taking deep lungfuls of air and squeezing the excess water out of her sodden hair. She watched Shelly performing a dainty breaststroke up the length of the slow lane and waved when she'd reached the end. Shelly beckoned her back in.

"We're the only ones in," she said, when Rose was treading water next to her.

"Great, isn't it? Where I go swimming, we fight to stay in the lanes, and there's always rowdy teenagers in, taking up the space." Rose lifted an elegant pointed leg out of the water. "This is heavenly."

"Wait till you see the Mediterranean." Shelly rubbed the water out of her eyes. "You will think you're in heaven."

Rose looked around; they were alone apart from a bored-looking lifeguard. "Fancy a dip in the jacuzzi?"

"I thought you'd never ask." Shelly dived under, kicking back her legs so vigorously that it created a wave and a froth of water that smacked Rose full in the face.

"Race you!" Shelly called as she flailed her arms forward.

Rose laughed, pulled her goggles back on and slid effortlessly into the water, propelling her lithe body underneath Shelly's and tweaking her on the waist as she passed. She waited at the top of the steps for Shelly to drag herself breathlessly out.

"I let you win that one," Shelly said with a smirk. "Now, let's go relax before we indulge in a well-deserved lunch."

Relaxation included a stint in the jacuzzi and steam room. Rose lay on the lower bench inhaling the eucalyptus oil which had been liberally dispersed.

"This is so nice." Shelly sighed with happiness. "Wasn't this a great idea?"

"Yes, but won't Harry be missing you?"

"Are you kidding? They've gone to Alton Towers." Shelly rolled onto her front, swinging her lower legs in the air. "Fin's idea. Last time I heard from him, they'd been on all the new roller-coasters and were doing a second circuit."

Rose shuddered at the thought of being flung about high in the air. "So Harry and Tom are adrenaline junkies, too?"

"Not really," Shelly said, with a dreamy sigh, "Harry just goes along with it. He's brave though, Rose, real brave. He did a bungee jump for children with cancer, ran a half marathon for people with Alzheimer's. Did I tell you that he rescued a neighbour from a burning house?"

"He sounds perfect." Rose inhaled deeply, longing to quiz her about Tom.

"He is," Shelly replied, but then frowned. "I mean, for a guy. He still drives me mad – leaves his pants all over the floor, never puts the toilet seat down and by God, he snores."

Rose started to laugh. "I'm sure you'll sort him out."

"It's a work in progress," Shelly admitted, just as her stomach let out an almighty growl.

"Come on." Rose staggered to her feet. "Let's get a shower and go grab some lunch."

Lunch consisted of a three course à la carte experience which began with a glass of champagne followed by finely cut slivers of salmon, cream cheese and chives. As they tucked into their food, Rose looked around the restaurant. It was a cosy room but the small space had been utilised well. There were a dozen or so tables spread out, the white tablecloths matching the walls and ceiling. Dotted around the room were pleasant paintings of flowers and landscapes. The wall nearest to them held a magnificent shot of the Eiffel Tower, next to numerous company accolades in gold-edged frames.

"Granny Faith would love it here," Rose ruminated, "she's been trying to get me to one of these places for years."

"Aren't you enjoying it?" Shelly asked, leaning across to take a wedge of bread out of the complimentary basket.

"Surprisingly, I am," Rose replied. "You know I was never really into hair and beauty, though."

"You always preferred living inside a book, that's why." Shelly gravitated her eyes into a roll. "It's time to start living in the real world, Rosie." She pointed her bread at Rose. "Tell me the truth, how many boyfriends have you really had?"

Rose swallowed and shifted on her seat. "No one serious." She winced at the look of incredulity on her friend's face. "I mean I've been on dates, of course... but they didn't progress into relationships."

Shelly leaned closer and lowered her voice. "You mean you've never... have you even kissed a guy?"

"Of course I have!" Rose peered around the restaurant, making sure the other guests and staff were out of ear shot. "It's not that I haven't wanted to have... it's just that the right opportunity has never arisen. It should be with someone special, someone you care for, someone you love... Don't you agree?"

Shelly's lips slid upwards into a naughty smile. "Oh, I don't know. There's something liberating about one night stands and don't judge me, Archer, this is the twenty-first century we're living in and women can act just as wantonly as men."

Rose ducked her head down. "Of course I wouldn't judge you. It's your life, Shelly and you're an adult..."

"Rose, stop." Gently, Shelly patted her hand. "I was also going to add that it is different when you meet that special someone. Sex can be magical, mind-blowing even."

"It is?" Rose's mouth hung open.

Slowly, Shelly nodded. "You are so sweet and naïve. So lovely and kind. Not all men are after one thing. What are you afraid of?"

"Just another phobia to add to the list," Rose said brightly.

"What, men?" Shelly chuckled.

"Not men per se." Rose gesticulated with her hands, trying to find the words to explain how she felt. "I like men. I guess I'm just scared of relationships, commitment, that sort of thing."

"You're scared of intimacy," Shelly said knowingly. "You're terrified of falling in love and letting your guard down and committing yourself to someone. Am I right?"

Without making a sound, Rose nodded.

"Well, that's going to change." Shelly's face erupted into a grin that stretched from ear to ear. "I'm going to show you how wonderful love can be."

"In ten days?" Rose said doubtfully.

"Yes." Shelly's tone was determined. "I will bet my last dollar that you will return from Majorca a changed woman."

She thrust her hand at Rose, who gingerly took it. "I think you'll lose the bet, Shelly, but I'm game to play along."

"Bring it on." Shelly thumped the table. "Bring it on!"

twelve

The afternoon consisted of a journey to the beautician's. Two smiling attendants, Julie and Jane, wrapped them in a sea salt scrub followed by performing a full body massage. Rose tried hard to stifle her laughter as they rubbed at her feet. She lay on her stomach and watched the clock ticking round as they pummelled her back and thighs.

"What does this do, exactly?" she whispered to Shelly, who had her eyes closed and a look of immense pleasure on her face.

"What?" Shelly opened one eye.

Fresh-faced Julie answered for her. "The scrub opens your pores and draws out any deep-down impurities, leaving your skin super clean and radiant."

Jane squirted a blob of translucent oil into the palm of her hand. "And the massage relaxes all your muscles and improves circulation and skin tone, creating a feeling of serenity and wellbeing."

"I'm that relaxed, I could fall into a deep sleep," Shelly said, with a contented smile.

Rose, being super ticklish, felt tense in comparison. Her body was acutely aware of Jane's feather- light fingers and was covered in goose bumps.

"Are you cold?" Jane asked, stepping away to check the wall thermostat.

"No," Rose said with embarrassment, "just super-sensitive."

"You're missing a man's touch," Shelly teased.

"I'm missing my clothes," Rose said through gritted teeth as Jane's expert fingers carried on their torment. "Oh, please don't touch my neck, that's the worst part."

Jane's hands fluttered back to her feet. "And my feet are really, really ticklish." Rose let out a sudden burst of laughter.

"It's okay," Jane said, with crisp professionalism, "I know how to handle this." In one movement, she had both of Rose's arms back in the air and pulled tightly. There was a resounding crack, which had Rose yelping with surprise. Shelly's face was pressed down onto the bed, her shoulders shaking with mirth.

"You think Granny Faith would enjoy this?" she managed to ask, in between the laughter.

"Probably." Rose winced as Jane began karate-chopping her back. "She's always been a bit of a masochist."

Then, to her horror, Rose developed a bout of loud hiccups. "I need to sit up," she said, scrabbling to her knees and swaying precariously on the padded bed.

"Would you like some water?" asked Jane, who was shaking her head with disapproval.

"Yes, please." Rose clamped one hand over her quivering mouth.

"You are so embarrassing, Archer," Shelly said, turning over to reveal an erect nipple. "Maybe we should stop?"

"Yes please," Rose said gratefully, taking a long sip of water. "Can we go and relax in our room now?"

"Not so fast," Shelly replied. "We're having a manicure and pedicure first."

Yikes, thought Rose, more bodily torture.

She shrugged on her dressing gown and waited for Shelly to join her in the adjoining room; an L-shaped structure with rows of bottles of nail varnish in a myriad of colours, a noisy ceiling fan and a row of marble foot basins.

Rose noticed with relief that Jane and Julie had decided to swap clients. Julie was the smaller of the two and friendlier. She had a winsome smile and a no-nonsense Northern accent. She practically pushed Rose into the seat, telling her to stretch out her hands and to "keep them still, lass."

Once comfortably opposite, Rose gazed at the perfectly made-up beautician with a baleful expression. "I've never had a manicure," she revealed.

Shelly guffawed. "She's a manicure virgin."

Rose threw her a warning look. A look which said 'don't you dare start on my virginity status'.

Julie inspected her nails. "They're in good condition and quite long. Did you want extensions?"

"No! Just a colour will do fine."

"I'll have extensions, please." Shelly beamed. "I want them pale pink with crystals – the full works."

Julie switched on the radio and extracted a filing stick from her very organised nail organiser. "This won't be painful, I promise." She ardently set to work and Rose was thankful that there was at least one section of her body that didn't squirm in defiance.

"Oh they look lovely." Shelly's head was on Rose's shoulder as she eyeballed her friend's nails. "Very natural."

Rose held up her lightly painted, white-tipped fingers. "I like it."

"French manicures are my favourite." Julie was packing away her tools. "Do you want the same on your feet?"

"Why not?" Rose was feeling happy and relaxed and settled herself on the black swivel chair. Julie set to work on her feet, cleaning and buffing; her hands were firm and Rose managed to suppress the giggles.

"You have lovely eyes, madam."

"Oh, thank you and please, call me Rose."

"Better without your glasses," called Shelly from across the room. "Please tell me you'll wear contacts when we're away."

"Have you ever considered having an eyebrow wax?" Julie said as she wiped Rose's feet. "It would really open your eyes; make them look bigger."

Rose chewed her lip. "I've never considered waxing anywhere, it sounds so... painful."

Julie smiled. "It's not too bad. I'm very quick."

"Do it, Rose," Shelly encouraged.

"Okay, I will." Rose watched as Julie carefully applied the nail polish on her toenails.

When she had finished and the colour had set, Rose followed her back into the other room.

"Hop on up," Julie patted the bed, "this will only take a few minutes."

Rose braced herself for the wax strip, but it wasn't half as painful as she had anticipated.

"Shall I do your top lip as well? You have a few wispy bits."

"Uh-oh." Rose pulled her mouth into a taut line. In two fluid movements, the unwanted hair had gone.

"Beautiful." Julie asked her where she was going and Rose told her briefly of the wedding plans.

"Sounds like you're going to have fun." Julie lowered the bed with her foot so Rose could hop off.

"You bet we are!" Shelly stood in the doorway. "How about we order room service for tea, watch some weepie movies and investigate the mini bar?"

"Perfect." Rose tightened the belt on her dressing gown and followed her best friend out of the beautician's and back up to their opulent room.

≈

It was raining the next morning but that didn't stop Shelly bouncing on her bed with excitement.

"Guess what I've got planned for us today?"

Rose groaned, rolled over and buried her head into the feather and down pillow.

"Not more exercise?"

"Nope," Shelly replied, sliding her mouth into a massive grin. "Well, I suppose it could be classed as exercise... but the enjoyable, cute sort."

"What have you done?" Rose lifted a tousled head.

"We are going horse-riding!"

"But," Rose's mouth flapped open, "the weather's awful."

"Doesn't matter." Shelly glanced at the rain beating against the windowpane. "A bit of rain won't hurt us."

"Can I go back to sleep first?" Rose rolled onto her side and snuggled underneath the duvet.

"Only for ten minutes while I have a shower." Shelly clambered out of her pyjamas, flinging them up into the air and whooping as she made a dive for the bathroom.

Rose's pony was a black filly called Moonbeam. After a shaky mount, the horse-riding instructor, Andy, led her slowly around the paddock, encouraging her to sit upright with her back straight. Rose clutched tightly onto the reins, closing her eyes when Andy broke the horse into a trot. Shelly, an experienced rider, had been left to her own devices and was galloping on ahead. Rose had visions of her friend being flung in the air and trampled on, thus ruining her wedding plans and her future with Harry, but Shelly seemed in her element.

"This is great, isn't it?" Shelly called, hair flying behind her.

Rose pulled at the riding hat which was cutting into her chin. "How much longer do we have left?" she asked Andy.

He looked up at her with amused eyes. "It's only a half hour session, it'll soon be over."

Rose breathed a sigh of relief as Moonbeam stopped to munch on a tuft of grass.

"You scared of horses?"

"A little," Rose replied. "I was bitten on the shoulder by one when I was a young girl."

"She won't hurt you," Andy said with a smile, "she's a gentle girl. You can help feed her afterwards if you fancy it."

Andy pulled the bridle and Moonbeam turned and made a slow amble back towards the stables.

"I'm drenched," Rose complained as she slid off the pony. Her lower legs were caked in mud.

"You had enough?" Shelly cupped her hands and shouted above the noise of the wind.

"I'm going to feed her," Rose yelled back. She followed Andy through a cobbled archway and into a stable which reeked of manure.

"She needs a clean-out," Andy said apologetically, "but I won't ask you to help with that."

"First of all we fill up her water trough." Andy passed her a bucket. "The tap's over there."

Rose filled the bucket with fresh water then poured it into the trough.

"What do you feed them?" she asked Andy.

"Hay mainly, along with the daily treat. Here." He passed her a box of apples and carrots and set to work forking hay into the container.

Rose held out a bent carrot. Moonbeam clip-clopped over to her, sniffed her hand and then devoured the vegetable. The animal's mouth was whiskery and cool on the palm of her hand; her chocolate brown eyes regarded her as she munched on the food. Rose delved in the box for an apple and listened as Andy explained how he'd come to work at a beauty spa looking after horses.

"I used to be a farm hand, helped in the fields up the road.

When they bought this place and advertised for help, I reckoned a more laid back existence would be right up my street."

"I love animals," Rose divulged. "I wanted to be a veterinary's assistant for years at school."

"So why didn't you?" Andy paused and lent on his pitchfork.

"I don't really know," Rose said quietly. "I needed a job at the time, wanted to earn my own money and I didn't fancy more years stuck in education. I guess I gave up on my dream."

"It's not too late," he said primly, shovelling more hay in. "There's a great animal care management course at the local college. I reckon you'd be good with animals."

Rose patted the filly. "Sometimes I prefer them to humans."

"There you go then. Follow that dream, love. You've got your whole life ahead of you. It would be a pity to weigh it down with regret." Andy began whistling, a merry tune that lifted Rose's spirits and bought a smile to her face. Outside, she could hear Shelly whooping with exhilaration and envisaged her friend free as a bird, living life to the full, raging against the mundane and the safe option. Taking chances and following her heart.

"Maybe I will," whispered Rose, "maybe I will."

thirteen

After another shower to wash away the grime of a sodden Saturday morning, Rose and Shelly made their way to the in-house hairdresser's. The salon was busy, full of women reading celebrity magazines while sitting underneath heat lamps, attended to by young weekend trainee staff who rushed around sweeping cut hair from the floor and making copious mugs of strong tea. Frederick, the head stylist, exclaimed his delight at seeing Shelly. It appeared they knew each other from their travels, Frederick had spent a summer stint on Majorca's neighbouring island, Ibiza. They had met on a boat party. Frederick and his partner, Stephan, had been enchanted by Shelly's fun-loving personality and her penchant for cocktails. They had bonded over Margaritas and gossip and had been firm friends ever since.

"Shelly!" He pulled her into a humungous hug which lasted a lengthy time. Rose was hanging behind them feeling like a spare part and clearing her throat to gain their attention.

"And who is this?" His gaze slid over Rose's petite frame.

"This is my best friend." There was no mistaking the pride evident in Shelly's tone. She pulled Rose close to her, sliding an arm around her waist. "Isn't she gorgeous?"

Frederick kissed his thumb and forefinger and exclaimed that she was stunning.

"I hear you're settling down!" cried Frederick, pulling out two swivel black chairs. "What has happened to party girl Shelly?"

"She is no more," Shelly sighed and held her engagement ring up for inspection. "I've met the most wonderful man, Freddy. He's a doctor and I'm head over heels in love."

"My darling girl – you're positively glowing." Freddy clapped his hands. "This calls for a celebration. Yvonne, open the bubbly."

Yvonne stopped sweeping to stare at her boss in surprise. "The posh bubbly you've been saving until you win hairdresser of the year?"

"Never mind that," Freddy grinned, showing a set of cute dimples, "this calls for a celebration. Tea will not do, not for the bride-to-be."

Yvonne passed him the champagne, which he opened with a resounding pop.

"I'm afraid I don't have crystal flutes."

"Mugs will do just fine." Shelly revolved in her chair.

"So, princess," he fluffed up her hair, smiled at her in the mirror, "what can I do for you?"

"Weave your magic, darling and not just on me. Rose, too."

"Magnificent!" Frederick's eyes shone with excitement. "I'll start with you while your friend decides what she's having done. Yvonne, give the girls the hair magazines – all of them."

Rose sipped her champagne and watched with wide eyes as Frederick set to work on Shelly.

"I think highlights and a good cut are what you need." He then proceeded to send one of his juniors to mix the colour and collect the foil strips.

Frederick then stood behind Rose, delving his hands into her thick curls. "This is natural?"

"Yes," Rose squeaked, "I really can't do much with it."

"It's beautiful," he replied, pulling out a ringlet. "People pay a fortune for natural curls. And it is in good condition, too. Often curly hair can be very dry."

Rose smiled, feeling pleased at the unexpected compliment.

"Are you a natural redhead?" He cocked his head on one side. "I mean, are you fiery by nature?"

"Erm... not really..." she trailed off lamely.

"She's not at all," Shelly cut in. "If anything, she's the opposite."

"Then this," he blew on her head, "must go."

Rose swallowed. "What... erm... colour were you thinking?"

Frederick twirled on the spot and held out his arms. "It's obvious, darling. You must go blonde."

Rose clutched her hands to her chest and sat like a frightened rabbit as a full colour was applied to her hair.

"Come on, sweetie," one of the juniors spoke to her like she was a small child, "let's get you under the heat lamp. More champagne?"

Rose nodded gratefully and held out her glass. Shelly was laughing uproariously with Frederick, reminiscing over fun times spent together. Rose delved in her bag, extracted her mobile and checked her messages. There were two from her mum, asking if she was okay and telling her that Marty had been caught in an amorous clinch with a married woman.

Rose clicked on the phone icon and after a few rings was connected to Fran.

"Hi, love." Her mum sounded breathless. "I've just finished hoovering, are you enjoying yourself?"

"Hi, Mum. I'm having a great time, thanks. What's going on with Marty?"

She heard an audible sigh. "He's been messing about with the butcher's wife. Did you know anything about it?"

Rose swallowed. "Erm... no. I mean, I knew he liked her, but..."

"Your dad has tried to have a heart-to-heart with him, but I think it's fallen on deaf ears." There was a pause. "Could you speak to him, love? He listens to you and you've always been close."

"I don't know what I can do about it," Rose replied. "He is an adult, Mum."

"Sometimes I wonder about that. What are you doing, by the way?"

"I'm in the hairdresser's." Rose lowered her voice. "I've been coerced into having a makeover."

"Whoopee! My girl is going to look even more gorgeous."

"I hope so, Mum, I really do."

"Send me a picture when you're all finished. Your gran will be happy, at least."

"I will," Rose promised. "I'll see you later this evening and Mum, don't worry about Marty."

"I'll always worry about my kids." Fran's tone took on a soft, whimsical quality. "You'll always be my babies. One day, when you have children of your own, you'll understand, Rose."

"'Bye, Mum." Rose cut the call with an eye roll.

For the next half an hour, Rose skimmed through a couple of magazines, wishing she had brought her book. People pay to read this junk? she thought, looking with distaste at a celebrity flashing her underwear. A few of the older women left, happy with their coiffured hair. Rose had to admit that Frederick was a brilliant hairdresser. She watched his fingers expertly wield the scissors to create beautiful styles on his customers. He was currently finishing Shelly's, but before he began blow-drying her friend's hair, he came over to inspect Rose's head.

"Yvonne," he clapped his hands, "wash this off now, please."

Yvonne, who was biting into a juicy red apple, led Rose to the wash basin.

"Is this warm enough for you?" she asked, sprinkling water onto Rose's scalp.

"Yes, thank you." Rose bit her lip. "Does it look... erm... okay?"

"Very nice. You are in for a big surprise."

Rose's stomach flipped with apprehension.

Shelly was giving her a big thumbs-up sign as Frederick plugged in his hairdryer and blasted her hair. Then Yvonne was massaging Rose's head and she forgot all her trepidation and relaxed back into the chair.

"All done." Yvonne dragged the comb briskly through Rose's conditioned hair. It smelt sweet like apples and was feathery soft to the touch. "If you pop over to Frederick, it looks like he's ready for you."

Rose clutched her cape round her neck and went to sit down in the styling chair.

"What do you think?" Shelly was inspecting herself in the mirror, tilting her head in different angles. The light caught her finished hair. Rose thought she looked beautiful.

"Stunning."

"Do you think Harry will like it?"

"I think Harry will love it." Rose turned away from Shelly and gazed at her own reflection. Gone were her red curls. Oh gosh, it was light and blonde and straight. Rose couldn't decide if she liked the colour, it was so different.

Frederick ambled towards her, scissors and brush in hand. "I'm feeling a Marilyn Monroe vibe going on here." He tilted her head, "I think a bob would look divine on you."

"What do you think, Rose?" Shelly asked, eyes twinkling.

Rose swallowed. "I agree with Frederick. I've had my hair in the same mid-length style for years. I want something totally different."

"Fantastic!" Frederick cried with excitement. "When I'm

finished, you will look like a star." He pressed exuberantly on the foot pedal and Rose slid downwards with a jolt.

Next to her, Shelly grinned. "You won't regret this, Rose. I promise."

~

"Are you sure it looks all right?" Rose and Shelly were sitting in the car, after lugging their packed weekender bags into the boot.

"Are you kidding me?" Shelly popped her gum. "You look gorgeous."

Rose pulled her mirror down and stared at the big blonde curls framing her face. "I think I'm in shock. I look so different."

Shelly slid her an exasperated look. "Don't you like it?"

Rose touched her hair in wonder. "I do," she said, "I think I actually love it."

"You do look like Marilyn Monroe," Shelly pointed out. "What was it Freddy called you? A blonde bombshell, sexy as..." She trailed off as Rose gave her a pointed look.

"I don't want to develop a reputation of being dumb."

"That's just a silly old stereotype." Shelly clipped her seatbelt into place. "Although it probably is true that blondes have more fun and you certainly could do with more of that. Let's have a selfie." Shelly flipped her phone onto landscape position and pulled Rose closer. "This is going on my Facebook wall."

"For everyone to see?" Rose's tone lifted in protest.

"Of course!" Shelly chuckled. "Are you still harbouring an aversion to social media?"

"It's not my thing," Rose replied emphatically. "I'd rather read a book."

"Well, for the next two weeks you can forget your books, because we are going to have fun with a capital F."

Rose started the engine and gave her friend a wry smile. "Don't you think we should get the wedding dresses first?"

"Absolutely." Shelly nodded. "Lead the way to the bridal shop."

Magical Moments was the only wedding dress shop in Twineham. It was a small establishment positioned at the end of the High Street, attached to a flower shop and opposite the quaint bookstore that Rose loved. She looked longingly at it as she pulled into a parking bay. Shelly was up out of the car, cooing theatrically at the glittery wedding dress in the window.

"Isn't that the cutest thing?" She pointed at an accompanying page boy's suit.

"A bit too small for Harry," Rose teased. "Has he got his outfit sorted, by the way?"

"Yes and it took him half an hour, apparently."

Rose frowned. "Didn't you want to match his outfit with the bridesmaids'?"

"Nope," Shelly said lightly, pushing on the shop door. "It's his choice."

Rose shook her head in amazement. "You are so laid back about this wedding."

"I told you, Rose, I'm not doing stress. This wedding is going to be simple and fun."

"Glad to hear it." Rose gazed at the rows of wedding dresses. The shop smelt deliciously sweet; vases of freesias and lilies were dotted around the room and bowls of potpourri added to the ambience. An immaculately groomed lady put down her pen and paper and strode towards them; the fabric of her trouser suit swished above shiny high stilettos which clacked on the wooden flooring.

"Hello, I'm Samantha." Her smile was wide and showed a set of perfect white teeth. "Welcome to Magical Moments. Please feel free to look around and let me know if I can help in any way."

She turned to fluff out the tulle skirt of a young child's bridesmaid dress. "Who is the bride-to-be?"

"That'll be me." Shelly held up her hand. "And this is my friend, she's my matron of honour."

"The bridesmaids' dresses are in the back," the shop assistant informed them, as she drew a calculator out of her desk drawer. "There's plenty to choose from so take your time browsing and just hang up any that you want to try on."

"Go and have a look," whispered Shelly. "I think we're going to be here a while."

Shelly started looking through the bridal gowns and Rose wandered into the back room.

There were dresses in all sorts of shape and colours. Rose began rifling through them, wincing at the garish pink and orange ones.

"Do you have a colour theme in mind?" she called, holding a pretty lilac satin dress up against her.

"You decide," Shelly shouted back. "Just remember you're buying for Marian, too."

"She really should be here," Rose mumbled. "Right now, I'm feeling the pressure."

She picked a light blue dress off the rails and went to hang it with the lilac one.

Rose held the sleeve of a yellow one against her arm. "Too pale," she decided.

"These dresses are beautiful." Rose's voice carried into the other room. "Are you having any luck?"

"Trying one on at the moment."

Jeez, thought Rose, I need to hurry up. Grabbing a few more, Rose ducked into the changing room.

She swiped back the curtain and struggled out of her clothing, deciding to try on the lilac one first.

Hmm, nice. She looked critically at her reflection. But would it suit Marian?

"Shelly!" she yelled. "What's your sister's favourite colour?"

"Blue," Shelly shouted back. "You haven't picked a pink one, have you? Marian hates pink."

"No!" Rose chuckled at the light pink satin puffed-out affair she'd quickly grabbed. She envisioned high-flyer, ambitious, workaholic Marian prancing around the beach in the overtly girly attire and the mental image made her laugh harder.

"Are you okay in there?" the shop assistant asked.

Rose abruptly stopped laughing. "I could do with a hand getting this zip up."

She pulled back the curtain, allowing the prim lady to fasten her up.

"It looks very nice," the assistant said.

Rose walked out of the changing room and went to look in one of the many full-length mirrors. She had changed out of the lilac one and into the blue. It was a simple dress; full length satin with thin straps and a sweetheart neckline. It clung to her body, accentuating curves Rose didn't realise she had.

"Wow, Archer, that's the one."

Rose spun round to gaze in shock at Shelly, who was dressed in the most exquisite gown, veil and tiara.

"That's the one," she echoed, tears in her eyes as she rushed forward to envelope her best friend in a tight embrace.

fourteen

Rose stood in front of her wardrobe, one hand on her hip while the other rifled through her clothes.

"Yes." She threw a daisy printed sundress on the bed.

"No," she decided, skimming past two pairs of navy work trousers and a collection of plain blouses.

"Need any help?" Fran's head peeped around the open door.

"I'm not sure what to take, Mum. Your advice would be most appreciated."

Fran smiled. "Why do you make everything so complicated, love? It's simple. You need to take light summer clothing and not them." She raised her eyebrows at the sight of Rose's favourite suede jeans, which had been lovingly folded and placed at the bottom of her suitcase. "You need cotton trousers. It's going to be hot in Majorca. I checked the weather app and it's creeping up to thirty degrees there."

Rose looked out of her window at the pale blue sky and the streak of wispy white clouds.

"Am I really going up there?"

"You sure are." Fran sank down onto the soft bed. "Why didn't you go to the doctor's, love? I'm sure he could have given you something for..."

"My nerves?" Rose pulled a t-shirt off the hanger. "I'm not taking pills, Mum."

"Okay, but maybe he could have helped you in a different way." The bed squeaked as Fran crossed her legs. "I mean all that new age stuff that your dad keeps calling nonsense. Meditation, deep breathing, distraction methods, chanting..." They both laughed at that.

"I'll be fine." Rose picked up her straw hat and tossed it into her case.

"It's quite common, you know."

"What?" Rose began counting out her knickers.

"Aviophobia," Fran said softly. "Your aunt Lesley was a terrible flyer. In the end, she had a course of hypnotherapy and now she jets off to Benidorm twice a year."

"It's a two hour flight," Rose said crisply, "and there'll be children on board and... and elderly people. How bad can it be?"

"Not bad at all. That's the spirit!" Fran stood up. "You might even enjoy it, especially with the delectable Sinclair brothers in tow."

Rose swallowed. "Maybe."

Fran placed a comforting hand on Rose's shoulder. "How will the folk choir cope without you?"

"They'll have to do accappella, or maybe Sabrina can step in and take my place." Rose smiled. "So shorts, sun dresses, underwear, sun cream, flip flops..."

"Bikinis." Fran gave her a cheeky wink.

"Bathing suits," Rose corrected. "And of course my matron of honour dress. How could I have forgotten?"

When Rose was finished, she dragged her suitcase into the bathroom and popped it on the scales.

"See? Plenty of room," Fran said over her shoulder. "Do you think you could bring me some duty-free perfume back?"

"Yes, of course." Rose carried her case down the stairs,

depositing it underneath the coat stand, then walked into the lounge. "Anybody else want anything from Majorca?"

"Ciggies." Marty had his feet up on the coffee table and was playing a game on his phone.

"Whisky." Her dad looked away from the TV screen, giving her a big smile.

Granny Faith woke from her afternoon nap, shooting Rose a gummy grin. "Sangria."

"Well, that's easy to remember – perfume, booze and tobacco." Rose sank down on the sofa, shoving Marty's long legs out of the way.

"What time's your flight again, love?" Rod said, with a scratch of his head.

"Seven in the morning," Rose yawned, "which means an early night for me."

Fran chuckled. "You won't sleep, love, with all the excitement."

"Aye," cut in Faith, "she'll be throwing her guts up."

Marty made a retching sound.

"I'm going to be absolutely fine." She took a deep, calming breath. "Now, can we talk about something else?"

"How about that new hairstyle of yours? You'll be fighting the men off now you're a platinum blonde."

"That's not why I had it done," Rose snapped. "I just wanted a change."

"You've certainly changed, love." Faith tore open her king-size fruit and nut bar. "A proper little bombshell." They all murmured with agreement.

Rose touched her head. "You don't think it's too over the top?"

"No!" her family cried in unison.

"It looks beautiful," Fran said warmly.

Marty waved the remote control in the air. "You just watch that Fin. I noticed him making eyes at you at Shelly's party. He seems a wild sort."

"Maybe that's what she needs." Faith wiped chocolate crumbs from her mouth. "Someone to bring her out of her shell, and hopefully she'll lose her virgi..."

"Mum!" Fran said with a cross tone. "Why don't you go and put the kettle on?"

Faith hoisted herself to her feet and left the room with the aid of her walking stick.

"So," Rose crossed her arms and decided to ignore her gran's personal remark, "speaking of wild! How is my little brother's love-life?"

"Eh?" Marty slid her a warning look. "I've decided to have a break from women."

"Not permanently, I hope," Rod said, with a chuckle.

"Have you taken a vow of chastity?" Fran teased.

"Ha-ha, very funny." Marty stretched his arms above his head. "I'm spending more time with my mates. Well, the few single ones I have left. Seems almost everyone from school has settled down and is busy popping out rug rats."

"You'll be the same when you meet the right woman." Rod nodded at his son. "I was like you once, vowed never to get tied down and now look at me. Married over twenty years, two kids, my own business and living with the monster-in-law." He looked at Fran apologetically. "And I'm the luckiest fella on the earth."

"Careful, love," Fran said, with a smile, "they'll be accusing you of being romantic next."

"Why don't we go out for tea?" Rod said, jumping sprightly to his feet. "The whole family – my treat. Call it a goodbye meal for our Rose."

"I don't think I'll be able to eat much." Rose touched her whirling stomach.

"You can have salad then." Marty switched off the T.V. "I, on the other hand, will be having the biggest T-bone steak on the menu. And seeing as Dad's paying, I think I'll squeeze in a pudding, too."

Rose was on the road early the next morning. Her dad drove her to the airport in his dusty white van, chugging up the slow lane, dodging the lorries. The windscreen wipers were on the fastest setting as a torrent of rain followed them up the motorway.

"Typical British summer weather, eh?" He offered her a stick of gum which Rose politely declined. "Have you remembered everything? Sun cream, passport, European Health Card?"

Rose opened her rucksack and peered inside. Nestled beneath her book and sunglasses, she could just see her passport and tickets.

"Yep. Got everything."

"What time are you meeting Shelly?"

Rose checked her watch. "In about half an hour. How much further is it?"

"Not long now. Don't worry." He slapped Rose's thigh. "I'll get you there in plenty of time. Look!" He pointed to a sign up above, which read AIRPORT in big white letters.

Rose switched on the radio. The weather man was talking of non-stop rain for the next twenty-four hours.

She swallowed. "This rain... It won't affect our flight, will it?"

Rod indicated and moved into the middle lane. "Of course not, love. Pilots are used to flying in all sorts of weather. It's the wind you have to watch out for."

A flurry of leaves danced in the air in front of them and the trees at the edge of the road were swaying back and forth. Rose briefly closed her eyes.

"So you and Mum are going on a mini-break while I'm away?"

"We're off to York." Rod grinned. "It will be nice, just the two of us."

"Gran will be home alone."

"Are you kidding? She's invited half the occupants from the

day centre. Said it'll be a quiet tea and chat afternoon, but I think it's secretly a party."

"I'll miss her," Rose said, with a sigh.

Rod glanced out of the corner of his eye at her. "You will be too busy having fun and your gran would be giving you a telling-off if she knew you were pining after her already. Now, find a station that plays music and cheer up, love!"

When they arrived, Rod parked in the short stay area and walked with Rose towards the main airport entrance.

"There they are." He pointed across the busy road, where Shelly was sitting on her suitcase surrounded by Harry, Fin and Tom. "Go on then, love, looks like they're waiting for you."

"'Bye, Dad." She turned to hug him, squashing her nose against his waterproof coat. "I'll text you when I get there."

"Enjoy yourself." He pulled back slightly. "And don't stress about anything."

"I'll try not to." Rose's laugh was shaky.

"I'll be here to pick you up in ten days' time."

Ten days – it seemed such a lengthy amount of time to Rose. She pulled up her suitcase handle and waved to her dad, before crossing the road and walking towards Shelly. The roar of an aeroplane stopped her and she stood for a moment watching the plane climbing into the air. *I can do this*, she told herself. *Be brave, Archer.*

"Rose!" Shelly was on her feet, waving manically. "I thought you'd changed your mind. I thought you weren't coming."

"I'm here," Rose said, with a forced brightness. She turned to say hello to Harry, Fin and Tom.

"You ready for the ride of your life?" Fin hooked his arm around Rose's shoulder. "Don't worry – I'll look after you."

An involuntary nervous laugh emitted from Rose's mouth. "So what happens now?"

Shelly took a step back. "I keep forgetting that you've never flown! We get rid of our cases, collect the boarding passes, go through security and then we can go grab some breakfast. Are you hungry?"

Quickly, Rose shook her head. "I could do with a cup of tea, though."

As they walked into the airport, Harry said to her, "Shelly's hardly slept."

"I'm excited!" Shelly squealed. "I can sleep on the plane. Now, where is my darling sister?"

"She's over there," Fin drawled, pointing to the end of a long line of checking-in passengers. "Does she always look angry?"

"That's her city high-flyer face. Hi, Maz."

Marian's gaze flickered over them all. "You're late," she snapped.

Shelly shrugged. "Motorway was busy."

"I managed to drive up here from London on time..." Marian's eyes slanted. "Oh, never mind, you're here now."

Shelly let out a whoop. "Let's get this party started!"

After checking in and going through the hand luggage and passport inspection, they made their way up a long escalator that branched out into a vast area of shops, bars and restaurants. Rose jostled through the crowds, walking quickly to keep up with Marian and Shelly, who were charging ahead.

Tom fell into step beside her. "You okay?" he asked, with a slight smile.

"I think so," Rose replied. "I didn't expect there to be so many people."

"Did you notice the line for America? Those jumbo jets have loads of seats. Must be where a lot of them are heading."

"Is that what you came on? A jumbo jet?"

Tom nodded. "Our plane was huge. Luckily, we managed to bag door seats, so I had extra room to stretch my legs."

Rose looked up at him; he had to be at least six foot two. "It must be uncomfortable at your height."

Tom shrugged. "I've got used to it."

"You fly a lot?"

Tom suddenly looked away. "Yeah... over the years."

Rose noticed he was wearing the same baseball cap. Every time she had seen him, it had been wedged on his head and she wondered why. Was it a fashion trend in Australia? He had a lovely head of thick dark hair, so it couldn't be that he was trying to hide a receding hairline.

"Shelly said this is your first time flying?"

"Yes and might be my last." Rose slid him a tight smile. "I like my feet planted firmly on the ground."

"You'll be fine. What seat number are you?"

Rose showed him her boarding pass.

"Next to me," he said lightly. "I've got the window seat, but we can swap if you want to."

Rose shook her head firmly. Any other time, she would have been glad to be sitting next to such an attractive man for two hours, but right now, an impending sense of fear was squashing any excitement she might have felt.

Up ahead, Shelly and Marian had stopped to peruse a wall menu. "Let's go in here."

Shelly decided.

They found a table and ordered food and beverages. Five full English breakfasts were brought out and a plate of toast, jam and a banana.

"I'm really not hungry," Rose said, as she unpeeled her fruit.

Fin pointed a forkful of sausage at her. "I read somewhere that bananas are radioactive when they're on a plane."

"What?" Rose's hand quivered.

"He's messing about," Tom said, throwing Fin a stern glance. "Quit it, bro."

"Will there be mosquitoes in Majorca?" Marian dabbed at her scarlet mouth.

"Bound to be," Fin replied. "You'll find them anywhere it's hot and humid."

Rose shuddered. "I hate mosquitoes. I got bitten all over my legs in Cornwall once. It was unusually hot down there one summer and they must have taken a liking to me."

"Don't worry, Rose." Marian reached across the table to pat her hand. "I've brought a full medical kit which includes insect bite cream."

"Did you bring a sunhat, Rose? They're some pretty ones over there." Shelly pointed to a nearby stand which was full of hanging hats and scarves.

"I did," Rose replied, glancing at Tom's baseball cap. "It's important, isn't it, to protect your head and face?"

"Talking of hair, I like your new colour, Rose. It really suits you." Marian and the others gazed at her head. Rose felt herself blush and mumbled a thank-you.

A woman's voice suddenly emanated from above, telling the whole airport that the departure gate for flight 815 to Majorca was now open.

"Hurry up, Shelly." Harry pushed his empty plate away and stood up.

"What about my breakfast!" Shelly cried.

"Leave it," Marian ordered. "We don't want to miss our flight."

Rose picked up her hand luggage and, with a deep breath, followed her friends.

fifteen

It seemed that their impromptu dash across the airport was unnecessary, as when they arrived at the departure gate they were the only passengers waiting and the door which would take them to their aeroplane was firmly closed. Shelly complained about having to leave her eggs, while Marian launched into a lengthy spiel extolling the professionalism of the London airports in comparison with the 'inefficient' Midland one they were currently in.

Fin and Harry stretched out on plastic seats and shared a packet of mini donuts. Rose dithered behind Marian. Her stomach was flipping with nerves and she felt quite sick. A lady pushing a stroller stopped beside her. Rose looked down at the strapped-in young child and her thoughts tormented her: see, there's a baby who's braver than you are. As Rose was grinning inanely, the baby bobbed his chocolate-smeared tongue out, and Rose moved away, stomach squelching at the sight.

"Rose." Tom was leaning against the window, beckoning her with his hand. She scurried over, thankful to be away from Marian and her incessant chatter.

"How are we going to cope with her for ten days?" Tom said,

with a shake of his head. "Shelly had warned me that she was hard work, but jeez..."

"You're the lucky one, I'll be with her all the time. You'll only see her for a bit of the holiday," Rose reminded him.

"Lucky me." He gave her a lovely smile which added to the motion of her rolling stomach. Only this movement wasn't quite so unpleasant. "Look out there," he said, mesmerising her with his gorgeous green eyes.

After a moment, Rose glanced away out of the window. There on the tarmac stood a fleet of planes.

"Which one's ours?" she asked, eyes wide.

"This one here." He pointed to a blue and white one with the words Premier Holidays emblazoned across its belly.

Rose swallowed. "How do they stay up in the air? I mean, there are so many people going to be on it and the cases... won't they weigh it down?"

Tom rubbed his chin. "I've no idea, but hey... let me search it." He fiddled with his phone. "So according to Google it's a combination of the airplane's awesome engines and wings working with the air flow that keep it in the air. Nothing to worry about – see?" He showed her the internet web page which explained it in more detail. As Rose was skimming the article, Shelly skipped towards them.

"I think this calls for a photo opportunity."

A shadow fell across Tom's face and his smile slid away. "I'll take one of you two," he said smoothly, taking Shelly's camera out of her hands.

Shelly pulled Rose close. They were both giggling as Tom snapped away.

"How about a selfie, Tom, the three of us?" Shelly grabbed hold of his arm and tried to pull him nearer, but he shrugged her off.

"No," he said firmly.

"You are such a grump." Shelly's mouth turned into a pout. "Tom hates having his photo taken."

"Leave him alone!" shouted Harry.

Rose glanced at Tom, who looked embarrassed and a little bit angry.

"It's okay," she said to him, "I hate my picture being taken, too." Her words were meant to make him feel less uncomfortable, but internally Rose was flummoxed as to why such a gorgeous man would hate having his photo taken.

Shelly had lost interest in teasing Tom and was seated on her fiancé's knee, leaving Rose feeling awkward.

"I think I'll sit down." She flashed Tom a small smile and slumped down in the chair opposite Marian and Fin. They were bickering over who should sit in the window seat.

"I've bagged the window seat," Fin said, with a hint of stubbornness. "It says so on my ticket."

"But surely a gentleman would relinquish his seat if a lady so desired?" Marian made an attempt at an eyelash flutter. "Please Fin. Unlike Rose, I love flying and I wanted to take a few shots of the clouds to put on my Pinterest account."

"Well, okay," he folded his arms across his chest, "but I get the window seat on the way back."

"Of course you do," Marian patted his knee, "and thank you for being so gracious."

The seats at the departure gate slowly filled up. Rose moved her hand luggage so an elderly couple could sit next to her.

"Been to Majorca before, love?" the gentleman asked her.

"It's the first time I've flown anywhere," Rose said with trepidation.

"You've never flown?" His wife leaned forward to shoot her a look of astonishment. "My Frank and I go to Majorca every summer. It's a wonderful island."

Frank had a full head of white hair that matched his bushy moustache. "Business or pleasure, love?" he asked.

"A wedding." Rose nodded towards Shelly and Harry, who were whispering sweet nothings into each other's ears.

"Ah, that's nice." Frank's wife let out a sigh. "Beats getting married in dreary Britain."

"Remember our wedding, love?" Frank chattered away and Rose was glad of the distraction. But twenty minutes later the tanoy was announcing that the plane to Majorca was now ready for boarding. Two airport attendants stood at the desk, checking passports and tickets. Rose was pushed along in the throng of excited travellers. Then she was walking down a corridor that took them to the opening of the plane, where an air steward welcomed her with a bright smile.

"You're near the front, right hand side, madam." Rose looked back once before stepping onto the plane. This is it, she thought. I'm going to fly to Majorca and I'll be absolutely fine.

Rose's seatbelt was clipped firmly into place as the thrum of the engines began and the plane slid slowly forward. Shelly was sitting two rows in front with Harry. Marian and Fin were somewhere behind. Rose popped a gum in her mouth; she had read in a magazine that the ascent could affect your ears, and she wanted to be prepared. From the row adjacent, a baby wailed, and Rose gripped tightly onto her armrests. The air steward was strolling down the aisle, closing the overhead bag compartments.

"Have you done this flight before?" Rose asked, her teeth chattering.

"Oh, hundreds of times." The air stewardess asked Tom to put his tray rest up. He moved his Kindle and did as he was asked. Rose took a swig of water before ferreting in her bag at her feet. She extracted a paperback book, a novel about sunshine and romance and happiness and opened the first page. Rose tried hard to concentrate, but the words swam in front of her eyes and, frustrated with her lack of concentration, she snapped the book shut.

"We're nearing the runway," Tom said gently. "Want to look?"

Rose shook her head furtively, took a deep calming breath and closed her eyes.

As the plane moved faster, the roar of the engines deafened the sounds of the crying baby. She was vaguely aware of her hand being held lightly, Tom's fingers caressing hers. A shiver ran down her spine. The plane paused for a moment, giving the cabin crew time to strap themselves into their own seats. Rose exhaled a shuddering breath; her heart was racing and her forehead felt clammy. Her mind was racing. Why did I agree to this? I wish I was back in Twineham.

"Tell me about Australia," she mumbled, turning her closed eyes in Tom's directions.

He twined his fingers through hers and spoke softly. He was so close that his breath fanned against her ear; he smelt of peppermint and of musky aftershave, a heady combination that Rose found very appealing. His words painted a picture of his homeland; vast desert and sparkling ocean, poisonous snakes, camels and kangaroos. As the plane whooshed up the runway, he told her about watching magnificent sunsets where the sky lit up the sea and turned it golden. Rose's breath caught in her throat as the plane lifted into the air. She visualised her parents sitting at home, Granny Faith in her rocking chair and Marty on his phone, all four of them joking and chatting. Her family; her loved ones.

"Open your eyes, Rose," Tom whispered.

Slowly, Rose opened them, to be greeted by a spectacular vision of white mist.

"You're in the clouds," Tom said, squeezing her hand.

"I'm flying," Rose murmured, "I'm really flying."

Once the plane had levelled out, the seatbelt signs were taken off and straight away there was a line for the toilets. Tom asked if she was okay and Rose replied that surprisingly she was.

"It wasn't as bad as I thought it would be," she admitted. "My legs are still shaking though."

"The worst bit's over." Tom pulled his cap over his eyes. "Wake me up when we get there." Rose's eyes slid surreptitiously over him. His muscular arm was touching hers and his thigh was pressed close against her own. He was wearing a tight-fitting white shirt and navy chinos that screamed designer. Dark stubble lined his cheek, adding an air of ruggedness. How could I have thought Jeremy was attractive? she thought, licking her dry lips. Tom Sinclair was in a different league.

The air stewardess paused by their seat with her trolley. "Drinks or snacks?" she asked.

"Not for me," Rose replied, pointing to her water.

"Would your boyfriend like anything?" The air stewardess was staring at Tom's sleeping form.

"Oh, he's not my, er, boyfriend," Rose whispered. "I think he's asleep."

"I'm dozing," Tom opened one eye, "and I don't want anything, thanks."

The air stewardess fluttered her false eyelashes before moving along.

"Would you like some of my water?" Rose offered, wanting to keep him awake.

"Great, thanks." He took the bottle from her and closed his lips over the lid. Rose stared at his mouth as he took a long gulp, wondering what it would feel like to kiss him. Her attention was diverted by the voice of the captain introducing himself and telling them how high they were. Rose's hands involuntarily gripped the seat rest at the thought of being so far from the ground. The nerves had returned, and in an attempt to abate them she began gabbling about the bridesmaid's dresses.

"Are your suits nice?" she asked, after she had been speaking for a lengthy amount of time with no interaction from Tom.

"They're okay," he replied, "for a wedding, I suppose."

A flurry of clouds shot by in her peripheral vision. Rose snapped her eyes shut. "Have you been to Majorca before?"

"Nope," came the monosyllabic reply.

Rose felt a rise of resentment towards Tom and his laid back approach towards flying. Relax she told herself. RELAX. There was a sudden bump and the plane shuddered.

"What was that?" she frantically quizzed.

"That'd be turbulence, nothing to worry about."

The plane jolted again and there was a sudden beep as the seatbelt lights were switched on. The cabin crew were still on their feet, swaying from side to side as they pushed their trolleys back up the aisle. Rose gasped as the plane plummeted down and then it was calm again. She let out a shaky breath and, as Tom slept next to her, she decided to try and distract herself again with her new novel. This time it worked and she was soon lost in a fictitious world of power struggles, love and lust.

The baby on the other side of the plane had finally stopped bawling and the rest of the journey was uneventful. As informed by the pilot, they reached Majorca on time and soon began their descent. Tom was still sleeping so Rose leant across and fastened his seatbelt. She had kept hers firmly in place for the whole of the journey and thankfully hadn't felt the need to queue up for the toilet.

Shelly turned around and gave her a wave, while asking if she was okay.

Rose informed her she was fine and as the plane began lowering, she managed to bypass the gorgeous Tom and direct her attention out of the window. Through the clouds, she could make out a brilliant blue sea and then land. It loomed closer and closer until finally they were zooming down the landing strip and, with one big bump, they were finally on the ground. Rose breathed a huge sigh of relief and mentally high-fived herself for psychologically surviving the trip. Now she could enjoy herself, she thought with an excited grin.

Tom finally woke as the doors to the aircraft were swung open.

"Are we here?" he asked sleepily.

"We're on Majorca," Rose confirmed. "Look at that sky."

She stood up, clutching her bag and cardigan, waiting for the passengers in front to exit the plane. As Rose walked down the steps, the heat hit her. Even though it was still morning, it was hot. Rose waited at the foot of the steps for Tom, Shelly, Harry, Fin and Marian to catch her up.

"We're here!" cried Shelly, rushing forward to embrace her. "The flight wasn't too bad, was it?"

"No," Rose gave her a watery smile, "apart from take-off and the turbulence. I think my nerves are okay."

"We should get our cases and find our coach," Marian said, with a cool air of bossiness, "and please stay together, everyone, we don't want anyone getting lost."

They hopped up on the bus, squashing close together as other people streamed on. Finally, when it was packed full, the bus moved away, passing other planes and Spanish men who were unloading cases.

After a bumpy ride, the bus pulled into the airport terminal.

"Get your passports ready," Marian instructed, waving hers aloft. The queue of people had slowed to a standstill as they neared passport control.

"Hola." A dark-skinned man sheltering behind a glass screen welcomed her.

"Oh, hola," Rose replied. She slid her passport through the opening and smiled as he glanced over her.

"Que tengas un buen dia." He waved her past and Rose tripped slightly as she scurried through the opening.

"I have no idea what he just said to me," Rose admitted to Shelly.

"Have a nice day, you wally." Shelly socked her playfully on the arm. "I thought you were going to invest in a crash course in Spanish."

"I didn't have time," Rose retorted, "what with the spa weekend, shopping and work, I've been super busy."

"Don't mention the 'w' word," Shelly said, with a shudder. "We're on holiday, remember?"

Rose nodded. "How did you manage to wangle all this time off, though?"

"I have an understanding boss." Shelly pointed to a winding conveyor belt. "Australia isn't like the UK, where everyone is stressed and worked to death. It's very laid back in comparison."

Rose sighed. "It sounds heavenly."

Marian pushed through the middle of them, clapping her hands. "Right-oh, folks, the plan is to grab our cases as quickly as possible and find our coach – agreed?"

She stalked off as the others trailed behind.

Shelly groaned. "Please tell me I'm nothing like her."

"I know what the problem is," Fin drawled, as he draped his arms across Rose and Shelly's shoulders. "Sexual frustration."

Shelly burst into laughter and Rose grinned ruefully. She's not the only one, she thought, with an appreciative glance at the gorgeous Tom Sinclair.

sixteen

The conveyor belt burst into life and suitcases appeared from behind a plastic flap. Rose waited with the other passengers for her case. Fin and Harry stood poised at the front of the queue, ready to grab everyone's luggage.

"Just point yours out, Rose," Harry instructed.

Rose opened her mouth to tell him she was quite capable of grabbing her own case but was poked in the ribs by Shelly.

"Isn't he a gentleman?" Her friend's face had a dreamy sheen to it.

"That's mine!" Marian stood on tip-toe, pointing to a blue and white spotty suitcase that was nearing the bend where Fin and Harry stood.

Fin dragged it off, mouthing to Marian to move it out of the way. Five minutes later, Shelly and Harry's luggage arrived, closely followed by Rose's.

"Just Tom's and then we can go," Shelly squealed with excitement. "I can't wait to get my bikini on and dive into the pool."

Tom was leaning casually against a stone pillar, messing with his phone, baseball cap wedged firmly into place.

"Why does he always wear that hat?" she whispered to Shelly.

Shelly glanced over at him and then shrugged. "Does he? I hadn't noticed."

"Are you kidding?" Rose stared at her friend. "He had it on all the time in England. Is it a fashion trend in Australia?"

"Er… yes, that would be it." Looking shifty, Shelly moved away.

"Then why doesn't Harry wear one?"

"Harry's a professional person, Rose, he doesn't bother about fashion."

"Fin then?" Rose placed her hands on her hips. "Surely fun-loving, trendy Fin would have one, too?"

Shelly pursed her lips into an exasperated exhalation of air. "I don't know why Fin doesn't wear one, too. It's just a cap, for goodness' sake, why are you making such a fuss about it?"

"It just seems odd," countered Rose, "that he always has it on. He seems to be surgically attached to it and my mum always told me it was bad manners to wear headgear indoors…"

She stopped as she noticed Tom staring at her.

"Leave Tom alone," Shelly whispered hotly, "he's just different, that's all and he can wear whatever he likes. Why are you so interested, anyway?"

"I'm not," squeaked Rose. "Sorry, forget I mentioned it." She slid the handrail up on her case and flashed a smile Tom's way. There was something going on with him, she thought, something he was hiding, and inquisitive Rose made a mental pledge to try and find out exactly what.

"Is that yours, Tom?" Harry called to his brother. "Typical that your case is the last one on the damned belt."

Marian threw up her arms. "The coach will go without us. COME ON!"

They hurried through the sliding doors of the airport. Marian scanned the crowd for a Premier Holidays representative and found her collecting her possessions together, looking ready to leave.

"Coach number twenty-seven." She pointed through the lines of cars and mopeds, where a fleet of dust-covered coaches waited.

"Everyone here?" Marian asked, as she led the way across the car park.

"Yes, Miss." Shelly rolled her eyes. "Keep up, you two."

Rose was lagging behind with Fin. She was feeling tired. Lack of sleep from the previous night was catching up with her and she felt uncomfortably hot; her skin and clothes were damp with sweat.

"I think I need my inhaler," she gasped, pressing a hand to her tight-feeling chest.

"Is it in here?" Fin took her rucksack off her shoulder.

Rose nodded.

"Wait up!" Fin shouted, as he rummaged through her belongings.

"Rose, what's wrong?" Shelly jogged back to them.

"The heat... asthma's playing up." Rose's chest shook as she coughed.

"Here, honey." Shelly pulled a blue inhaler from the inner pocket and passed it over. After a few puffs, the tightness in Rose's chest dissipated and her breathing returned to normal. "I'm not used to this heat." She felt embarrassed that Tom had witnessed her asthma attack. "I know it can get hot in Britain, but the sun feels different here. More intense."

"I'll have to keep an eye on you." Shelly looked at her with concerned eyes. "I don't want you being poorly."

"I'll be fine." Rose smiled. "Looks like this one is our coach and we're just in time."

Rose watched the Majorca countryside flash by, marvelling at the greenness of the land. She had expected it to be barren and dry, but it was lush and colourful with wooded hillsides and towering mountains. The passengers on the coach had burst into a rendition of "We're all going on a summer holiday" and the atmosphere was happy and upbeat. Next to the friendly driver, a holiday rep spoke into a microphone, reeling off interesting facts about the biggest of the Balearic Islands.

Rose pulled her phone out of her bag and proceeded to snap pictures of the beautiful scenery that they passed by.

"Wait till you see the beach." Shelly applied a thick layer of lip gloss. "Ten days of lazing by the pool and sea. Now can you see why I wanted to get married abroad?"

"Yes, I can certainly see the attraction. Majorca is beautiful." Rose turned to her friend. "But I'd like to see more of the island than just the beach."

Shelly snapped the lid of her lipstick back on. "If it's adventure you're after, stick with Fin, he'll have you doing all sorts. Do you like water sports?"

Rose smiled. "That wasn't what I was thinking of. I meant sightseeing, walking, boat trips."

"There's plenty to do here." Shelly lowered her tone. "Marian is planning an itinerary. Whereas I just want to relax and get a great tan for my wedding."

"We can do both." Rose sighed and gazed out of the window. "It's my first time abroad and I'd like to experience Majorcan culture."

"Something to tell the knit and natter club about?" Shelly smirked.

Rose laughed. "Anecdotes to share with everyone," she patted her phone, "along with hundreds of photos."

Shelly leaned towards her, eyes twinkling. "I have a feeling that this holiday is the start of something new for you, Rose, something big. Your life is going to change, and for the better."

Rose settled back and enjoyed the rest of the journey. In no time, they were pulling off the main road and onto the smaller resort roads. After a few stops, they entered Sa Coma. The coach trundled to a stop outside The Majestic Palace Hotel.

"Is this ours?" Rose pulled her earphones out and peered through the window at the opulent-looking hotel.

"This is our home for the next two weeks, honey." Shelly stuffed the uneaten sweets back into her bag and stood up.

Tom waited in the aisle so she could follow Shelly off the coach. The driver had hopped off ahead of them and was busy hauling their cases out of the bowels of the vehicle.

"It looks amazing." Rose smiled at the sight of the neat, landscaped gardens and a gushing water fountain.

"It looks all right, I suppose," Marian flicked her hair out of her eyes. "Is it five star?"

"Yes," Shelly sighed, "it's an adults-only deluxe hotel."

"Even better." Marian nodded. "No screaming brats to interfere with my sunbathing."

Rose touched Shelly's arm. "It must have cost you a fortune. Can I give you something towards the cost?"

"Nope," Shelly said, with a firm shake of her head. "Tell her, Harry."

"It's all taken care of." Harry grinned. "All you have to do is enjoy yourself."

"But..." Rose frowned.

"No buts, Archer." Shelly wagged her finger. "If I'd have got married in Blighty and had a big church wedding, it would have cost a hell of a lot more than this. Anyway, my love can afford it."

Harry nodded his agreement.

"You're both very generous. Oh, thank you... I mean gracias." She took her case off the cheerful driver.

He touched the brim of his sunhat. "Enjoy your stay in beautiful Sa Coma."

They walked up a winding path and through a set of revolving doors that took them into a sumptuous reception area. It was a large, open-plan space dotted with trailing green foliage and colourful flower baskets. Marble, whitewashed walls, polished floor tiles and the gentle sound of classical music created an ambience of style and class. There were staff attired in black and white hurrying back and forth and guests lounging on cool leather sofas. Towards the left of the foyer stood a reception desk, where a line of holidaymakers waited to be checked in.

"I could murder a beer," Fin drawled, wiping his perspiring brow with the back of his hand.

"Let's find our rooms first," Marian said, in an authoritative tone, "and then we really should unpack."

"I vote we dump our cases and explore the hotel." Shelly cast her sister a mutinous look. "We can unpack later when it's cooler."

Everyone's hand shot up except for Marian's.

"Democratic decision made." Fin winked at Marian. "You can help me with my unpacking later if you want to, though."

"I'm not your mother," Marian said, with a snort.

Rose stifled a giggle at the image of Marian sorting Fin's underwear into a neat pile. She noticed that Tom was laughing behind his fist and her stomach soared. He had the loveliest smile that crinkled his eyes and took away the frown lines from his forehead.

The receptionist greeted them warmly and, after filling in some forms, they were given room keys.

"Looks like you're sharing with me." Marian jabbed at the lift button.

"Great." Rose tried her hardest to inject a tone of enthusiasm into her words.

The lift doors slid open with a hiss and a porter backed out, pushing a high luggage trolley. He wished them a good day and Rose exclaimed how friendly the staff were.

They squashed in with their cases and were soon on the fifth floor.

"Our rooms are all next to each other," Shelly hurried up the plush, carpeted corridor, "521, this is ours, Harry. So we dump the cases, get changed into swimming gear and meet back in reception – yes?"

There was a series of whoops from Fin as he followed Tom to their room.

Marian was fiddling with the door key. "Well, I hope this room is okay."

Rose waited for her to swing the door open. They walked into a bright, spacious room with two beds and an assortment of bedroom furniture. While Marian went to inspect the size of the wardrobe, Rose was drawn to the sliding patio door that took her out to a good-sized balcony and a sublime view of the sea.

"Wow!" she muttered, holding onto the rail and looking out at the vast expanse of blue.

"Is it nice?" Marian came to stand next to her.

"It... it's breath-taking." Rose's eyes swept over the golden beach and the children playing in the bubbling surf.

"It is nice," Marian conceded, "so I suppose we should dig out our bathing costumes and go join the others."

Reluctantly, Rose turned away. "Let's do it."

Seventeen

After a speedy tour of the inside of the hotel, they wandered outside into bright, hot sunshine and a patio which led to an impressively large pool. Shelly grabbed them all towels while the others searched for vacant sunbeds.

"Is it warm, do you think?" Marian was on the edge, dipping her toe into the ripple of water.

"Want to find out?" Fin pulled his t-shirt off and advanced towards Marian with a wicked gleam in his eye.

"No!" Marian held her hands up, a look of dawning horror on her face as she backed away.

"Yes, Marian. We all think you need cooling off." With one swift movement, Fin had her over his shoulder and took a giant leap into the pool. There was an almighty splash and they both disappeared underneath the water. The poolside erupted with laughter. People lying on their backs reading novels sat up and looked over at them with interest. Tom, Harry and Rose were clutching their sides as they laughed.

"What have I missed?" Shelly asked, her arms full of fluffy white towels.

Harry pointed to the pool, where a drenched Marian had surfaced and was doggy-paddling back towards the edge.

"Not funny, Fin," she threw back at Fin, who was now doing handstands in the water.

Harry helped her out and she sat on the side, kicking water in Fin's direction.

Shelly stepped out of her playsuit. "Last one in is a loser!" She ran at the side, tucking her legs up and cannonballed into the pool.

Rose undid her shorts and shimmied out of them, trying not to gawp at the sight of Tom's bronzed, muscular chest. She executed a graceful dive, slicing into the water and touching the floor of the pool. This is heaven, she thought as she slowly surfaced and flipped onto a back crawl. The pool was quiet and Rose crossed the length with no interruption. She stopped at a palm tree island, smiling at the sight of Harry and Shelly kissing and hugging in the shallow end.

Fin was teasing Marian, flicking water into her face. She looked around for Tom and watched a line of bubbles dancing in a line before his face appeared directly in front of her.

"You can swim," he said, with a grin.

"I can."

"I thought I might have to rescue you."

"It's more likely to be the other way around," Rose said tartly. With a flick of her legs, she had gone, swimming away from him to the other end of the pool.

She could hear him following and sped up. Rose clung onto the side and turned to face him.

"You can really swim. You're faster than Fin!"

"Does that surprise you?"

"Yes." He flicked his wet hair off his forehead. "You're full of surprises, Rose Archer."

And you are moody and enigmatic and gorgeous and mysterious, Rose thought, as she gently trod water.

"I'm glad you're here." Tom was staring directly at her, making her stomach flip and her bottom lip tremble.

"Ditto," she returned, colouring slightly.

"Hey, you guys." Shelly waved them over. "Fancy an ice-cream?"

The sun dipped slowly in the sky and a fresh breeze cooled the land. After an afternoon of sunbathing, they went back to their rooms. Rose sat on her bed, waiting for Marian to finish using the shower. She Facetimed her mum, assuring her she was okay and having a great time.

"The hotel is lovely." Rose stood up and swept her phone over the room.

"It's raining here." Fran pulled a sad face. "I suppose it's gloriously hot in Majorca."

"Well, we have air conditioning, so it's actually quite cool. I burnt my shoulders."

"Rose! I warned you to be careful in the sun. You're a redhead, remember. What factor are you using?"

"Thirty. Maybe I should up it to fifty."

"Yes, do that." Fran smiled. "Your gran wants to know if you've met any handsome Spanish men yet?"

Rose tutted. "No and I'm not looking, thank you very much."

"There's plenty of time." Fran puckered her lips at the screen.

"Mum, what are you doing?"

"Just sending you a kiss from us all." She could hear her dad shouting in the background that he was missing her.

Marian had stopped singing and the sound of the shower had tailed off.

"Mum, I have to go but I'll call you in a few days, okay?" Rose blew kisses at her phone. "Love you all. See you soon."

Marian came out of the bathroom clad in a towel and with her hair wrapped up, turban-style.

"Watch the hot tap, it comes out really strong, almost scalded me."

"Will do." Rose threw her phone on the bed and, scooping up her toiletries, closed the bathroom door firmly behind her.

"What do you think of this dress?" Marian asked a while later. She was holding up a blue strapless maxi dress made of pure cotton.

"Very nice," replied Rose. "How about mine?" She pointed to the white sundress hanging from the picture rail.

"Very Fifties goddess, especially now you've had your hair cut and coloured."

Rose gazed in the mirror at her bobbed blond curls, freshly washed and smelling of apple conditioner. She leant forward and carefully applied silver liner underneath her eyelids.

"Rose," Marian began, suddenly looking shifty, "does Fin have a girlfriend?"

"I have no idea." Rose snapped the top back on the pencil crayon. "I hardly know anything about the Sinclair brothers."

"Me neither."

Rose turned to face Marian. "He seems a really nice guy, though."

"He is." Marian's cheeks flushed and she looked down to fasten her sandals. "He's younger than me, though."

"Not by much," countered Rose. "Do you...?"

Marian sighed. "Yes, I like him, but I'm not sure if the feelings are reciprocated. Fin is... well... he's friendly to everyone, isn't he?"

"You should tell him." Rose stood up and passed her by to unhook her dress.

"I couldn't do that!" Marian shook her head fervently. "What if he rejects me or laughs?"

Rose stared at Marian. For such a high-earning, confident woman, Marian's vulnerability surprised her.

"Maybe you should get to know him a bit better," she advised. "Enjoy yourself and see what happens."

Marian flopped on the bed. "My life is like being on a treadmill of constant pressure. Work is mad, I have almost no social life and, between you and me, I'm lonely, Rose. Nobody knows how

I'm really feeling, of course. They all look at me and think I'm a slick high-flyer who has it all, but I don't... I really don't."

"Then this holiday is just what you need." Rose placed a comforting hand on her shoulder. "But Fin will be going back to Australia soon."

"I know. I was just thinking of having a no-strings holiday romance. Some light-hearted fun. Does that make me sound shallow and selfish?"

"Of course not," Rose replied. "It makes you human."

"Good!" Marian grinned. "I'm glad I have your blessing. Shall we go and meet the others, if you're ready?"

"Let's go."

The six of them strolled slowly along the seafront. Even though it was evening, the beach was still busy. Rose could see people bobbing in the water and a large group were playing volleyball on the sand. They stopped outside an open-air restaurant and perused the menu.

"This sounds nice," Marian said, pointing to the chicken section. "Shall we eat here?"

"I thought we could go to the bar I used to work at. They have live music and sell food, too." Shelly was pointing to a restaurant built into a rocky outlet further up.

"Sounds good, angel." Harry hooked his arm around Shelly's waist, pulling her close.

The restaurant was busy, but when the manager saw Shelly he came rushing over.

"Shelly, is that really you?" He put his pad and pen down on the nearest table and pulled her into a rough embrace.

"Hello, Darius," Shelly kissed both of his cheeks, "it's good to see you."

"Come, come." He ushered all of them inside and led them to a large table overlooking the sea. "What are you doing back here? Surely you're not after a job?"

"No," Shelly laughed, "I'm on holiday and I'm getting married here."

"What?" Darius swept one hand through his caramel-coloured hair. "Who is the lucky man?"

"This is Harry," Shelly said proudly, "my husband-to-be."

Darius clapped Harry on the shoulder. "You are one lucky fella. I always hoped she'd settle down with me."

"You joker." Shelly tossed her hair back. "How is Carmella?"

"She is here. I'll go and get her."

"She still works in the kitchen?" Shelly sounded surprised.

"She is my finest cook. But you might be surprised when you see her." Darius turned and hollered for Carmella to come out. A small Spanish lady appeared in the kitchen doorway, holding a whisk and clad in a white apron. As she neared, Rose noticed her protruding stomach. At the sight of one another, Shelly and Carmella squealed.

"You look well," Carmella gushed, "it is lovely to see you again, my English friend."

"Are you pregnant?" Shelly asked as they embraced.

"What do you think?" Carmella rolled her eyes. "Please do not presume I am now fat!"

"Our baby is due soon." Darius placed his hand on Carmella's stomach.

"No more partying for me," Carmella said, "now I have swollen ankles, piles and stretch marks!"

"We had some good times," Shelly said, her eyes misting over. "Can you remember going skinny-dipping with those Germans?"

"Hush!" Carmella laughed. "Do not give all my secrets away to Darius."

As the two girls reminisced, Rose picked up the menus and passed them around.

"What a cracking view," Fin drawled. "I vote for a beach day tomorrow. What do you reckon, Rose?"

"Urm, yes." Rose nodded, aware of Marian looking at Fin longingly.

Darius snapped his pad open and asked what they would like to drink.

"Shall we share a bottle of wine?" Marian suggested.

They ordered Prosecco for the ladies and beer for the men.

"Who are all these people?" Carmella asked, looking at them with interest.

"Fin and Tom are Harry's brothers. They've travelled from Australia just for our wedding. This is my big sister Marian, and this ..." she hooked an arm through Rose's, "is my best friend."

"You are all very welcome in Sa Coma," Darius bowed theatrically, "so relax and enjoy the beautiful scenery and our fine food." He ushered Carmella away, back into the kitchen.

"This really is heaven," Rose sighed, gazing out at the undulating sea.

"The view is stunning." But Tom wasn't looking at the sea, he was staring straight at Rose. She held his gaze for a moment then averted her eyes to Marian, who was sloshing wine into three crystal flutes.

"A toast," Marian held her glass aloft, "to Shelly and Harry."

Pint glasses were chinked against wine glasses and in the background, the sun slid slowly down a blood-red evening sky.

eighteen

Rose woke to the sound of an early morning tide crashing against the rocks. Hair had fallen across her face and was tickling her nose and upper lip. She rolled onto her back and stared up at the grooves in the ceiling. The patio curtain arched inwards, caught in a strong gust of wind. From outside, she could hear the distant sound of a rumbling truck and workmen who shouted jollily to each other. Rose fumbled for her glasses and found them on the bedside table next to her phone, which informed her it was seven-thirty. Her thoughts wandered to last night; a lovely meal, followed by a few drinks in the hotel bar. It hadn't been a late night; everyone was weary after the journey and the alcohol had intensified the tiredness. This morning, Rose felt fresh, and excited for what lay ahead: the beach.

The door swung open and Marian came speed-walking through it. She was wearing fitness clothes and running shoes and her hair was tied into a high ponytail which bobbed from side to side.

"Did you wonder where I was?" she asked cheerfully.

Rose cleared her throat. "I presumed you were in the bathroom. Have you been running?"

"Yes, along the sea front and it's beautiful out there." She pulled off one shoe. "Do you mind if I have a shower first? I'm dripping with sweat."

"Go ahead." Rose flopped back onto her pillow and reached for her book as Marian deposited a line of clothes across the floor and disappeared into the bathroom.

Rose decided to sit and read on the patio. Sunlight streamed on her feet and thighs as she settled herself on one of the wicker chairs. She watched a man playing frisbee with his dog on the beach and a young couple roller-skating hand in hand. The ocean sparkled in the distance; a vast expanse of shimmering blue, it kissed the cloudless sky, where birds ducked and dived, singing to the world. It was so beautiful it took Rose's breath away. She reached for her phone, took a few snaps and then forwarded them onto her mum; a digital postcard all the way from Majorca.

"It's all yours." Marian craned her head around the doorway. "Enjoying the view?"

"It's stunning." Rose got to her feet and padded into the bathroom where she stood underneath the shower, enjoying the feel of the cool water on her bare skin.

Once she was clean and dry, she dug in the drawer for her bathing costume, shorts and t-shirt. Rose gathered her hair into a short bun and then applied a layer of lip gloss.

"Shall we have breakfast?"

Marian nodded. "I'm famished. I suppose the others are still asleep. Shelly always was a lazybones."

Rose picked up her phone. "I'll text her when we're in the restaurant."

It was a surprise to see Shelly already there, sitting with the Sinclair brothers, drinking coffee.

"You're up!" Rose hugged her briefly before sliding into a vacant seat.

"Don't sound so surprised," Shelly replied with a laugh, "I'm an early bird now. Up early every morning at the radio station."

"Are you missing Australia?" Rose reached for the coffee pot.

"I'm missing the people, my friends and the dog, of course, but I'm happy to be back here. I've missed this place."

"Maybe I could visit you in Australia," Marian sliced into a croissant, "and Rose could come with me."

Rose gulped. "That's a long flight."

"It would be so cool if you did." Shelly let out an excited squeal. "You wouldn't have to pay for digs, of course."

"Good. I'll pencil it in my things-to-do section of my planner," Marian said, with a small smile.

Rose glanced at Fin, trying to gauge his reaction, but he was looking down at his fried breakfast.

"And I'll have to have a think about that," Rose cut in. The thought of such a long flight had sent a cold shiver running up and down her spine, even though the morning was already bright and hot.

A smiling waitress brought Rose a plate of delicious-looking bacon and eggs and Rose tucked into it, listening to Shelly chattering about their eventful midnight caper.

"I swear the spider was this huge." She made a large circle with her hands. "Harry chased it round the bedroom a couple of times before he caught it in a cup."

"Did you squash it?" Marian looked up from her toast.

"Of course not," Shelly replied. "We chucked it out of the window."

"You should see the spiders in Australia," Fin drawled. "They stare at you with attitude." Everyone laughed at that.

"I hope you managed a good night's sleep after that," Rose said, mopping up her runny egg.

"Nope, because then a moth flew in and it was big and hairy." Shelly shuddered. "Ugh! I think I hate moths more than spiders."

"The bed was comfy, though," Harry said, with a cheeky grin. "How did you sleep, Rose?"

"Good," Rose swallowed her food. "I went flat out, no problems."

"She was sleeping like a baby when I went for a run."

Fin looked at Marian with surprise. "I hadn't got you down as the sporty type."

"Oh yes," said Marian, with a flick of her head. "Keeping fit is important to me, a healthy body, healthy mind outlook."

Fin nodded with approval and Rose smiled at the way Marian was gazing at him.

She turned to Tom, who was staring moodily out of the window. "Is your room nice?"

Rose gulped as he directed his penetrating gaze at her.

"It's okay. I've stayed in a lot worse." He stretched his arms above his head and Rose noticed the ripple of taut chest muscles beneath his shirt. "The bed was lumpy. How was yours?"

"Mine was... soft and comfortable, perfect."

Tom raised an eyebrow at her. "I'm glad you like your bed."

A hotness spread into Rose's cheeks. "I do. I mean it's great to sleep in."

"What else could you do in it?" His lips curved into a smile and Rose felt her pulse quickening.

"Excuse me," Shelly was on her feet with her hands on her hips, "if you two have finished talking about beds, can we go get this day started?"

Rose decided to apply her sun cream in the room before they emerged into the hot sunshine.

"I have to be careful in the sun," she said to Marian, who was filing her toenails. "I burn easily."

"You're a typical redhead in that respect." Marian waved her filing stick in the air. "Do you tan?"

"Eventually. You must tan really easily." She glanced at Marian's bare legs, which were already an enviable light brown.

"I rarely burn," Marian agreed. "I can sit in the garden at home all day."

Rose pointed the nozzle at her leg and a squirt of sun cream shot out, missing her and hitting the bed sheets with a squelch. She tried again and this time she was successful. Vigorously, she rubbed it in.

"Want me to do your back?" Marian asked. Rose passed her the bottle with a "please".

"Oh, that's cold!" She squirmed at the feel of the cool sun cream.

"Maybe Tom could rub some in for you later," Marian teased.

"Tom?" Rose winced as Marian's hands pummelled her back.

"I've noticed the way he looks at you, Rose."

"He's just being friendly."

"I think it's more than that. Fin told me he's single." Marian lowered her voice to a whisper, although there was no need as the dividing walls were super thick. "Apparently he was engaged and had his heart broken."

"Is that why he's so quiet... so moody?" Rose queried.

"Probably." Marian shrugged. "Maybe what he needs is a bit of light-hearted fun like the rest of us."

"I'm not interested in a holiday fling," Rose said firmly. Silently she added, and I definitely don't want my heart broken.

"Sometimes these things just happen when you least expect them to," Marian picked up her beach towel and squashed it into her bag, "and I definitely wouldn't say no to a bit of slap and tickle with Fin."

Her words made Rose laugh. "Then I think you should make a move before the holiday's over."

They strolled slowly through the hotel and out onto a main road, where coaches trundled past, spewing out dusty clouds and people on scooters whizzed by, papping horns and shouting good morning.

"The people are really friendly here," Rose commented, as they dodged across the busy road.

"That's partly why I stayed so long," Shelly agreed.

"How long did you live here?" Rose asked.

"Two years. When the holiday season finished, I worked on Darius's family's farm." She lowered her voice. "I had a whirlwind romance with the head waiter at the time, but it fizzled out and last I heard, he was studying business and economics in Barcelona."

"You've had such an exciting life," Rose said wistfully, "seen so many places."

"But there's no place like home," Shelly said, as they neared the beach.

"Where is home?" Rose cocked her head to one side as she regarded her friend.

"Right now it's Australia and Britain, I can't decide which I love the most."

Sand was invading Rose's flip flops. They walked around a low wall onto the beach and she stared with excitement at the sea. Fin dropped his towel and pulled off his t-shirt.

"We can't stop here!" Marian berated him, "we need sunbeds and shade." She pointed to a cluster of sunbeds with palm trees for shade.

They carried on, nearer to the sea.

"We came at the right time," Marian continued, with a satisfied nod, "there's plenty of room."

The beach was quiet, apart from a handful of people who were sunbathing. Rose watched a couple of young children jumping in the surf and a dog chasing through the gentle waves.

"This is idyllic," she said, rolling her towel onto one of the sunbeds.

"So," Shelly raised her arms above her head and pulled off her playsuit, "who's coming in the sea with me?"

Fin sprang up. "Race you." Then he was off, sprinting down to the water with Shelly in close pursuit.

Rose turned to Harry. "You're not going in?"

Harry was watching his wife-to-be with a smile. "I'm going to work on my tan for a bit." He stretched himself face-down on the sunbed. "Shelly tells me you're a great swimmer."

"I'm not too bad." Rose sat down, burying her toes in the soft golden sand.

"And she said you're modest." Harry ran a hand through his ginger hair. "It's been good for her, seeing you again. Shelly hasn't got many friends – real ones, I mean. A lot of the people we hang around with are on the celebrity circuit. Wannabes, spoilt and shallow. It's the not so glamorous side of Shelly's job."

"And what about your job? Have you always been a doctor?"

Harry shifted and leant his chin on his forearms. "I originally trained as a vet but had a change of heart. Now I'm wondering if I made the right decision. Human patients can be so ungrateful, so mistrusting. Whereas animals, when they're sick, they're the opposite."

Rose nodded in agreement. "I love animals. Maybe one day I'll follow my dream to work with them."

"Why not do it now?" Tom suggested. "You're wasting your life in that call centre."

Rose glanced across at him, feeling irked. "I wouldn't call it a waste. It pays very well."

"Does it fulfil you, though? Does it challenge you? Do you honestly love going into work every day?"

He was standing at the foot of her sunbed, smiling lazily down at her.

"No. To all three," Rose admitted. "But it's not that simple to switch careers. You're talking a major life decision here."

"I reckon you should just go for it." He picked up a ball and twirled it expertly on his finger. "D'you think you could challenge me to a game of water volleyball? Or is that too extreme for you?"

Rose's eyes narrowed behind her sunglasses; for someone so good-looking, he sure had an attitude.

She jumped swiftly to her feet and darted behind Tom, catching him unawares. The ball was in her hand and she was running across the hot sand. "I think that's a point to me already," she shouted tartly.

nineteen

In the end, the whole group was in the water, batting the ball with their hands from side to side. It was women versus men to start, but after the girls found themselves losing, Marian took charge and mixed them up. Rose hit the ball high, splashing Tom in the face as he dived to return it. After an hour in the warm water, Marian acknowledged her team's defeat and they called a halt to the game.

"Look over there," Fin said to Rose as she swam languidly on her back.

"Hmm?" She was gazing up at a beautiful clear sky, daydreaming about what she could wear tonight.

"More water fun." He splashed her in the face, making her leap bolt upright onto her feet. Rose shielded her eyes as she looked in the direction he was pointing. Further along, she could make out a group of people with life vests, swimming towards a man in a speedboat.

"It's an inflatable sofa," he said, before she could ask, "they're loads of fun. Fancy a go?"

"Are they safe?" she asked dubiously.

"Sure," Fin grinned. "You're not chicken are you, Rose?"

"Don't listen to him," Shelly swam towards them, "he'll have you doing all sorts of daredevil crazy things."

"I'm not scared of the water," Rose said, with a determined smile. "Anyone else want a go?"

"I will!" Marian's hand shot up. "It actually looks fun."

Rose and Shelly both stared at her in surprise.

"Who is she trying to impress?" Shelly mumbled.

"What about you, Tom?" Rose called, but he was swimming away from her with Harry, back in the direction of their sunbeds.

"Looks like it's just us three then." Marian began swimming in the direction of the pay kiosk. "Come on, then."

The attendant checked their life vests were firmly in place before telling them, with a broad grin, to have a blast.

"Wait for me," Marian spluttered, as Fin and Rose cut swiftly through the waves.

They hauled themselves onto the rubber sofa, positioning Marian in the middle.

"Hey, guys," Marian waved at the men in the speedboat, "go easy now." The two men gave her a thumbs-up and a laugh which, to Rose's ears, sounded quite sinister. Rose noticed that Marian was gripping onto the hand rails so hard you could see the whites of her knuckles.

"Relax," Fin said with a laugh, "let your body go with the movement of the sea."

"Okay." Marian's teeth were chattering and Rose was overwhelmed with a foreboding sense of worry. Maybe this wasn't such a good idea, she thought fleetingly as the inflatable began moving.

It started gently enough, but then the boat propelled its engines to fast mode. The sofa began rocking, then bouncing, then lifting high into the air.

"Jesus!" screamed Marian. "This is horrible!"

Next to her, Fin and Rose were being flung about, but both were laughing and enjoying the thrill.

The speedboat executed a sharp turn and they swerved to the right, bouncing high into the air.

"Let me off!" Marian had turned a puce shade and was hanging on for dear life as she was flung about.

"Woo-hoo!" yelled Fin. "Go faster, mate."

The skipper of the boat put his thumb up in acknowledgement and sped up a notch.

The inflatable swung upwards. Rose was screaming with laughter and exhilaration but next to her, Marian was sobbing. Then suddenly, a wave appeared out of nowhere and as they came crashing down on top of it, all three of them were flung out of their seats and into the water with a resounding splash.

Rose surfaced, looking frantically around for Marian. She had been propelled further out and was bobbing up and down on the ocean swell. Fin reached her first.

"I got you," he soothed, taking her in his arms. Marian clung to him, tears running down her ashen face.

"Are you all right?" Rose panted.

"No. I'm bloody not alright. That was the most horrible experience of my life. Please don't tell me you enjoyed that."

Rose was grinning.

"I think she's a closet adrenaline junkie," Fin said, with satisfaction.

"You guys okay?" The men in the boat were hanging over the edge, looking at them with concern.

Fin held his hand up. "All okay, but I think this one's had enough inflatable fun for one day."

"Do you want us to tow you back in?" the speedboat captain asked.

"No," snapped Marian, "I'm not getting back on that thing."

They swam slowly back, Marian complained the whole way.

"My arms are aching," she said.

"That'll be because you were gripping on too tightly."

"I had no choice," she retaliated. "Did you two really enjoy that experience? I'd hardly describe it as a thrill."

"I'd rather go on that than a plane," Rose said consolingly. "I'm terrified of heights."

Marian sniffed, looking completely bedraggled. "Well, I won't be partaking of any more water sports. From now on, my feet are staying firmly on the beach."

"Looks like it's just me and you then." Fin slid a teasing glance at Rose and then their feet were on the ground and Shelly was racing towards them, asking if they were all okay.

For lunch, they walked into the centre to dine at a British pub and karaoke bar.

"What shall we do next then, Rose?" Fin asked, as they ate their food.

"I think I'm going to have a lazy afternoon," Rose replied, with a laugh.

She noticed Tom glancing slant-eyed from her to Fin, but his brother appeared oblivious to the sudden attention.

"I noticed they have a banana boat as well as parasailing. Fancy that?"

Rose pulled a face. "Not sure about parasailing, as you know I don't like heights, but the banana boat sounds fun."

Marian shuddered. "There was nothing fun about that experience."

"Since when did you become such a daredevil?" Shelly pointed her fork at Rose. "I'm seriously impressed, Archer."

"I'm feeling brave," Rose replied. "Maybe the sunshine's gone to my head."

"And maybe it was there all along," Shelly said, with a fond smile, "hiding beneath all that hair and shy demeanour."

· · ·

Later on in the afternoon, Fin managed to talk Rose into going on another inflatable. This time it was just him and her, lying flat on their stomachs as the speedboat whizzed and flipped them across the sea.

"That was awesome," Fin said, as they swam back to shore.

"I'm feeling a bit sick," Rose grimaced. "Food and inflatable rides do not mix."

"I'll let you relax for the rest of the day then," Fin grinned, "get a tan on that gorgeous body of yours."

Rose's thoughts were immediately on Marian. "Shelly's sister's a nice girl, isn't she?"

Fin frowned. "I guess so."

"I mean, underneath all that high-flyer façade, she's really down to earth and... nice."

"Nice?" Fin ducked his chin into the water. "Not a trait I usually find appealing in a woman."

Rose tried a different tactic. "But she can be hot-tempered. Passionate, even and I know she likes men who are a little bit wild and dangerous."

Fin spluttered with laughter. "Is that a hint? I already know that she likes me, Rose. Harry told me and I've noticed the way she's been looking at me."

"But are the feelings reciprocated?" Rose glanced sideways at him, but his expression was deadpan and unreadable. "Sorry, that was nosy of me, I didn't mean to pry."

"I know what your intentions are – to fix me and Marian up. Am I correct?"

"Would a holiday romance be such a bad idea?"

Fin flicked water at Rose. "I could ask you the same thing."

"Oh, I'm just here for the water sports," Rose laughed, but her eyes searched the beach for Tom.

"Yeah, right." With a sudden movement, Fin pushed Rose under the water. When she resurfaced, he was executing a fast front crawl away from her. But then he turned around.

"Be careful of my brother, Rose. He's the one who's really dangerous."

He flicked his legs, disappearing under the waves and Rose was left contemplating what exactly could be dangerous about the quiet Tom Sinclair.

Rose was pleased when she looked in the mirror later that evening. The redness and soreness on her skin had abated, and a faint brown colour had begun to cover her body. Apart from her stomach and lower back, which remained a pale white colour.

"Why don't you wear a bikini?" Marian suggested. "You could borrow one of mine."

Rose chewed her lip. "I feel more comfortable in a swimsuit."

"But you'll never tan your stomach." Marian sounded horrified at the idea of a white midriff. "At least try one on."

It would be easier to give in, so Rose nodded her agreement.

Marian twirled on the spot. "How do I look?"

"Beautiful." Rose smiled at her polka dot playsuit and high wedges.

"And you look stunning." There was a note of envy in Marian's words. "I don't think Fin is interested in me, he seems to be seriously into you."

"I don't like Fin," Rose replied quickly. "Well, not in that way."

"You don't?" Marian was staring at her suspiciously. "I wouldn't blame him or you, you have so much in common and me... well, I hate all that adrenalin junkie shit."

"I'm nothing like Fin," Rose cried, "I'm shy, serious, a nerd."

"You were," Marian corrected, "until you got back with my sister. She has this knack of bringing out the hidden extrovert in all of us."

"The sea has done something to me." Rose crossed to gaze out of the window. "It's magical."

"It's beautiful," Marian agreed, coming to stand next to her. "Are you glad you're here, Rose?"

"Yes." Rose reluctantly turned away to pick up her diamante clutch bag. "So shall we go meet the others."

Marian nodded. "Let's see what tonight brings."

twenty

"Fancy a curry?" Shelly stood at the entrance to the restaurant, hands on hips, looking expectantly around at the group.

"As long as it's not too spicy," Marian replied crisply. "Indian food gives me terrible heartburn."

"There's plenty of mild dishes on here." Fin cocked his thumb towards the menu.

"What would you recommend?" Marian sidled over to him, fluttering her lashes flirtatiously. The two of them wandered into the restaurant and were immediately accosted by a smiling waiter.

"Looks like we're eating here then." Harry hooked his arm around Shelly and led her inside, where two waiters were busy pushing tables together to accommodate the party.

"Do you like Asian food?" Rose looked up at Tom, who looked brooding and handsome in a black shirt and cut off shorts.

"I do," he replied, "and I'm starving after a hard day lazing on the beach."

"Lazing for some!" Rose grinned. "I'm worn out after those inflatable rides and I've got the bruises to prove it."

She lifted the hem of her dress and they both stared down at the purple blotches on her knees.

"That's what happens when you hook up with Fin." Tom shrugged.

"Oh no, I haven't hooked up with him." Rose's eyes widened. "I mean, he's a friend – that's all."

"Really?" Tom lifted one eyebrow. "The way he was speaking, my brother seems smitten."

Rose swallowed. That's probably because we both share a platonic love of the water."

"Well, maybe you should let him know and stop leading him on then."

"I haven't led him on!" Rose protested quietly. A feeling of anger sparked in her stomach as she glared at Tom. "And it's really none of your business, anyway. Excuse me." She flounced past him and towards the others, who were seated.

"Rose!" Fin patted the empty chair to his right and flashed her a sparkling grin. Marian was on the left of him and Harry and Shelly were opposite, which meant that Tom would be sitting opposite her. He slid into the empty seat as the waiter fussed around them, taking the drinks order.

"What are you having, Rose?" Shelly asked.

"I'll have a cocktail," Rose replied firmly, "whatever you're having."

"Woo-hoo!" Shelly lifted her arms into the air. "Let's get this party started!"

Tom glanced up from the menu. "You said you're not a drinker. Those cocktails can be pretty potent."

"Chill out, Tom," Fin drawled, "Rose is on holiday and can have whatever she wants." He patted her knee and Rose stiffened. Shelly looked from Fin to Tom and then back to Rose, with suspicious eyes. "You sure you're up for it? Tom's right, they're strong if you're not used to them, and I wouldn't want to make you sick."

"I'll be fine," Rose tossed her head and reached for a menu, "so can you please stop fussing?"

"All right, then." Shelly skimmed over the starter section, satisfied that she had done the sensible thing and given her best friend fair warning.

The smiling waiter appeared back at their table a few minutes later, carrying an oval tray high above his head.

"Beer for the men," he set the pint glasses down, "and cocktails for the beautiful ladies."

Rose admired her drink. It was presented in a pretty crystal flute with sugar iced around the rim and a pink umbrella poking from the top. She took a long sip through the straw, then began coughing.

"Whoa!," Rose's eyes were watering. "That sure has some kick to it."

"Mmm, it's lovely." Marian offered her straw to Fin. "Want some?"

"Nah, thanks." Fin picked up his pint glass. "Beer and cocktails are not a good combination."

"Don't you think you should slow down?" Tom said, with a pointed look at the almost empty glass in Rose's hand.

Rose sucked harder and siphoned up the remains of the liquid. "Another one!" She motioned to the waiter. Then she turned cool eyes on Tom and said, "We're here to have a good time and you're not my father."

A muscle pulsed at the side of Tom's jaw as he answered, "Don't say I didn't warn you."

Shelly ordered poppadoms for everyone while Rose perused the menu. After deciding on onion bhajis as a starter and a bhuna with garlic rice for her main, she relaxed back and listened to Fin telling Marian about his life back in Australia.

"I get that you're an adrenaline junkie," Marian said, in between mouthfuls of cucumber salad, "but what do you do as a day job?"

Fin shrugged. "I work in bars mainly, do a bit of security in the night clubs."

Marian coughed. "Don't you have a career, I meant?"

Fin looked confused as he took a swig of his beer. "The ocean's my career."

This statement had Marian in peals of laughter. "But where's your ambition? The sea's beautiful but it doesn't pay the bills, does it?"

"Ah," Harry pointed his fork, "that's where you're wrong. Fin's a serious surfer, and he's made quite a bit of money from it."

"How?" Marian asked. "Do you have a sponsor?"

"No, nothing like that. I enter competitions, I travel a lot – America, South Africa, Hawaii. I've even been to Cornwall."

"I bet that wasn't very glamorous," Marian said waspishly.

"It was great," Fin smiled as he recollected surfing on Fistral Beach, "although not so much fun when I trod on a weaver fish and poisoned my leg."

"In England?" Shelly sounded surprised.

"Yeah. You have to watch out for the jelly fish there, too."

"Cornwall's not too far from my place in London," Marian said enthusiastically. "Maybe we could go down there together? You could show me how to surf."

Rose winced at Marian's bolshiness and surreptitiously glanced at Fin. But he seemed as relaxed as ever and unperturbed by her obvious infatuation. He asked Marian about her job in the capital and they began chatting in quieter tones. Shelly and Harry were whispering sweet nothings to each other, which left Rose no other choice but to instigate a conversation with Tom.

"So," she began brightly, "you're an electrician?"

Tom looked up from his food, startling her with his green gaze. Gosh, he is gorgeous. Rose gulped with the realisation of how attracted she was to him.

"Er... yep." He looked away and attraction was replaced by irritation. What was his problem? Rose wondered. Why did he come across as being shifty and moody all the time?

"Have you done it for long?" Rose persisted, through gritted teeth.

"Since I left school," he replied quietly.

"It must be handy having a trade. My dad's a painter and decorator and he's never been out of work." Rose smiled, trying to lighten the tense atmosphere between them.

Tom sucked in a breath as his gaze roamed over her face. "I suppose it is."

Rose looked away and broke off another piece of poppadom. "You're a great swimmer."

His impromptu compliment surprised her. "Thank you."

"I was thinking of hiring a car," he continued. "Would you fancy exploring a few different resorts with me?"

The words were out of her mouth before she had chance to think about it. "I'd like that very much."

Tom grinned. "Great! I'll organise it tomorrow."

Rose grinned back at him. "Fab."

"Tell me about your family. You seem close. Do you miss them?"

Rose nodded. "I am missing them. I've been on holiday with them every year since I was born. We've travelled all over England, and Wales, too. But I've never been to Scotland..." She trailed off as his warm fingers brushed a stray curl out of her eyes.

"Carry on," he prompted.

Rose swallowed. "We're a close family, I can tell my mum and dad anything."

Tom's eyebrow lifted. "What about your brother?"

"He's annoyingly protective. But I wouldn't be without him."

"And your gran?"

"... is a darling and definitely the family matriarch."

"She was good fun at Shelly's party. I love old people and their 'no inhibitions – don't give a crap' attitude."

"Me too," Rose said softly. "I guess when you've lived ninety years, not much bothers you anymore."

"I guess not."

The waiter re appeared then and asked if they were ready for their starter.

When he had taken away their empty plates, Rose leant towards Tom, eager to continue their conversation.

"What about your family? Are there any sisters?"

"No, just my mum."

"Oh." Rose dabbed at her mouth, wondering why he hadn't mentioned his dad.

A plate of steaming bhajis were placed down in front of her.

"My dad left us. For a younger woman." Tom picked up his fork and stabbed at his shish kebab.

"I'm sorry." Rose looked up. "That must have been difficult to come to terms with."

Tom gave her another of his intense, knee-trembling gazes. "Not really. It was more a case of good riddance. He was a waster. Think Fin and magnify it by ten, with none of the warmth or kindness."

"He liked surfing too?" Rose swallowed.

"No, he didn't like much of anything apart from the beer. He was a drunk, although he denied he had a problem. Couldn't hold down a job, spent Mum's housekeeping in bars. The police were forever picking him up when he was inebriated. I haven't seen him for over ten years."

"But how did your mum cope? Alone with three boys."

"She's got four sisters. They helped out a lot and then there's the community where we lived. My hometown is a tiny, close-knit place, where everyone knows each other's business. The neighbours would babysit while Mum worked her three jobs. They'd bring round meals for us, help with DIY, that sort of thing."

Rose smiled and sipped her drink. "It sounds a nice place to live."

"It is if you're a ten-year-old. But not much to do for a bored teenager."

"So you no longer live there?" Rose finished her starter and laid her cutlery neatly together.

"Nope." Tom leaned back in the chair and stretched his arms behind his neck. A move which accentuated firm, well defined arm and chest muscles. "I live four hours away. But I go back to visit whenever I can and sometimes Mum comes to stay in my apartment." He dug one hand in his pocket, extracting a battered-looking wallet. "This is her." He passed over a passport-sized photograph of a laughing, dark-haired lady.

"She looks like you!"

"Thanks," Tom replied.

The breeze ruffled Rose's hair as she turned to watch one of the waiters pushing a trolley laden with steaming food. "I hope I can eat my main, that starter was filling."

"I'm sure that I can help if you're struggling." Tom grinned, showing a set of even white teeth.

"Don't encourage him, Rose," interjected Harry, "he eats like a horse and unlike me, who has to watch my weight, he never seems to carry excess fat."

I can see that, Rose thought, as her eyes roamed with appreciation over Tom.

"I love every chubby bit of you." Shelly pinched Harry's cheek between her thumb and forefinger.

Talk turned to the upcoming nuptials. Shelly reeled off the itinerary for the day of her wedding.

"The hotel has been fantastic. They've organised everything. All we have to do is show up!"

"And what about the hen-do?" Marian commented. "I take it you can tear yourself away from Harry for one night?"

"Of course," Shelly replied, "but I'm leaving that up to you and Rose to organise."

After the main meals were consumed, Harry paid the bill – a move which seemed to outrage Tom.

"You can't pay for everybody! Let me!" He slapped a credit card down on the table.

"No," Harry said, raising one hand, "I can afford it, Tom. I'm a high-earning doctor, remember."

"You need your money for your new house," Tom replied, "and for those sprogs you're planning."

Rose felt all warm and gooey at the thought of miniature Shellys running amok.

"We want to enjoy married life first," Harry chuckled. "There's plenty of time for kid-raising."

"And in the meantime," Shelly hooked a seductive finger around Harry's chin, "we'll have plenty of fun practising." She deposited a lingering kiss on his mouth.

"Oh, pur-lease!" Marian balled her napkin. "Save it for the bedroom."

"Nothing wrong with being affectionate in public," Shelly returned. "We're in love, and we don't care who knows it."

"Love is overrated," Marian said, with slanted eyes. "What do you think, Rose?"

"I wouldn't know," Rose replied, heat colouring her cheeks.

She could feel Tom's eyes upon her and squirmed with embarrassment.

"That's the spirit!" Marian's eyes flashed at Fin. "Men only break your heart. Steer well clear and invest in a cat – that's my advice." She laughed as she pushed back her chair. "So, are we going on a pub crawl or not?"

The main resort consisted of a small strip of shops, restaurants and bars. It was a busy evening and the street was full of holidaymakers. They stopped outside a brightly lit store which seemed to sell everything from beach towels to groceries.

Marian turned to her sister. "I must say I'm surprised that you picked Sa Coma to come to. I would have thought Palma Nova or Magaluf would have been more your kind of thing."

"I told you I worked here," Shelly replied, "and I wanted a quieter resort."

Rose paused by a row of swimwear to admire a pretty red bikini.

"You should get that." Shelly placed her hands on Rose's shoulder. "The colour would look amazing on you."

"Yes, treat yourself," Marian urged, "and get some colour on that milk bottle belly of yours."

Rose glanced at the price tag. It was relatively cheap, so, mind made up, she picked it off the rails.

Fin whistled as she passed him by. "You wearing that tomorrow?"

"No," Rose replied, with a touch of sarcasm, "I thought I'd buy it just to look at."

As she waited at the till, she noticed Tom staring at her in that unnerving manner of his and her skin prickled in response. A glance at her watch told her it was past nine-thirty. The sun had set and the sky was dark, but it was still hot. Rose loosened the belt around her midriff and fanned her face with one hand.

The shop assistant placed her purchase in a bag and gave Rose back her change before wishing her a pleasant evening.

They resumed a slow stroll, chattering amongst themselves.

"Excuse me, ladies." A well-proportioned African lady, dressed in a striking lime green tunic, beckoned them over. She was sitting on a stool, next to a board which advertised her hair-braiding skills. "You have in hair?" She pointed to a picture showing a multicoloured row of beads twined on a model's head.

"Yes!" Shelly plonked herself down on a facing stool and cocked her head to one side as the hair lady set to work.

"You have pretty hair." The African lady beamed a smile at Rose. "You have beads also."

"Okay," Rose nodded, "but one row only."

"It's a rip-off," Tom whispered in her ear, "I could do it for free."

Rose laughed lightly. "Somehow I doubt that."

"I'm very good with my hands." He folded his arms across his chest as they both watched the woman's fingers working their magic over Shelly's head.

Rose swallowed. "I would hope so, you being an electrician. Hair, on the other hand, might be a different story."

"What are you two whispering about?" Marian demanded to know.

"Nothing," Rose squeaked, "just talking hair."

Marian looked at them suspiciously. "Fin's decided he wants a bead as well, so we might be here for some time. Will you come and look around the shops with me, Rose?"

"But I was next!" Rose protested.

"You can go after Fin," Marian snapped bossily, "we won't be long. I, er... just need to get something."

"Okay." Rose picked up her bag and followed Marian across the road.

"I need some pain relief." Marian winced. "Headache from hell."

"Oh, you should have said. I bought a first aid pack with me."

"It's come on all of a sudden and I don't want to be a party pooper and have to go back to the hotel early." Marian lowered her voice. "I think I'm on the verge of getting lucky with Fin. He's been paying me compliments all evening."

"That's great, if you're sure that's what you want." Rose spotted the paracetamol and they headed towards it.

"What do you think of him?"

Rose answered slowly, "I think Fin's a nice guy."

"He's hot as hell," cut in Marian, "have you seen his pecs? And he smells divine. How are you getting on with Tom?"

"What d'you mean? Nothing's going on between us, Marian!"

Marian slid her a knowing glance. "Not yet, but wouldn't it be fun if we all hooked up?"

"I don't think a holiday fling would be fun." Rose passed her the pills and followed her to the till. "Just be careful you don't get your heart broken."

Marian snorted. "You are such a worrier, Rose. I'm not going to propose to the guy. I need some stress relief, that's all. My life is so structured… so staid. A summer of passion is just what I need."

Rose cleared her throat. "It sounds like a summer of madness to me."

"Ha! Sometimes we all need a little madness in our lives, including you, Rose Archer." Marian gave her arm an affectionate pat and, as she turned away to pay, Rose was left thinking that maybe Marian was right, after all.

twenty-one

Once the braid was firmly in her hair, Rose paid the cheerful woman and they headed towards a pub-restaurant which was blaring live music. Rose felt her spirits deflate as she read a sign signifying there was karaoke every night at this particular establishment. But Marian, Shelly and the guys seemed excited by the idea of embarrassing themselves in front of a large group of strangers. Except for Tom, who was looking like she felt – aghast at the prospect. They settled at a pale plastic table which was chipped and covered in minute pieces of rock salt. A waitress sped walked towards them, disinfected cloth in hand.

"What can I get you guys?" she shouted, above the din of the live disco.

The women decided on another round of cocktails, while the men ordered bottled beer. A quick flick of her cloth and she was gone, taking the ketchup and salt pot with her. Around them, people were still eating. The smell of greasy food permeated the air and Rose felt her stomach squelch.

Marian wound her way around the tables and came back with a song list.

"How about it? Us three girls up there together?"

"Oh no," Rose held up her hand, "I don't do public singing.

"Spoilsport." Marian gazed at Shelly expectantly. "Tell me my bubbly sister is up for a song or two?"

"As long as it's not I Will Survive." Shelly ran one manicured finger down the playlist. For the next five minutes they bickered about the song choice, but then decided on an Eighties track which oozed the proverbial cheese.

They settled back to watch a stream of people crooning an assortment of songs from the Sixties through to modern day. The atmosphere in the pub was happy. People were clapping along and swaying in time with the tempo.

"And now, ladies and gents, we have two sisters from England. Come on up now, Shelly and Marian."

There was a spattering of applause. Rose flipped her phone onto its side and pressed record. The karaoke machine burst into life as Shelly and Marian opened their mouths to sing.

"They are awful," Fin said, as the two sisters were pelting out the last notes.

"Hey! That's my wife-to-be up there," Harry protested, socking his brother on the upper arm.

"Be honest, bro, they cannot sing."

"How about you then, Fin?" Rose interjected. "Could you do any better?"

"Is that a dare?" Fin grinned widely.

"Yes!" Rose picked up the pencil. "Name your tune."

"And if I get a standing ovation," Fin said swiftly, "you owe me a kiss. Done." He reached across to shake Rose's hand. "Put me down for New York, New York."

Rose gaped at him with surprise and noticed Tom frowning and shaking his head.

"Oooo-kay," she replied, "that's a hard song to sing, though."

Fin rubbed his hands together. "I love a challenge. Same goes with my women." Rose was disconcerted when he winked at her. "Here's Marian," she said firmly.

. . .

"Was I okay?" Shelly draped her arms around Harry's shoulders.

"You were great," Harry replied, pulling her onto his lap. "Both of you."

"Fin's going to have a go," Rose said brightly. She scraped back her chair and walked over to the DJ. When she came back, another round of drinks had been placed on the table.

"What is that?" Rose eyed the yellow frothy cocktail warily.

"Banana Daiquiri," Shelly announced. "I've made hundreds of these on my travels. They sure like them in Asia."

Rose sipped some of the liquid through the straw. "It's lovely," she acknowledged, "but I really should slow down, my head's feeling a little woozy."

Tom frowned across the table at her. "Would you like some water?"

Rose nodded. "That's a good idea."

The waiting staff were busy, so Tom went over to the brightly lit neon bar. Rose followed him, pausing underneath a rapidly whirring ceiling fan.

"It's so hot," she said to him, tempted to wrap her whole body around the cool metal bar handrail. "I'm so glad I left my suede jeans at home."

"You were going to bring suede jeans?" Tom chuckled. "Did you think the climate would be the same as in England?"

"I didn't quite know what to expect," Rose replied, tucking a damp curl behind her ear, "but it is hotter than I anticipated."

"It's good that we have fully-functioning air conditioning in the rooms, otherwise you wouldn't get much sleep."

"I can imagine." Rose signalled to the bar attendant by pointing to the bottles of water in the fridge.

"Have you ever slept on a beach, Rose?" Tom stared down at her.

"Um, absolutely not." She shook her head. "Aren't there tons of creepy crawlies on the beach at night?"

"You might see the odd crab or two," he replied, "and maybe in Australia you could be lucky enough to see turtles, but here in Majorca the beaches are very clean and it's an unforgettable experience to be sleeping right next to the ocean. Better than any inflatable ride thrill."

Rose was struck with the crazy notion that Tom might be a tad jealous of the fun day she had spent with Fin.

"We should do something... tomorrow."

"Like what?"

"The banana boat?" she said lamely. "It looks fun."

"Let's see how we feel tomorrow," Tom said smoothly. "Too many more of those cocktails and bouncing about will be the last thing on your mind." He cleared his throat. "I apologise, that sounded rude."

Rose laughed. "It's okay, I know what you meant." She glanced shyly up at him. "You know, you don't come across as a traditional Australian male. You seem more British, as your manners are impeccable."

"Really?" Tom lifted an eyebrow. "Now I'm intrigued! What do you view as a typical Australian male, and are you saying we have no manners?"

This time it was Rose's turn to be apologetic. "Sorry, that was rude of me. I just always envisaged Australian men as beer-swilling male chauvinists. Which I have wrongly gleaned from the press and media."

Tom sucked in a sharp breath. "Ouch. No, Rose, we're not all like that, as I suppose not all Englishmen are football hooligans. Fin likes a drink, as you've probably noticed, but Harry and I can take it or leave it. I guess growing up with a drunk means you become immune to the positives of alcohol."

"I'm sorry," Rose touched his arm, "that was insensitive of me."

"You don't need to apologise." Tom's smile created a flipping sensation in her stomach. "You look beautiful, by the way."

"Thank you." Rose grinned, feeling ridiculously pleased with the compliment. "I guess we should rejoin the others."

Tom picked up the bottles. "Lead the way."

Fin's rendition of New York, New York was surprisingly good. In fact, as the song wore on, he seemed to gain in confidence and belted out the notes with ease. He also executed a dance move that was sort of a combination of Tom Jones's hip swings combined with Prince's sexy gyrations. The women in the bar began to cheer and whoop and one bold middle-aged lady even sidled up to him and ran her hands up and down his chest.

Marian's face turned thunderous. "How tacky," she hissed.

But Fin seemed to enjoy the attention and finished the song with his arms wrapped around two complete strangers.

Rose was disconcerted to notice the women in the pub pushing back their chairs to stand and clap. Fin caught her gaze and winked salaciously before heading towards her. From the corner of her eye, she was aware of Marian throwing one of her formidable glares in her direction, and she internally willed Fin to kiss her instead. No such luck. Fin had set a path towards her, with a determined look on his face.

"I think you owe me a kiss, Rose."

Rose was embarrassed and growing angrier by the second. Fin knew that Marian liked him romantically, so why was he playing with her affections? Was she a game to him? Rose wondered, glancing at Marian with sympathy.

When he aimed for her lips, Rose turned her head and murmured in his ear to stop fooling around.

He pecked her cheek and drew back. "Sorry. I must be the wrong brother, huh?"

Heat flamed in Rose's cheeks. "I like you as a friend, Fin, and that's all." She mumbled the words, hoping that the others hadn't overheard.

"Fair enough." He plonked down on the chair and took a long swig of beer.

There was an awkward silence, which was broken by Harry asking everyone what they would like to drink next.

~

They left the karaoke bar and walked slowly back to the hotel.

"The entertainment isn't bad," Shelly said. "There's a magician tonight and an Abba tribute act later on in the week."

"What's going on over there?" Marian pointed to the beach where a group of men were hauling lights and speaker systems onto a makeshift stage.

"Looks like a beach party," Fin answered, "let's check it out."

Rose clambered over a low wall and then her feet were sinking into soft sand.

"Howdy," Fin said to the men, who had paused to catch their breath, "is this a private party or is anyone allowed to join?"

"The more the merrier," a sandy-haired muscular man said. "It'll cost you, though."

"I'll pay." Tom dug in his pocket for his wallet.

Rose opened her handbag. "Can I give you something towards it?"

"No," Tom snapped, "let me treat you."

"Then I'll pay for the drinks." Rose stuck out her chin.

"Has she always been this stubborn?" Tom asked Shelly.

"Yep." Shelly wrapped her arms around her friend. "And she's perfect just the way she is."

"Yes, she is." Tom had said the words so quietly that Rose thought she may have imagined them.

They were distracted by the booming sound of music and a flurry of activity as people began piling onto the beach. Once Tom had paid, a man wearing a ripped vest and Ray-bans stamped the back of their hands with red ink. Which meant they could leave and re-enter tonight's beach party as many times as they wanted.

"Let's dance," Shelly cried, pulling off her shoes and grabbing Rose by the arm. Fin, Harry and Tom went to the makeshift bar to purchase more cocktails. As Shelly and Rose began swaying in time to the disco beat, Marian plonked down on the sand and looked around with distaste.

"We're the oldest ones here," she grumbled.

"Oh, c'mon." Shelly beckoned her to join in. "How often could you do this in dreary Britain?"

"Actually, I went to a proper beach party in Brighton one summer," Marian sniffed. "There were thousands there."

"Wasn't that when you were offered drugs most of the night and fell over in a pool of vomit?"

"What?" Marian blinked as remembrance dawned. "It was fine after the police raid!"

Shelly sighed. "This is a family resort, Marian. Just enjoy it for what it is."

"I still think we should have gone back to the hotel." Reluctantly, Marian clambered to her feet. "How am I going to get lucky with Fin with all these other women around?"

"Me and Rose have told you to make the first move," Shelly advised. "Fin loves confident women. He won't do the chasing, Maz."

Marian stuck out her bottom lip. "He was willing to chase after Rose."

"He was just joking," Rose said quickly. "We're inflatable ride buddies, that's all."

Marian squinted across at Fin who had his back to them. "You think he likes me?"

"Only one way to find out. Here," Shelly reached across to pop open two buttons on her sister's blouse, "go and seduce him girl."

"Okay," Marian grinned, "but first I'll pop to the toilet. Hitch up my skirt and reapply my lip gloss." She wandered off, kicking sand behind her.

"Are you sure we should be encouraging her?" Rose asked nervously. "What if he turns her down?"

"I doubt he will," Shelly shook her head, "but in the unlikely event of this happening, we'll just have to fix up my darling sister with some other male."

"You don't mean..." Rose swallowed. "Not Tom?"

Shelly gaped at her. "Of course not Tom. What a ludicrous idea." She threw back her head and laughed.

"Why? What's wrong with him?" Rose inhaled sharply. "He's not married, is he? Or... gay?"

"No to both," Shelly replied, her eyes twinkling in the darkness. "He's just not Marian's type, that's all. She'd scar him for life."

Rose chuckled. "She is pretty intense. Poor Fin."

"Oh, he could handle Marian. He's an expert at relationships with difficult women."

They were both sniggering when the guys returned with the drinks.

"What's so funny?" Harry asked, passing their drinks over.

"Your brother is in for a treat," Shelly whispered, "a Marian experience that he will never forget."

"Looks like she's too late," Harry replied, pointing backwards. "He's got talking to a chick from Yorkshire."

Rose and Shelly turned around. Fin was swaying diagonally across the sand with his arm around a woman who was wearing the shortest skirt Rose had ever seen.

"Oh, my sister sure is going to be mad!" Shelly laughed even more.

"Ssh, she's coming back." Rose glanced at Fin, who was now standing cradling his beer while the Yorkshire lass began a slow, provocative dance directly in front of him.

A burst of lager erupted from Harry's mouth. "Is that a mating ritual?"

"What's going on?" Marian stalked towards them, throwing daggers in Fin's direction.

Harry shrugged. "She's from Yorkshire."

"Yorkshire?" Marian screeched. "What the hell is he doing with some Northern strumpet? They have no class and they're tight as a duck's arse. Not to mention their common accent."

Yorkshire chick turned around. "You talking about me?"

"No. I was referring to that post behind you." Marian's tone dripped with sarcasm. "Of course I'm talking about you! There's no one else around here chatting with a bizarre accent."

"Actually," Yorkshire lass pointed, "there's a whole crowd of us over there."

Marian's face drained of colour as she spotted a lairy group of revellers, many of which consisted of muscular men who were staring their way.

"What's your problem, anyway?" Yorkshire lass continued. "Is this your fella?"

Marian's lips snapped into a tight line.

"They're friends," Rose gabbled, wanting to diffuse the tense situation. "Come on, Marian, let's go and look at the sea." She took hold of her hand and tugged her away. "Fin really isn't worth all this aggro," Rose said, as Marian shrugged her off and stalked on ahead.

"He is!" Marian snapped. "I really like him. Why doesn't he like me?"

"I'm sure he does," Rose replied, in the most soothing tone she could muster, "but Marian, I'm afraid he comes across as a bit of a player. You may have had a lucky escape there and sometimes not getting what you want can be a blessing."

"How would you know? Shelly said you've never had a serious boyfriend, so why should I take romantic advice from you?"

"Go back then," Rose shrugged, "go and throw yourself at him if you're that desperate. Yes, it's true I've never had a serious relationship, but at least I have self-respect!"

"Oh God, I'm sorry." Marian buried her face in her hands. "I'm a sharp-tongued bitch sometimes, and I've made such a fool of myself."

"Fin's the fool," Rose said softly.

"Jeez, my ears are burning." Fin's voice wafted through the darkness. Rose turned to watch him jogging towards them, but Marian stared resolutely at the ocean.

"Marian, I'm sorry," Fin began, "I've acted like a dick."

"Yes, you have," Marian retorted. "Go away."

"I'm all yours if you still want me," he said breathlessly.

"What about your new admirer?"

"She's gone." He hooked an arm around her waist. "It's you I like."

"Really?" Marian's lower lip trembled as she looked up at him.

"Yeah, really," he drawled, before dipping his head and kissing her.

Rose backed away. "I'll leave you to it."

"Rose..." Marian's face was luminous with happiness in the moonlight, "thank you."

"No problem." Rose smiled and headed back to the others with a happy spring to her step.

twenty-two

"What are those two doing?" Shelly asked, an hour later. "Actually, forget I asked that. Do I really want to know?"

"Probably best not to," Rose replied lightly.

"So they're really getting it on at last?" Shelly mouthed, peering through the darkness.

Rose nodded. "It seems that way."

Shelly touched her arm. "You aren't pining for Fin yourself a little?"

"Absolutely not." Rose drained the last remnants of liquid from her glass. "Want another?"

"Lead the way!"

Rose picked up her bag and walked towards the bar, swaying slightly. "Those cocktails sure are nice."

Shelly caught hold of her as she stumbled. "Why don't we have a mocktail next?"

"Actually, I was thinking more of a sex on the beach. What's in that?"

"Vodka mainly," Shelly replied drily. "So now we've got my darling sister hooked up, how about you?"

"What?"

Shelly sighed. "Isn't there anyone who's caught your eye?

Surely you must have noticed the waiters giving you admiring glances and then there were a few fit men I noticed looking at you around the pool yesterday."

"Not my type." Rose waved the idea away. "Tom's nice."

Shelly stopped walking. "Did you just say our Tom?"

"Yes." Internally, Rose was aware that she shouldn't be disclosing this information, but the alcohol was doing strange things to her inhibitions and loosening her tongue.

Shelly looked alarmed. "Rose," she said slowly, "get that idea right out of your head. Tom is..."

"Gorgeous," finished Rose, hiccupping slightly.

"And scarred emotionally."

"What d'you mean?" Rose gazed at her, bleary-eyed. "Lots of people go through break-ups."

"It's not just that." Shelly shook her by the shoulders. "He's too dangerous for you, Rose. You're way too innocent for the likes of Tom Sinclair."

"Well, maybe I want to be corrupted." Rose winked. "Besides, he's been the perfect gentleman."

"Rose," Shelly said urgently, "there are things about Tom you don't know..."

They were interrupted by a charging Harry, who lifted Shelly from the sand and threw her over his shoulder.

"Us guys are dying from thirst. What's taking you so long?"

Rose laughed at the sight of Shelly; hair flowing, beating her fists on her husband-to-be's back.

The DJ abruptly stopped the dance track which had been playing. "Shall we slow it down?" he hollered. A large cheer erupted from the crowd.

"Do you want to dance?" Tom's hand was a gentle pressure upon her shoulder. Rose turned to face him.

"Say no if you want," he said, grinning, and Rose felt her pulse quicken.

"I'd like that." She slipped her hand in his and followed him to the sectioned-off dance area.

"Fin and Marian have reappeared." Tom nodded to the amorous couple who were sitting with their limbs entwined on the sand.

"Finally they get it together." Rose smiled at the sight of Marian's smeared lipstick and ruffled hair.

"Good to see." Tom's breath was warm on her ear as he pulled her closer. "I was worried for a while that you might fall for him, too."

Rose cleared her throat and swayed a little. "Actually, I like somebody else."

"Oh yeah?" His warm hands rested on her hips.

Rose's hungry gaze locked on his. "I like you," she murmured, "a lot."

He pulled back a little, a teasing smile playing on his lips.

"But I've been warned off you," she continued, "and I have no idea if you feel the same about me."

She looked down at the sand, embarrassed by her outburst, but his fingers lifted her chin.

"I'm no good for you," he said huskily, "but right now I want you, Rose."

"Let me be the judge of that," she said firmly, as his head dipped down, "and oh..." her stomach flipped over, "I want you, too."

Then they were kissing, slowly at first and then with an intensity that took her breath away. It seemed to last forever, that first kiss, and all the while it was happening, it felt like there were a thousand fireworks detonating in Rose's stomach.

"Jesus!" Tom said shakily, stepping away abruptly.

Rose gazed up at him, her eyes like molten lava.

"Don't look at me like that," he rasped, "we shouldn't be doing this."

"Why not?" She grabbed hold of his hand, pulling him back.

"You're drunk for a start," he replied, "and I don't take advantage of inebriated women."

"I want you to take advantage of me," she implored, "and I'm perfectly capable of making my own decisions. I'm not a child, Tom."

"We should stop, Rose," he pushed a curl off her forehead, "this isn't a good idea."

"It's too late," she mumbled throatily, "it's already started."

Feeling bold, Rose hooked her arms around his neck, drawing him down again. This time she was in charge of the kiss and it was even more intense. When they finally drew apart, they were both gasping.

"The music's stopped," Tom commented. They both looked around. People were starting to disperse, leaving a trail of debris all over the beach.

"What a mess!" Rose bent to pick up an empty beer bottle. "The beautiful beach."

"Leave it, Rose," Tom said, "there are staff paid to clear up. By the morning, you'll never know there was a party here."

"Where's everyone gone?" Rose hiccupped.

"Looks like Fin's gone back to our room." Tom hooked an arm around her waist as they began heading towards the lights of the hotel. "He asked me if Marian could stay in our room for the night. Which means I've been usurped from my bed."

"You can stay in my room," Rose said quickly, "it has three beds."

"What about Shelly? She won't be happy when she finds out we've slept in the same room."

"Shelly's my best friend, not my mother. I'm twenty-eight, Tom, not four and..." Rose stopped as bile rose suddenly in her throat, "I think I'm going to be sick."

She felt herself being steered quickly towards a bin that was lining the promenade.

She was vaguely aware of him holding back her hair as she retched.

"Please go," she mumbled, "you don't need to see this."

"I'm staying," he said firmly. "Here..." He passed her a napkin.

Rose wiped her mouth. "Sorry. You were right about those cocktails, I shouldn't have drunk so many."

"You're on holiday," he smiled, "and like you said, you're not a child."

"I feel terrible," Rose admitted miserably.

"Let's get you back to the room."

They walked slowly along a tree-lined path. Tom fumbled in his pocket for the gate card which would take them back into the hotel grounds.

"The pool looks beautiful." Rose gasped at the sight of the serene water, lit up with floor lights.

"It's a nice hotel," Tom said, as they passed hundreds of sunbeds, vacant for the night.

"Is madam okay?" A waiter holding a tray of drinks paused by the side of them.

"Madam is fine," Tom replied.

The lift seemed to forever to reach the ground floor, and all the while Rose's stomach squelched uncomfortably.

"I think I'm going to throw up again." A feeling of panic engulfed her.

"We're nearly there."

Rose slunk down in the corner of the lift as it rose steadily to the fifth floor. The doors whooshed open. Then Tom was pulling her to her feet and leading her quickly down the corridor.

She clamped one hand over her mouth as Tom inserted the card in the door. Once it was open, she hurried past him and into the bathroom, firmly closing the door. Then she sank down next to the toilet and retched again.

Thoughts tumbled through Rose's mind; Tom's strong arms around her and that scorching kiss. How typical that she had spoilt the evening by drinking too much alcohol.

"Are you okay in there?" There was a gentle rap on the door.

"Um, yeah... just give me five minutes." Rose staggered to her feet and glanced in the mirror. My word, she looked a mess! Her hair was sticking up, her make-up was smudged and one of her earrings was missing. Her pearl set which had been a gift from Granny Faith. Rose sighed and then swilled her face with cold water, before brushing her teeth vigorously.

Then she unlocked the door and told Tom about her bare left ear.

"I doubt you'll find it," he said sympathetically. He patted the bed and she noticed he'd turned down the sheets and plumped the pillows.

"Where are you going to sleep?" She swayed across the room and flopped on the bed.

"Right here on the sofa bed." Tom passed her a large tumbler of water. "Drink this, it will help stop a hangover."

Rose took the glass gratefully. "Sorry again. I'm not used to alcohol. I only usually drink it at Christmas. I look and feel like a complete mess."

"A good night's sleep will rectify that." He pulled off his shirt and Rose gulped at the sight of his muscular chest.

"Lie down," he instructed. "On your side."

Rose did as she was told, aware of his fingers loosening the straps of her sandals.

"Tom, about that kiss..."

"Ssh." He placed a forefinger softly over her lips. "We can talk in the morning."

Rose struggled to sit back up. She wanted to tell him how much she liked him, that it wasn't just because she was drunk, but he was pushing her gently back down and telling her to go to sleep, in that sexy voice of his. She closed her eyes and the sound of the rolling sea pulled her into a deep slumber.

The sound of shouting woke Rose early the next morning. Bleary-eyed, she turned to face the open patio door. The curtain remained still, signifying there was little wind, but it was hot, so hot already. Rose's body, covered in the white bed sheet, was damp with perspiration. She shifted and rose groggily to her feet. A quick look around told her that Tom was still sleeping, lying on his side, his broad back uncovered. She crept to the patio door, peeking her head out. The bright sunshine hurt her eyes and instinctively she shielded them with her hand. There were people in the sea already, she could see their figures looking like distant matchstick men, bobbing in the waves.

Rose padded back inside, pausing by the mini fridge to pour herself a large glass of water. As she gulped it down, a flashback of last night assailed her: the lovely meal, fun karaoke and then the beach party. The passionate kiss she had shared with Tom. It all came flooding back and Rose's mouth gaped open slightly as she relived the delicious feeling of his mouth and his strong arms around her.

As she was gazing at him, he stirred, turned onto his back and stared directly at her.

"Morning," she said softly.

"You're up," came his surprised reply.

"I couldn't sleep... the heat."

He raked a hand through his tousled dark hair. "How are you feeling?"

"Okay, I guess, a little dehydrated."

Tom chuckled. "Water for you today, Missy."

"Yes." Rose smiled and there ensued a silent pause, which was broken by a loud rap on the door.

"If that's room service, tell them to come back." Tom hooked the sheet over his face and Rose glanced at her watch. It wasn't even seven o'clock. She padded to the door and was confronted by a worried-looking Shelly.

"Thank goodness!" Shelly bustled in, eyes scanning sharply over Rose's mussed-up bed and Tom's prone frame. "I'm really angry with Marian for doing this. She should be here with you, Rose! I presume she's with Fin?"

"Good morning, sister-in-law." Tom peeled back the sheet to reveal his grinning face.

"Is it?" Shelly snapped. "Poor Rose, having to bunk in with you."

"Oh no." Rose stepped forward. "Tom looked after me last night."

"I bet he did!" Shelly's eyes gravitated into a roll. "Well, I suppose I should go and get dressed. Shall we meet for breakfast in an hour?" She flounced out of the room, the ties of her silk dressing gown trailing on the floor.

Rose folded her arms across her chest and glanced shyly at Tom. "I'll shower and get ready, then."

"Okay." Tom flipped onto his side. "Wake me up when you're ready."

After a lengthy cool shower, and a change into her new bikini and sundress, Rose was ready to face a new day. She tiptoed round the room while Fin slept, picking up discarded items of clothing and rearranging the shampoo bottles in the bathroom. Rose watched him for a while and then, feeling overwhelmed with longing and worried that she was adopting serious voyeuristic tendencies, she went out onto the patio and swept up the grains of sand that she and Marian had brought into the room. She leant against the glass railing, the sun warming her face as she watched a rotating sprinkler soaking the beautiful bougainvillea and myrtle.

The patio door slid open and she looked over her shoulder. Tom flashed her the loveliest smile, which had her stomach flipping and her skin prickling.

"Are you hungry?" he asked.

"Famished." Rose coloured slightly. "Apologies for last night again. I don't know what came over me. I'm usually so sensible."

"I had a great time," he said casually, "and you don't need to apologise, you didn't do anything wrong."

Oh, but I did, Rose thought. I let my guard down big time!

"You must be hungry, too," Rose looked up at him, "and I hope the bed was comfortable."

"Are you always so concerned for others?" he asked, stepping closer.

"I suppose I am..." Rose cleared her throat, "when I care about them."

He twined his fingers through hers. "You are so lovely," he said softly, his head lowering. Rose closed her eyes and waited. But the sudden rapping on the door had them springing apart.

"Yoo-hoo!" Marian burst into the room like a mini whirl-wind. "Only me. Shelly's sent me up to come and get you, they're all waiting in the restaurant. Did you guys have a clean-up? It's tidy in here."

"Hi, Marian." Rose stepped back inside the room. "We were just... er... coming."

"Well, come on then." Her bossy tone had Rose quickly pulling on her flip flops. "Tom, you need to put a t-shirt on, you can't go in the restaurant with a bare chest."

"I'll get a clean one." Tom stepped past them.

When he'd gone, Marian linked her arm through Rose's. "Did you have a good night then?"

Rose blinked. "Nothing happened, Marian."

"What? You mean you had a room together, alone, and you slept in separate beds?" Marian looked incredulous.

"I mean I was drunk and sick. Tom was the perfect gentle-man," Rose picked up her sunglasses, "and I'm not going to discuss my personal business with you, anyway."

"Fair enough," Marian's face creased into a wide smile, "but I can disclose that someone got lucky last night and it was heaven." She skipped up the corridor. Behind her, Rose scowled, kicking at the carpet as she ruminated when and if she was ever going to be the girl who got lucky.

twenty-three

After breakfast, they trooped down to the beach with their bags and inflatables.

"Whoa, it's hot!" Fin flopped down onto a vacant sunbed.

"Darling, before you get comfortable, can you rub some cream onto my back?" Marian passed him the bottle and with a sigh Fin rose back to his feet.

"Is this what the rest of the holiday is going to be like," Shelly whispered in Rose's ear, "darling this and darling that?"

"And I thought you were the loved-up ones," Rose replied ruefully.

"Fancy a swim?" Shelly turned towards the ocean. "There aren't too many in at the moment."

"Sure." Rose tugged off her sundress, revealing her new red bikini. She noticed Tom's gaze roaming the length of her and felt suddenly awkward and shy. She picked up the inflatable lilo, holding it against her bare midriff, before walking briskly down towards the water.

Shelly jogged to catch up with her. "Everything okay between you and Tom?"

Rose flopped her lilo down on the water. "Yes, of course, but I'd rather not talk about him."

Shelly looked hurt. "You used to tell me everything."

"There's nothing to tell... really. We just kissed, that's all, and I haven't forgotten how you tried to warn me off him last night."

Shelly swallowed. "I'm just looking out for you. Tell me to mind my own business next time."

"Okay." Rose grinned as she pushed her inflatable past the breaking waves. "Now comes the fun bit."

After a struggle with the lilo and numerous falls into the water, Rose managed to pull herself on. She lay on her stomach, watching Shelly with amusement as she battled to get on hers.

"Finally!" Shelly manoeuvred her arms over the side until she reached Rose.

"This is heaven," Rose said sleepily, reaching out to grasp Shelly's hand.

Lazily, they floated past an amorous couple with their limbs entwined, a father snorkelling with his young son and a group of lads playing catch with a beach ball.

One of the men shouted something at them in a foreign language.

"What did he say?" Rose murmured.

"No idea. I don't understand German." Shelly raised her head to look at them. They were wolf-whistling and waving.

"Didn't you visit Germany on your travels?"

"No, that's one place I didn't stay. Oh no, they're coming over."

Rose struggled up onto her elbows and watched the four men swimming towards them.

"Guten morgen," the fair-haired man shouted, "bist du Englisch?"

"Ja!" Shelly shouted. "English."

"Nice to meet you," one of the other men said in perfect English. He then went on to introduce himself and the others.

"We have visited England many times – London, Liverpool,

York. It is a great country." He smiled at Rose. "Have you been to Germany?"

Rose shook her head. "This is my first time abroad, ever."

"Wow." Hans splashed water over his dark curls. "So, you like?"

"I love," Rose made a heart symbol with her hands, "although flying – not so much."

"She likes water sports, though," Shelly said, with a grin.

"Ah yes." Hans nodded. "Have you tried parasailing?"

"What?"

"You know, up there?" He pointed to the sky.

"No," Rose said hastily, "I don't like heights."

Hans flicked water at her playfully. "You should try. I could come, too, hold your hand."

Rose blushed and shook her head, a movement which made Hans laugh. "You prefer to play with a German ball?"

"What?" Rose spluttered, aware that Shelly and the others were laughing at Hans' cheeky flirting. "No, but thank you... I'm just relaxing with my friend."

"Ah, okay, I see you are not interested, but if you change your mind..." He trailed off, giving Rose a wink. Then the four of them were gone, back to their game and no doubt to torment other unsuspecting women.

"Thanks for your help dealing with that," Rose said hotly to Shelly.

"I thought you wanted me to mind my own business," Shelly replied lightly. "Besides, I knew you could handle a randy German, it's an Australian I'm more concerned about."

Rose told her to shush, but her eyes were bright with good humour.

"I'm just going to have five minutes," she said sleepily, as she closed her eyes and the background noise slowly faded away ...

"Rose! Rose! Wake up." Shelly was shaking her arm frantically.

"What's wrong?" Rose mumbled, her face warm and salty from the sea lapping against it.

"We've drifted!" Shelly yelled.

Rose was immediately wide awake. "Where's the beach?"

She looked in all directions, but all she could see was vast blue sea.

"I don't know," Shelly sobbed. "Oh Jesus, we're going to drown and my hen night and wedding and honeymoon…"

"Stop!" Rose shouted. "We're going to be all right. Sit up, Shelly."

Rose helped her into a sitting position. "We need to stay calm." Carefully, she turned on the lilo, cupping her hand above her eyes. "I can see land. There." She pointed and Shelly craned her neck, following her line of vision.

"Yes, you're right. I can see the beach, but we're so far away." Shelly licked her lips. "What are we going to do?"

"We'll have to get in the water and swim," Rose replied calmly. "We're drifting further away from land. We need to start now, Shelly."

Rose slipped off her lilo and into the water.

"I can't." Tears were pooling in Shelly's eyes. "I'm terrified of deep water and I'm not a good swimmer like you are."

"Stay on here, I'll pull you." Rose flashed her a wobbly smile. "It'll be okay."

"But what can I do?" Shelly wiped the tears away with the back of her hand.

"Paddle in the direction I'm going, that will help get us to the beach faster."

Rose began swimming with one arm, kicking her legs with all her might and pulling the lilo with the other.

She made slow progress, cutting through the gentle waves, passing a line of plastic buoys bobbing on the surface. From far away Rose could hear the sound of rumbling engines.

"Oh no," she said.

"What's wrong?" Shelly asked tersely. "Rose?"

"We're right in the middle of the speedboat zone. We need to get out of here fast." Rose spoke quickly. "Get in the water, Shelly and swim. NOW, Shelly!"

"Okay, okay I'm in." Panic was evident in Shelly's tone. "Surely they'll see the lilos? They're pink, for goodness' sake."

"I don't want to take that risk," Rose said with determination. "Come on, swim as fast as you can."

Shelly moved her arm frantically, holding tightly onto the inflatable with the other. Rose kicked her legs fluidly, quickening her pace. She could see the other line of buoys signifying the safe swimming area. If they could reach there, they'd be okay.

"Come on, Shelly," Rose urged, "swim faster."

"I can't," spluttered her friend. "Oh my God, there's a speedboat!" Shelly screamed. "It's coming straight for us."

"Move your ass, Shelly!" Rose shouted. She was swimming so fast that her muscles were throbbing, and the hot sun was beating down, burning her nose and already parched lips.

The sound of the speedboat loomed closer and closer. Rose and Shelly swam with all their strength, kicking in unison.

"I don't want to die!" screamed Shelly. "I want to marry Harry. I love him so much."

"Then tell him, Shelly." Rose surged on through the water, gritting her teeth. "Tell him how much you love him. Don't you give up! Keep moving."

They were almost at the buoys. Rose puffed and panted as a thunderous noise wrapped all around them. Then there was yelling from the beach as people noticed what was occurring. A bloodcurdling scream erupted from Shelly's mouth and Rose felt herself being sucked under the water and there was no more noise. Peace overcame her.

Whoosh! Water erupted from her mouth, her ears and her nose as she was pulled from the sea. She gazed up at the bright sun, her body racked by a coughing fit.

"Shelly!" she said weakly, reaching out a hand.

A dark-skinned man appeared above her, blocking out the sun's rays.

"You're going to be okay," he said, with a kind smile.

"My friend." Rose turned onto her side, trying to clamber to her knees. She looked around her at the deck of the speedboat, where two other men were bent over a prone figure. "Is she okay?"

She had never felt so relieved to hear Shelly coughing. On her hands and knees, Rose crawled towards her.

"Shelly," she whispered, "are you okay?"

"What's up, Archer?" Shelly turned her pale face towards her and held out her arms. "That was fun, huh?"

They sat on the deck, arms wrapped around each other as the speedboat bumped them back towards the shoreline. Rose could hear Harry calling for his wife-to-be and then, amidst the hullabaloo, she heard Tom's voice carrying over the sea. Rose peered over the edge of the boat. To her total surprise, all their party was in the sea and swimming towards them. Even Marian, who looked worried to death.

Harry lifted his strong arms up, reaching for Shelly as she slowly backed into the water.

"My legs are shaking," she said, burying her face into Harry's neck.

"I gotcha." He rained kisses over her face. "Are you all right? Nothing bruised or broken?"

"No," Shelly replied, "they checked us on the boat, we're both fine. Just swallowed a stomach full of water."

"Let's get you outta the water." He began to tow her the short distance back to the shore.

"Wait! Rose!" She looked behind her.

"I'm coming," Rose shouted, "carry on."

Marian and Fin were treading water next to the boat. "D'you need us to tow you back to the beach?" Fin asked.

"I'm okay," Rose replied, her gaze rested on a concerned-looking Tom.

"You sure you're okay?" he asked, as she backed into the warm water. He wrapped his arms around her and looked down at her.

"Yes, just a bit shaky."

"That was one extreme thrill ride, huh?" Fin said, with a wide grin. "Tom was frantic with worry."

"You were?" Gingerly, Rose placed her feet down, thankful to feel the firm sea-bed.

"Of course." The water dripped from Tom's shorts as he walked through the waves. He took hold of her hand, lifting it to his lips for a kiss. "I knew you'd be okay, though. It was Shelly that was the real worry."

"Eh, Rose," Fin nodded towards a banana boat which was just taking off, full of people, "fancy a go on that?"

"Maybe later," Rose said, with a weak smile. "For now, I think I'm going to lie still and sunbathe."

When they got back to the sunbeds, Marian wasted no time in giving Rose and Shelly a dressing-down.

"I told you those inflatables were dangerous. You drifted out to sea and there nearly wasn't a wedding!"

"It's fine, Marian," murmured Shelly, "no harm done."

"No harm done?" Marian spluttered with anger. "I was literally sobbing, and poor Harry was white with worry. Please, don't ever go on those things again."

"She's right," Rose said. "It could have ended very badly. We were lucky."

"Okay," Harry held up his hand, "I think the girls have got the message. Now, who's for an ice cream?"

twenty-four

Rose spent the next few hours sunbathing, reading and surreptitiously ogling Tom from behind her sunglasses. She watched him playing football with Harry, wondering what, if anything, was going to happen between them. Or had their kiss been a mad, spur of the moment, drunken madness? She decided to play it cool and let him do the chasing. With her mind made up, Rose immersed herself in a fictitious world and was currently in the boudoir of a Scottish Highland knight, complete with a feisty heroine. Rose gasped as, in the book, Connor pulled off Heather's corset, and flung her onto the four poster bed.

"Any good?" Tom asked breathlessly, flopping down next to her.

Rose coughed. "Very entertaining."

"What genre is it?" He tried to peer at the cover. "Let me guess. You're reading a classic novel, something like Jane Austen or the Bronte sisters?"

Heat flooded into Rose's cheeks. "Er... it's a historical novel."

"Oh yeah?" Tom swiped the paperback out of Rose's hand.

"Give it back," she squeaked.

He glanced at the cover. "The Knight's Wanton Bride?"

Tom's eyebrows shot up. "It doesn't sound like a classic read. Let's see where you'd got to."

Rose struggled to her feet as he began reading aloud.

"Connor lifted Heather's skirt. His fingers were cool on her thighs, making her pulse quicken. Their lips met in the darkness; passionate and searching..."

"Whoa, Rose." Shelly peered over the rim of her sunglasses. "I didn't know you were into erotica!" The others started laughing and, after a slight hesitation, Rose smiled good naturedly.

"It's a historical romance, actually and it's a... erm... fun summer read."

"Sounds pornographic to me." Fin shrugged and pulled Marian into an embrace. "Maybe it could give us some tips." Marian burst into girlish giggles and Rose rolled her eyes.

"Please give me back my book." she looked enquiringly at Tom.

"Actually, Rose, I was thinking maybe we could do something together." He tossed the book on top of her beach bag.

"What did you have in mind?" Rose swallowed as he came to stand directly in front of her.

"Will you come parasailing with me?"

"You mean up there?" Rose pointed to the sky. "I'm scared of heights, Tom."

"It's not as scary as it looks," Fin said, as they all turned to watch a couple being pulled across the sky by a speedboat.

"Do it, Rose!" Shelly urged. "The only way to overcome a fear is to confront it, and Tom will look after you, won't you?"

"Sure!" Tom's eyes flashed as he took hold of her hand. "But if you want to go back to your book, that's okay."

Rose dithered. She desperately wanted to spend some time alone with him, and he was looking at her with those deep green, gorgeous eyes of his, so how could she say no to him?

"Okay," Rose said decisively, "but if I hate it, will you make them stop?"

"Absolutely." Tom strode off, tugging Rose behind him.

"Oh heavens, I can't believe I'm doing this!" Rose blew out a long, shuddering breath and gripped tightly onto the handrails. "Are you sure this is going to be okay?"

"Can I let you into a secret?" Tom whispered. "I've never done this before, either."

"What?" Rose's jaw dropped in surprise. "But I thought..."

"It'll be fine," Tom interjected. "You need to stop reading about life and start experiencing it, Rose."

"Parasailing hadn't been invented in the novel I was reading," Rose said hotly.

"I wasn't referring to that." Tom flashed her a sultry smile. "I meant the lovemaking."

Heat flooded her cheeks as Rose racked her brains, trying to think of a suitably witty reply. But there was no time, as the man at the front of the speedboat was giving his colleague a thumbs-up and the engine was rumbling to life.

"You guys ready?" The Spanish man gave the apparatus a final check and flashed them a wide grin. "Get ready for the ride of your life!"

"That was amazing!" Rose and Tom had sailed through the air for twenty minutes and were now bobbing in the sea, waiting for the speedboat to pick them up.

"It was fantastic." Tom was still holding her hand and staring at her with a huge smile on his face. "You were brave. I thought you might hate it – and me, for making you do it."

"I wanted to try it," Rose replied simply. "It's something else I can tick off my bucket list and it wasn't that stomach-flipping rollercoaster feeling you get, either. It was... well, like flying. I felt like a bird up there. I felt free, no worries, no hassle..."

Suddenly, Tom reached across and pressed his lips to hers. Rose kissed him back, wriggling in the water so she could move closer.

"I've been wanting to do that all day," he murmured, cupping her face in his hands.

"Don't stop then," Rose replied huskily.

"I want to be alone with you. I've hired a car... for tomorrow. Will you spend the day with me?"

"I'd love to." Rose touched his stubble-lined face. "But what about the others?"

"What about them? They'll be fine without us and they're all aware that we like each other, so it won't be a surprise if we sneak off together."

"You like me?" Rose teased, splashing water at him.

Tom splashed her back. "Just a bit. I suppose someone has to." He dived into the water. "Last one to the boat's a loser!" he threw back over his shoulder.

With a determined grin, Rose set off in pursuit.

Rose spent the remainder of the day sunbathing and swimming. They went back to their rooms late afternoon to freshen up and after a group vote, decided to spend the evening at the hotel. It was disco night and the atmosphere was upbeat and lively.

Shelly pulled the men up to dance, giving Rose the chance to ask Marian a few questions which had been playing on her mind all evening.

"How are you and Fin getting on?" she began tentatively.

"Great," came the reply. "Want some?" Marian pushed the sharing cocktail bowl towards her.

Rose winced. "No thanks, I'm sticking to pop tonight."

"Want a clear head for tomorrow, eh?" Marian winked.

"Shelly told you?"

"Of course! So where are you going with the delectable Tom?"

"I don't know," Rose shook her head, "I guess we'll decide in the morning."

"Or he will." Shelly gave her a knowing look. "Tom likes to be in charge, apparently. Fin told me he can be quite domineering and he's real fussy about women, too, Rose. Seems like you're highly honoured."

"Lucky me." Rose glanced at the dance floor where Shelly was limboing, her hair trailing behind her.

"You bought protection?" Marian sucked her drink noisily through her straw.

Rose coughed. "I didn't think to plan ahead. I had no idea anything would happen between us."

"Oh well, I'm sure Tom will be prepared."

"Marian!" A sudden image of Tom's naked muscular body had heat stirring in Rose's stomach.

Marian slid her a sly glance. "Sorry, Rose, I know you're shy and haven't had much experience with men. Just take it slowly, okay? From what I've heard, Tom can be pretty intense."

"I'll be absolutely fine," Rose scoffed. "So anyway, where are you sleeping tonight?"

"Sorry to disappoint you, honey," Marian patted her hand, "I'm back in with you."

"Oh." Rose's tone was laced with disappointment.

"Blame Shelly," Marian explained. "She threw a hissy fit over me bedding in with Fin and leaving you alone to fend off Tom, so now it's back to us girls only. That's at the moment, anyway. I'm sure we could change her mind if we gang up on her."

"It wasn't like that at all," Rose tutted. "We slept in separate beds and I was fully clothed throughout." Rose noticed Tom gazing at her and swallowed a nervous lump. "Maybe Shelly is right."

"About what?" Marian pulled a strip off the beer mat.

"About the fact you hardly know Fin and I hardly know Tom and oh..."

"My sister's forgotten how tempestuous she used to be," Marian cut in, "now she's all settled down and sensible. Doesn't mean you and I can't have a bit of fun, eh? Now come on, let's stop worrying and go enjoy ourselves on the dance floor."

After a good night's sleep, Rose woke feeling fresh and excited. Sunlight streamed through the open window as she dressed and applied a light layer of make-up.

"Why are you up so early?" Marian struggled to rest against the headboard. "It's only seven."

Rose stooped to pull on her sandals before replying, "We want to make an early start."

"Does Shelly know you're going to be gone all day?" Marian rubbed at her eyes, creating black smudges on her skin.

"Yes and I told her last night not to worry about me. What are you planning for today?"

"Lazing around the pool." Marian wrinkled her dainty nose. "The beach looks nice but it's so messy, especially when you're trying to apply sun cream, and today I'm seriously working on my tan."

"Well, have fun." Rose squashed items into her beach bag: a large bottle of water, a towel and an unopened bottle of factor 50. She glanced at her reflection, adding a floppy straw hat and a pair of sunglasses to her ensemble.

Marian plumped up her pillows and snuggled back down in the bed. "Have a nice day then."

"Thanks," Rose paused with one hand on the door handle, "and tell Shelly not too worry and that I'll text her."

"Will do," came the mumbled reply.

Rose closed the door softly and made her way down to the restaurant.

Tom was already seated at a white-linen-covered table. Two glasses of orange juice were set in front of him.

"Morning," Rose greeted him cheerfully.

"Morning." He looked up, startling her with his deep green gaze. "Did you sleep well?"

Rose slipped onto the chair. "I did, thanks, and you?"

"Flat out for seven hours."

She regarded him over the rim of her glass. She noticed he'd shaved, combed his usually ruffled hair and he smelt fresh and musky.

They both spoke at once. Tom grinned. "You first."

"I was just going to say it's another beautiful day."

"And I was just going to tell you how beautiful you look."

Rose smiled and looked down at her hands.

"Shall we get breakfast?" Tom stood up. The scrape of his chair sounded loud in the quiet restaurant.

Rose followed him to the buffet station. Numerous waiters passed her by, bidding her good morning and casting her appreciative glances. She lingered besides the hot food counter, watching as he piled his plate high with bacon, sausage and eggs. Rose didn't fancy a cooked breakfast. Her stomach felt fluttery and she didn't feel too hungry. She opted instead for croissants and cereal and made her way back to the table with them.

Tom called a waiter over, asking for fresh coffee.

"Oh, I'll have tea, please." Rose smiled as she sliced into her warm croissant.

"So what do you think of your first holiday abroad?" Tom thumped the base of a ketchup bottle.

"I'm having a wonderful time," Rose replied, "Majorca is stunning."

"Have you got the bug then?"

Rose swallowed. "D'you mean the travelling bug?"

"I mean, would you like to see more of the world Rose?"

"Absolutely. Not sure I'll ever be a fan of flying, but I think I've mostly conquered my phobia of air travel."

Tom leant his arms on the table. "So where would you like to go next?"

"My dream's always been to visit Italy." Rose took a sip of her juice. "I like churches, historical ruins and Italian food is my favourite. Have you been?"

"I've been to Northern Italy. Milan. It was very cosmopolitan, but Paris is my favourite."

"Is it really the most romantic city in the world?" Rose looked at him inquisitively, wondering who he had gone there with.

The smile slipped from Tom's face. "I suppose that's up to personal preference."

There followed a silent pause.

"So…" Rose wiped her mouth with the napkin, "how long are you going to stay in England?"

"We're due to fly home in a few weeks' time."

"Shelly and Harry too?"

Tom looked at her with a puzzled frown. "Yes. Their lives are in Australia."

"But… Shelly wasn't sure. She was thinking about moving back to England permanently."

Tom shrugged. "Harry loves it there. Australia's his home. Maybe, once they're married, they could visit a few times a year?"

Rose looked down at her plate, engulfed with disappointment. "And you'll be going back, too?"

"Yes," he said softly, "although England is growing on me. It has a unique charm and attraction."

Rose looked into his eyes and felt her pulse quicken. "Maybe I could visit Australia, although I'd probably have to knock myself out before the flight."

They both laughed, then Tom's face grew serious. "I like you a lot, Rose." He placed his warm hand over hers. "Shall we get to know each other better and see how things progress?"

"That sounds a good plan." Rose twined her fingers around his as sunlight streamed through the window, bathing them in a golden hue.

twenty-five

Rose was pleased that the car was air-conditioned. She fiddled with the knobs, turning the thermostat to the chilliest setting and settled back in the seat as Tom pulled away from the hotel and onto the road.

"Where are we heading?" she asked, resisting the urge to place her hand on his exposed knee.

"I thought we'd start at the neighbouring resort, Cala Millor."

"Great." Rose opened a bottle of water and took a sip.

The road was busy; with automobiles and mopeds zooming past, and people on pushbikes wobbling precariously.

"I'm glad you've hired a car," Rose said happily. "It's good to explore and see other resorts."

"I'm glad you approve." Tom flashed her a grin. "It's good to finally get you on your own."

He pressed a button on the dashboard and music erupted from a local radio station.

"They even speak English on the radio," Rose commented, after they'd listened in companionable silence for a while. "I feel inadequate not knowing their language. Maybe I'll take a Spanish class when I get home."

"Is that as well as the animal care course you'll be doing, too?"

"I'm not totally sure on that," Rose replied. "It will be a big step to give up my call centre job. The money is good and it's all I've ever known since finishing my A- levels."

"But do you like it?" Tom flicked water onto the window screen, blitzing the dust which had settled there. "There's more to life than money, Rose. Seems to me you're stuck in a rut, and there's a big wide world out there, just waiting to be explored."

"Yes, you're right, of course. I haven't been happy there for a long time. I guess I got scared of taking chances and trying something new, but I'm going to change. I don't feel afraid anymore."

"Shelly's influence?"

"Possibly." Rose laughed. "It's so great to have her back. She's so full of life, and I missed her. Really missed her."

"Shelly's lucky having such a caring friend." Tom cleared his throat. "I already knew that I'd like you from the way she described you – kind and caring. I just didn't expect you to be so..."

Rose cocked her head. "So what?"

"So damned attractive. Why are you still single?"

Rose blushed. "They call me the ice maiden at work. Not to my face, of course, but I've heard the gossip."

"What?" Tom sounded genuinely surprised. "You're anything but that. You're warm and friendly."

"I'm too fussy, apparently." Rose sighed. "I love going to church, reading... I'm a nerd and not many people my own age are into the same kind of things."

Tom gripped the steering wheel. "You're perfect. It's refreshing to meet a woman like you."

Rose's stomach fluttered at his words. Internally, she warned herself not to fall for him. This was obviously going to be a holiday fling. Tom would be going back to Australia and she would be going back to her safe, cosseted life in Twineham. They would be millions of miles apart and she might not see him again. Rose reminded herself to live in the present, try not to worry about the future and enjoy the few days she could spend getting to know the gorgeous Tom Sinclair more intimately.

They arrived at Cala Millor a short while later. After a quick whizz round, Tom found a parking spot beside the entrance to the beach.

"This is a bigger resort." Rose looked at the busy beach and the stretch of shops and bars behind it.

Tom took her hand. "What would you like to do? We could look around, spend some time on the beach?"

"Actually I'd like to do that." She pointed in the distance, where a boat was chugging towards the pier.

"The glass bottom boat?" They watched it for a while as it stopped and a stream of people alighted.

"Come on, let's go get tickets."

They spent the next few hours cruising around. The boat was full, but they managed to bag prime seats on the upper outside tier, which gave them a magnificent view of the sea and craggy coastline.

"Look at the colour of the sea!" Rose peered down at the undulating blues that were lapping against the side of the boat.

A woman who was sitting next to her asked Rose if she could take a photograph. Rose clicked the phone, taking shots of the young family.

"Thank you." The woman introduced herself as Hannah from Birmingham. "I'm guessing you're from the Midlands, too?"

"Twineham," Rose replied with a nod of her head.

Hannah from Birmingham shot her a puzzled look.

"It's a village not far from Birmingham, about a forty minute drive." Rose smiled at the baby wriggling on Hannah's lap. "This is Tom, he's from Australia."

"No way!" Hannah turned to her husband, a broad-shouldered man with a shock of dark curly hair. "Pete's from Australia, too."

"Whereabouts, mate?" Tom asked, holding his hand out for a firm shake.

"Perth, mate."

"Ah, the sunniest city in Australia, possibly the world." Tom rested his hand lightly on Rose's thigh. "I'm from Sydney."

"Cool." Pete nodded. "I've got family there."

"I take it you're not there anymore?" Tom said.

"Nah, mate, met the sheila while working in London, been in England now five years." Pete paused. "I'm sure I've seen you somewhere before."

Rose noticed Pete scrutinising Tom, his forehead creased.

Tom quickly wedged his baseball cap firmly onto his head. "I don't think so, mate. Sydney's a fair few miles from Perth."

"You look familiar," Pete persisted. "Not famous, are you?"

Tom's laughter sounded strange to Rose's ears: strained somehow.

"I'm an electrician, nobody special."

Rose looked at him sharply. He was edging away from her and looked uncomfortable.

"Fancy a drink?" he said to Rose, digging in his shorts for euros.

"Lemonade, please," Rose replied quickly, "I'll come with you."

She followed him down the steps to a bar. "Are you okay?" she asked, touching his arm.

"Yeah, fine. Think the sun was getting to me up there. Shall we sit in the shade for a bit?"

"Yes, of course." Rose took the can of lemonade and they sat down on some nearby seats. The wind ruffled her hair as she sipped her drink.

"So," she said brightly, "have you always wanted to be an electrician?"

"Um... I guess."

"And you're happy with your career choice?" Rose looked away from the sea and into his eyes.

"Never mind that." Tom lifted her chin. "Would you mind if I kissed you right now?"

A quick scan of her surroundings told Rose they were alone. "I wouldn't mind at all," she whispered.

"Good." He dipped his head, pressing his lips softly onto hers. He was gentle at first, but as the passion between them intensified, the kiss became fervent and Rose opened her mouth to deepen it. Tom's arms wound around her, holding her tight as she clung onto his shirt.

"I want you," he mumbled against her mouth, "I don't think I can wait any longer."

"Me too," Rose said huskily, sliding her hands around the nape of his neck.

"Are you sure?" Tom frowned, "I don't want you to feel pressured. You need to be certain, Rose. I..."

"Ssh," Rose placed one finger over his delectable mouth, "I'm absolutely sure."

"Later then?" His eyes bore into her.

"Later," she replied shakily.

The boat chugged to a stop and there was a mad dash towards the downstairs viewing area. Rose squashed onto the bench next to Tom, watching the colourful fish swimming by. Her mind, however, was distracted by indecent thoughts; the anticipated feel of his naked body and his lips caressing her all over. She was troubled by her own lack of experience and a little bit fearful of what he would expect from her. As if reading her thoughts, Tom kissed her hand and told her not to worry. Then he was pointing out an eel which had darted past and a shoal of fish weaving around tall, swaying seaweed.

After a while, they headed back to land. The boat made an impressive U-turn, creating a swell in the sea which had them rocking up and down.

"What next, m'lady?"

Rose laughed at Tom's attempt at a Cockney accent. She leant against him, feeling happy. "You decide."

When they returned to Cala Millor, the beach was full. Tom took her hand, helping her from the bobbing vessel.

"I'm hungry," he said. "Fancy a pizza to share?"

Rose nodded and fell into step beside him.

They found a quiet eatery down a side street. It smelt of freshly baked dough and was decorated with trailing plants and seaside pictures.

"Fancy a cocktail?" Tom wiggled his eyebrows, making her laugh.

"Not on a lunchtime," Rose replied. "I'll be no good for the rest of the day."

"Well, we can't have that." Tom ordered two sodas and a family-sized margarita pizza.

They chatted as they ate it. Tom told Rose about all the different places he'd travelled to.

"Thailand was my favourite," he said, grinning. "I was all set for finding a Thai bride and staying there, but Harry persuaded me to come to England."

"Is it your first visit?" Rose asked, pulling off a triangular-shaped wedge.

"Er... no, I've been to London."

She wondered why he'd ducked his head at her question.

"Was that with friends or a girlfriend?"

"With mates." Tom cleared his throat and pointed to a busker who was strumming a guitar outside the restaurant. "He plays good."

"Entertainment while we eat." Rose smiled. "Thank you for asking me today. I'm having a great time."

"I should be thanking you," Tom replied, gazing at her in that unnerving way of his. "I feel like the luckiest bloke on Majorca, having you with me."

"Ah, you are sweet." Rose looked down at the sharing plate. "I suppose I'll let you have the last piece of pizza for that comment."

"That's what I was hoping for." Tom winked and their laughter bought a smile from a hovering waiter.

After lunch, they walked around the resort, ducking into the many shops that lined the streets. Tom bought Rose a new hat, which she had pointed out and labelled as "cute." They took selfies while eating ice cream and had a ride on a horse and carriage. It took them back to the beach, where they spent an hour sunbathing.

"Want a go on the banana boat?" Tom pointed to a long yellow inflatable bobbing in the sea.

Rose sighed. "Another inflatable ride?"

"Not scared, are you?" Playfully, he scooped sand over her feet.

Immediately, Rose was up, dusting the sand off her hands. "Come on then."

They hopped over the hot sand, sinking their scorched feet into cool seawater.

Tom paid the man at the kiosk and they struggled into bright orange life vests. They swam out to the inflatable and Rose grabbed onto the rope as Tom pushed her up from behind.

There were half a dozen other people on the banana boat and a few of them were children. An angelic-looking girl with big blonde curls sat in front of Rose and two adolescent girls sat behind Tom. Rose could hear them giggling, no doubt excited by the close proximity of such a hunky bloke. The speedboat's engines revved and slowly, the inflatable began moving.

"Hang on!" Tom reached forward to kiss the nape of her neck and a shiver ran down Rose's spine.

Rose prepared herself to be flung about, but this was different from the inflatable sofa. It was a gentler ride, apart from the constant, annoying spray of water in Rose's face. The boat tugged them out to sea and Rose could see the shoreline becoming smaller. They passed a few other boats, waving to the people on deck.

"This is great, eh?" Tom's excitement was infectious.

The girl in front of Rose was whooping with delight and Rose was disconcerted to notice that she had let go of the handles and was waving her arms above her head.

"You need to hold on," Rose shouted.

Too late. The girl tipped to the side and then fell into the sea with a resounding crash. Without thinking, Rose dived in after her, closely followed by the girl's father and then Tom.

"Are you all right?" Rose grabbed hold of the girl.

"That was awesome!" The girl punched the air and Rose sighed with relief.

"She's a daredevil," her dad explained as they hoisted her back up.

Rose turned to Tom. "Why are you in here?" She splashed water at him.

"I thought you needed saving." He pushed her onto the inflatable before pulling himself back up. Then they were off again, bouncing over the water, heading towards the horizon, where the cloudless sky kissed the sea.

Rose squeezed the excess water from her hair as they walked along the beach. The sea lapped gently at their ankles as they passed hordes of sunbathers.

She had stuffed their belongings underneath a cerise pink towel, which she picked up to dry herself off.

"Fancy going to a different resort?" Tom was wiping droplets of water from his bronzed chest. Rose tried not to stare.

"Um... yes, but can we get some more water first?" Her throat was parched and her lips were dry and sore from the saltwater and hot sunshine. She slipped on her flip flops and they exited the beach and made their way back to the car via a quick stop at a nearby grocery store.

"I'm tired." Rose yawned as she buckled her belt into place.

"Lie back and relax." Tom flipped a switch and her seat reclined back. Soft music swooned around her and as Tom sang softly along, Rose leant her head against the window and closed her eyes.

twenty-six

She woke much later, when the sun was dipping and clouds were accumulating in the sky.

"You should have woken me." Rose stretched, her spine unravelling like a languid cat. "How long have I been asleep?"

"About an hour." Tom smiled. "You looked so peaceful. I thought you could do with the rest."

Rose thought of Granny Faith and her afternoon naps and was struck by a sudden sense of homesickness. She rummaged in her bag for her phone and fired off a message to her mum, asking if they were all okay.

"Everything all right?" Tom asked, slowing down at a roundabout.

Rose noticed numerous messages in her inbox from Shelly and deftly ignored them.

"Everything's fine," she replied firmly. "Where are we, by the way?"

"Almost at Alcudia." Tom paused at a set of traffic lights and they watched a group of tired-looking people disembarking a coach. "Looks like new arrivals."

"You must be used to this heat?" Rose turned towards Tom.

"Actually, this time of year is the chilliest in Sydney. January and February are the hottest months."

"Oh, really? That's usually the worst time of year in Britain."

Tom slapped his forehead. "Damn! I've succumbed."

"To what?"

"The British etiquette of small talk – talking about the weather."

Rose laughed. "What would you like to talk about then?"

"What I'd like to do to you." He was staring ahead but Rose noticed the flex of his jaw.

"I'd rather you show me." Her voice shook as she spoke.

Tom cleared his throat. "So while you were sleeping I found an Italian restaurant."

"Oh, great." Rose slipped her hand over his. "Is it far?"

"It's in the centre." He lifted his fingers off the gearbox, caressing her hand. "We can have a look around first, grab a few drinks."

"Sounds heavenly." Rose pulled down the mirror and eyed her reflection. "I've burnt." The tip of her nose and cheeks were pink, but her eyes were twinkling with happiness.

"There's some aloe vera after sun in my rucksack." He nodded towards the rear of the car.

"Thanks." Rose leaned behind her seat and extracted the small tube. As Tom reversed the car into a parking bay, she quickly rubbed the cooling gel onto her face.

The resort of Alcudia was much bigger than both Sa Coma and Cala Millor. The streets were full of holiday revellers, walking up and down the main centre strip. Rose held onto Tom's hand as they passed shops and restaurants. A friendly Spanish man wearing a smart shirt and trousers stopped them outside his steak-house, trying to entice them inside.

"Sorry," Tom said firmly, "we're eating later."

"Another time then," the man called after them.

"Let's go down here." Tom turned down a side street, which took them to a cluster of bars.

"There's an Irish bar." Rose pointed to an emerald green painted pub which blared pop music.

A woman was standing at the entrance, giving out flyers which promised 2-for-1 drink deals. Her eyes lit up when she saw them and she led them to an outside table.

"Hello, beautiful couple, what would you like to drink?"

Rose ordered wine and as Tom was driving, he asked for cola.

The pub was busy. Many of the patrons were eating meals and there was a man wedged in the corner playing a piano and warbling into a microphone. Rose and Tom chatted as they drank, watching the world go by.

Time flew by and they moved onto another bar and then, when Rose's stomach was grumbling with hunger, decided to make their way to the restaurant. It was a sumptuous dining experience; attentive waiters and white linen tables decorated with flickering candles. As they ate their starter, they watched a violinist walking between the tables. He stopped at theirs, giving Rose a single red rose.

"Is your food good?" Tom asked, as he speared a scallop.

Rose nodded. "The mushrooms are delicious." Underneath the table, her phone beeped to signify an incoming message. Rose put down her fork to retrieve it.

"Shelly again," Rose sighed. "I suppose I should answer her."

"She's worried about you being alone with me, isn't she?"

"She'd worry about me being alone with any male." Rose took a sip of the delicious wine. "Shelly is full of contradictions. She wanted me to have a wild romance in Majorca and now I... er... am interested in someone, she goes all mother hen on me."

Tom wiped forcibly at his mouth. "Maybe Shelly's right. Maybe I'm no good for you, Rose."

"Why not?" Rose's lip trembled. "You're lovely."

Slowly, Tom shook his head. "You don't know me, Rose, I'm not who you think I am."

"I know you've been hurt," Rose gabbled. "It doesn't matter, whatever's happened is all in the past."

Tom opened his mouth to speak but Rose cut in. "Please don't spoil the day. I know we haven't known each other long, but I like you so much..." She trailed off as he leant across the table and kissed her.

"Are you sure?" He gazed into her eyes, making her breathless with longing.

"Yes." She squeezed his hand. "I've never been surer of anything in my life."

Rose took her sandals off and sighed as the warm sea water lapped against her ankles.

"It's so quiet." She watched Tom as he skimmed a pebble across the sea. Night had drawn in and a full moon hung low in the darkened sky.

"We're the only ones on the beach," Tom said, taking her hand. "Come and sit with me."

They walked across the beach, feet sinking in the moist sand, to a secluded spot hidden by a section of rocks. Tom sank onto the ground, pulling Rose with him.

"I'm covered in sand now," she said, with a laugh.

"Lie back," he instructed.

"Are you always this bossy? I'll get sand in my hair, too."

In one swift move he had pulled off his shirt and was bundling it beneath her head. His chest glistened in the moonlight. It reminded her of a scene from Twilight, and Tom Sinclair was just as gorgeous as Robert Pattinson, she thought dreamily.

She waited with bated breath; surely he would kiss her again? But he lay still, on his back, staring up at the sky.

"Look at the stars," he said softly. Rose looked up. The sky was full of them, glittering soundlessly.

"It's beautiful." She exhaled and inhaled deeply, feeling

incredibly serene. They fumbled for each other's hands. Tom raised hers to his mouth, kissing her fingertips.

"You. Are. So. Beautiful." He shifted onto his side and Rose's pulse raced.

"Tom," she whispered.

As he dipped his head, her ears were full of the sound of the ocean, ebbing and flowing. His fingers moved to her blouse. Gently, he opened the buttons, pushed the fabric apart and then he rained soft kisses on her breasts and collar bone. Rose arched her back, wrapped her arms around him and succumbed to the intense feelings of pleasure.

Afterwards, she lay in a dazed stupor, her chest rising and falling as she drew in air.

"Are you okay?" He touched her hair, pushing it behind her ear.

"That was... amazing." Rose struggled to sit up, clutching her blouse against her bare chest as she looked around.

"There's no one here," Tom said softly, "don't worry."

"I can't believe I've just had sex on a beach." The words that fell from her mouth were shaky.

"Neither can I." Tom grinned. "It's a first for me as well." He pulled her back down, and she snuggled against him. The sound of his heartbeat thudded in her ear. She slipped her hand onto his chest, running her fingers through the silken hair.

"We should be heading back," Tom whispered.

"Do we have to?" Rose was comfortable, happy and reluctant to leave.

"Shelly will be out of her mind with worry." As if on cue, Tom's phone beeped. "That'll be Harry, checking I haven't had my wicked way with you."

"Too late for that!" Rose kissed his torso, moving upwards towards his neck. "Let's stay a while longer. I want to experience more of you..."

"You're insatiable," Tom chuckled as he moved on top of her. Rose parted her thighs and drew his face to hers, kissing him lovingly, overcome with longing.

～

"I want to hear everything." Rose was sitting beside the pool the next morning as Shelly clutched her arm. "Did you...?"

"Yes." Rose slipped her sunglasses over her eyes. "It was a fantastic night and that's all I'm saying on the subject."

"You were late for breakfast," Shelly sniffed. "I suppose you didn't get much sleep."

"We didn't get back to the hotel until well after twelve and I had a good night's sleep, thank you very much."

Shelly shifted on the sunbed, covering her arm with sun cream. "Was it gentle, or wildly passionate?"

"Shelly!" Rose tutted at her friend. "Please don't pry."

Shelly held up her white, sticky hands. "Sorry. Harry and I were concerned, that's all. You didn't answer my texts, Archer."

"I was fine." Rose stretched her arms above her head. "Tom was the perfect gentleman."

Shelly gave her a look, which Rose ignored. Her body felt different this morning after a night of lovemaking. She felt sated and happy, so happy. She watched Tom, Fin and Harry fooling around in the pool and pulled out her phone to take a snap of them.

"Shelly," she began, "why did you try to warn me off Tom? I don't understand. He's lovely."

"Did I?" Shelly snorted. "Well, it's too late now. Just don't fall for him too much, okay?"

"Because he'll be going back to Australia?" Rose ventured.

"Beeeecause he's different from you, Rose." Shelly swallowed. "He's experienced and a little bit jaded. Everything you're not."

"I think he's pretty perfect, actually."

"Oh boy, you have got it bad." Shelly touched her forehead. "Yep, definitely lovesick."

Rose batted her hand away. "Says the most loved-up person I know! How are the wedding plans coming along?"

"Great." Shelly grinned. "I spoke to the manager last night. Everything's organised. All I have to do is show up."

"What are you two gossiping about?" Marian advanced towards them, holding a drink which looked suspiciously like a cocktail.

"Isn't it a bit early for that?" Shelly pulled down her glasses and gave her a disapproving look.

"Are you kidding me?" Marian rolled her eyes. "There are a whole group of Scottish blokes in the pool drinking half pints of whisky."

Rose pulled a face. "We were just discussing Shelly's impending nuptials."

Marian flopped down on Shelly's sunbed, batting her sister's feet out of the way, "What about the hen night? We haven't made any arrangements for that yet."

"This," Shelly swept her arms in an arc, "is one big hen night."

Marian gave her a withering look. "You have to have a hen night! And a stag night for the men, of course. Doesn't Harry want to celebrate one last night of freedom?"

"Of course he does! And I need to celebrate, too. So what do you two have planned?"

"Nothing yet," snapped Marian. "I thought about bundling you in a taxi to Palma Nova or Magaluf, but it's miles away and would cost a fortune to get there."

"I'd rather stay here, anyway," Shelly replied, with a wrinkle of her nose.

"Well, that means that the guys have to go to a different resort then. We can't have you bumping into each other on your hen night."

"How about they go to Cala Millor?" Rose piped up helpfully. "It's a nice place and not too far away."

"That could work." Marian nodded. pausing to suck on her straw. "Leave it to me, and Shells, don't fret, we'll organise a hen night to remember."

Shelly sighed. "I just want simple, no fuss, pur-lease. I've spent years partying. It doesn't interest me anymore. I prefer the quiet life nowadays, like you, Rose."

"You were saying only yesterday that Rose needed to liven up," Marian said waspishly.

"What was that?" Rose coughed.

"Nothing," Shelly said quickly. "Okay ladies, I'll leave it all to you, and in the meantime, I am seriously working on my tan." She slid flat on the sunbed. "Wake me up when it's lunchtime?"

twenty-seven

The next few days were spent participating on trips around the island. They visited the Caves of Drac in Portocristo and spent a fun-filled day at a water park. On the morning of Shelly's hen night it rained, a brief reprieve from the scorching sunshine. By mid afternoon, the sky was cloudless again and the rain puddles had dried up. Shelly said a teary goodbye to Harry, wrapping herself around him next to the waiting taxi.

"Have fun," she sniffed, "be careful. Tom, look after him for me."

Tom had his arms around Rose, kissing her tenderly. They had been inseparable since their day out together.

Rose looked up at him. "I'll miss you."

"Ditto." Above her head, he assured Shelly that Harry would be fine.

Marian and Fin came out of the revolving hotel door. She looked angry, but Fin looked as laid back as ever.

"Just behave, okay?" she said to him. "No chatting up other women."

Fin slung his arm across Marian's shoulder and told her to chill.

The taxi driver poked his head out of the open window and

informed them he had to get going. The guys clambered in and Rose, Marian and Shelly waved as the car swerved off.

"So shall we go get ready?" Rose put her arm across Shelly's shoulder.

Marian hooked her arm around the other one. "Let's make the bride-to-be beautiful. It's your hen night, sis, let this party officially commence."

An hour later, Shelly looked stunning in a strapless silvery sequin number.

"Sit still," Marian instructed her, as she gave her freshly curled hair a spray of lacquer.

"Has anyone seen my other shoe?" Rose asked, as she looked underneath the bed for the third time.

"Try my side of the wardrobe," Marian replied.

Rose slid open the door and peered inside. "Why would it be in here?"

"Ah," said Marian, looking sheepish, "I might have borrowed your shoes when you weren't here the other night."

"You should have asked!" Shelly shook her head with disbelief at her sister's cheek.

Rose pulled the shoe out of the dark depths of the wardrobe. "It's all right," she mumbled, "no harm done."

She swiped a ball of fluff away, before slipping them on.

"Can we go now?" Shelly picked up her handbag, making for the door.

"Wait up!" Marian squirted perfume onto her neck, wrists and torso. "Now I'm ready. Let's go, girls."

Rose wobbled in her high heels, following Marian and Shelly into the bar. After ordering drinks, they slipped onto bar stools, watching the barman shaking a chrome cocktail mixer exuberantly.

"Ladies, you all look very beautiful." He smiled widely. "I am Manuel, but you can call me Manny."

"I'm getting married, Manny," Shelly divulged. "Got any tips on how to make a long, happy marriage?"

Manny slid a bowl of complimentary nuts towards them. "The woman is always right. This has made my marriage very happy. Here, have those cocktails for free as a wedding gift from Manny. But please do not tell boss."

"Thank you!" Rose sipped the peach Bellini. Her eyes flickered over the busy bar. It was a posh hotel which stipulated smart clothes for the evening dining experience. The men looked well-groomed and the women looked elegant.

"Are we eating here?" Shelly asked, grabbing a handful of peanuts.

"Nope." Marian tapped the bridge of her nose. "I've organised something, but it's a secret."

"I hate surprises." Shelly scowled. "Can I message Harry? Make sure he's okay?"

"No!" Rose and Marian said in unison.

"Why don't we have a little game?" Marian grabbed hold of an empty beer bottle. "Truth or dare. Here, Rose, spin the bottle."

"I hate this game," Rose mumbled.

"Get on with it, Archer, don't be such a grouch."

"Okay then." Rose laid the bottle on its side, giving it a spin. It stopped, pointing at Marian.

"Ask me anything." Marian tossed her head.

"Erm..." Rose thought for a moment, "are you really happy in London?"

Briefly, Marian closed her eyes, then flicked them open again. "This is too deep. Okay, no I'm not."

Shelly sat up straighter. "I thought you loved life in the big city?"

"It's a great city, gorgeous sights, thousands of people... funny thing is I've never felt so alone. Everyone hates me at work, they call me the boss bitch. Yes, I make loads of money, can pretty much buy whatever I like, but, I've got no real friends, no family... no man to hug me after a hard day. My life is shit, really."

Rose slipped off her stool, placing her arms around Marian. "I'm sorry you're unhappy, but you can change your life, Marian."

Shelly swirled her drink. "Jeez, sis, I had no idea how unhappy you were. I thought you had life all figured out."

"Who, me?" Marian blew out a shuddering breath. "I'm just muddling through, trying my best to make it a good one."

Rose hovered at the side of her, searching for words to make her feel better.

"Anyway," Marian continued, "it's my turn... so let me spin it." She gave the bottle a twirl and this time it landed on Shelly.

"Oh no." Shelly covered her eyes.

"So, sis," Marian said accusingly, "why didn't you call or write in the past ten years? Why did you jet off without a thought for your one and only sister?"

Rose looked nervously from one sister to the other. "Maybe we should play another game?"

"No, I'll answer the question." Shelly stuck out her jaw. "From what I can remember, you were never interested in me, or Mum, come to think of it. You just upped and left after Dad died, ran away to London town."

"It was grief!" Marian's eyes twinkled with tears. "When Dad passed and Mum went to pieces, I just couldn't cope. I needed a fresh start, like you did too, Shelly – am I right? And Twineham was so close-knit, so suffocating. Everybody knowing each other's business – bloody ridiculous. Now I've got the opposite problem, now nobody gives a crap. I am truly insignificant."

"Don't say that." Rose twiddled with the rings on her fingers. "It's not too late for you and Shelly to... to make up properly and forget about the past. You're sisters and I know you love each other. So... make friends, okay? Life's too short – right?"

Shelly stared at her. "My friend the eternal optimist. This is why I love you. This is why I came back."

Marian sniffed, "You're sweet, Rose and don't worry about me and my sister. We've been bickering since we could talk."

"Okay." Rose smiled and slipped back onto the seat.

"Now it's my turn." There was a mischievous glint in Shelly's eyes as she twisted the bottle round fast. It skidded across the table, landing in Rose's lap.

"Oh. Do you want to spin again?" Rose gabbled.

"No. I think that's a sign and it's definitely your turn, Rose." Shelly pressed her finger to her lips.

A few minutes passed. Rose waited with bated breath.

"Come on," said Marian impatiently.

"I'm thinking." Shelly exhaled noisily. "Okay. This might be obvious, but, have you fallen for Tom?"

Rose opened her mouth, then closed it again. "I..."

"Of course she has," snapped Marian.

"I was going to say, I like him very much."

Shelly popped a peanut into her mouth. "You like Jeremy, too. Which one do you prefer, Rose?"

"Jeremy and I are just friends, whereas with Tom it's different... and that's two questions, Shelly." Rose coughed.

"You mean you've been doing the horizontal tango with him?" Marian eyed her curiously. Is it just lust between the two of you then, like it is with me and Fin?"

"No." Rose sat up straighter. "It's more than that, much more."

"I knew it." Shelly pushed the bowl of nuts away. "It's the curse of the Sinclair brothers, drawing you in, captivating you. You love him, Rose, don't you?"

A sinking feeling weighed heavily in Rose's stomach, with the fear that Shelly could possibly be right. She tried to laugh it off. "I hardly know him. I'm going to spin the bottle and... and..."

Shelly pressed her hand over Rose's. "It's okay to admit you have feelings for a man, Rose."

"I know." Rose shook her head, dispelling thoughts of him. "Here goes."

The bottle landed on Shelly again.

"Right," Rose said brightly, "what's his secret?"

"Who?" Shelly looked blank.

"Tom, of course. I know there's something... not quite right. Call it intuition, so answer the question, Shelly."

There was silence. Marian raised an eyebrow, drumming her fingers on the polished bar.

"This is truth or dare, right?" Shelly said with discomfiture. "I ask for a dare, Rose."

"So you refuse to answer the question?"

"Yep." Shelly shook her head vigorously. "Dare me, Rose."

Rose's mouth tightened with disappointment. She looked around at the busy bar, an idea forming in her mind. "I dare you to kiss a strange man and return with an item of his clothing."

"Do I have to?" Shelly sighed theatrically, leaning her head on her arms.

"Yep and you have..." Rose glanced at her watch, "five minutes to do it. The alternative is answer the question!"

Shelly shot off her seat.

"I've never seen her move so quick," Marian observed. "It's almost like she's desperate."

"Hmm." Rose watched her friend dart around the room, stopping beside an elderly couple. She had her back to them and was bent slightly over as she chatted.

"She'll never do it," Marian said with a snigger. "Not in five minutes."

Rose watched her friend keenly. The couple were listening attentively, then the man delved in his pocket and extracted something. Moments later, Shelly was kissing him on his cheek and striding back towards them with a triumphant smile.

"There." A piece of white fabric floated out of her hand.

"A handkerchief?" Marian giggled. "Hardly an item of clothing."

Shelly crossed her arms. "I completed the dare. Isn't that right, Rose?"

"I suppose so." Rose sighed and patted the empty stool. "Sit back down then."

Manny the waiter was leaning against the optics watching them, with his arms folded. "You English are strange," he said with a chuckle. "Now, can I have my bottle back?"

And that was the end of truth or dare.

twenty-eight

There was a rainbow arching its colourful trails above them as they left the hotel. They skipped in fresh puddles, soaking their feet and lower legs. A car slowed down at the kerbside, the driver asking where they were going.

"You want to come to a party?" The spiky-haired man had an accent and a Dutch football t-shirt to match.

"No thanks!" Shelly shouted, stretching her arms wide. "This is my hen night. I'm getting married in two days' time."

"Lucky guy," the man replied, before winking and zooming away in a cloud of smoke.

"We need to eat," said Marian, tucking her arm through the crook of her sister's. "I've booked us a lovely table and you might get a surprise or three."

"Huh?" Shelly looked at her with suspicious eyes. "What have you done?"

"Wait and see," Marian patted her hand.

The sound of the sea was loud this evening. Rose looked out at the rolling breakers and inhaled the smell of salt, seaweed and freshness. They walked along the edge of the beach, pausing to watch an energetic volleyball game and a large family playing a relaxed game of cricket.

"I can understand why you wanted to live here," Rose said. "Majorca is truly stunning."

"Does that mean you'll be coming every year now, Rose?" Shelly cocked her head to one side.

Rose nodded. "I'd definitely come back. Mum and Dad would love it here and Gran would be in her element with all these half naked men about."

Shelly chuckled as they swerved around a woman walking six collie dogs.

"We're eating there." Marian pointed in front of them at a steak house restaurant which overlooked the sea.

"This looks lovely," Rose said with approval, as they stopped outside it. A dark-haired man in a well-cut grey suit welcomed them inside.

"I've booked a table. Your best one."

Rose wondered if Marian used the same authoritative tone at work.

"Ah yes, the hen party." He bowed slightly. "Please, come this way."

They followed him through the restaurant to their table.

"There are too many seats," Shelly said, as they sat down on the softly cushioned chairs. "Why are there six chairs, Maz? Are the boys coming back?"

Rose's body prickled with excitement at the prospect of seeing Tom.

"Of course not," Marian pulled three drinks menus out of the table holder, "but there are some other people coming to celebrate with you. And here they are."

Rose looked around. There was a face she recognised and two she didn't.

"Carmella?" Shelly jumped to her feet. "Maria, Isabel?" There was a squeal and a flurry of cheek-kissing and hugging. "It's so lovely to see you." Shelly patted the empty seats. "Sit down."

The three women joined them at the table. Rose glanced over them. They were undeniably Spanish. All three had jet black hair, dark eyes and glowing olive complexions. And they were all beautiful.

"You're here for my hen night?" Shelly was bouncing on her seat with excitement.

"That's right." Carmella placed her hand on her protruding stomach. "Darius gave me the evening off, but he tells me to be very careful."

"I'm so glad you could come." Shelly patted her hand then turned to the other girls. "How did you know I was here?"

The smaller of the two, Maria, began speaking. "Carmella rang us. She say crazy Shelly from England is back and that you are getting married. Isabel and I did not believe it. It is true then?"

"Yes," Shelly laughed. "I met Harry in Australia. As soon as I met him, I knew he was different from all the other lads. We started seeing each other, fell in love, Harry proposed and now here we are."

"You came here to get married?" Isabel's eyes were wide. "When you are surrounded by the beauty of Australia? Now I know you are still crazy."

"I came back for my sister and my best friend," Shelly replied. "This is Marian and Shelly. You've met Carmella, but Isabel and Maria are sisters." The four girls smiled at each other.

"How are you feeling?" Rose eyed Carmella's baby bump; she was so big, she looked as if she could give birth at any moment.

Carmella batted away a mosquito. "The baby has dropped. His head is in place. Now it is just a waiting game."

Rose swallowed. "You know the sex?"

"Not for definite," Carmella patted her stomach, "but we followed all the traditional Spanish advice to make a boy. Now Darius is convinced and has chosen the name Roberto."

A waiter ambled towards them, notebook and pen in hand. "Drinks, madams?"

Shelly ordered two pitchers of Sangria which were brought out promptly, along with six glasses.

"So how did you meet Isabel and Maria?" Rose asked, as Marian poured the drinks.

"We all worked at Darius's bar," replied Shelly. "Are you still there, girls?"

"No," answered Isabel, "we both now live in Madrid. I am a beautician."

"And I," cut in Maria, "am a fashion designer."

Shelly sipped her drink. "So what brings you back here?"

"We still have family here," Isabel replied, "and we wanted to see Carmella and her soon-to-be-born bebe." She turned to look at Rose, who was staring wistfully at the sea. "You like the island of Majorca?"

"I like," Rose replied, "it's... hermosa."

"Ah," the three Spanish women clapped, "very good."

Maria leant forward and gave a conspiratorial wink. "Shelly? She no want to learn our language. She is, how you say, English snob."

"Hey!" said an affronted Shelly. "I know loads of Spanish. Soy una buena chica."

Maria, Carmella and Isabella laughed.

Rose looked at Shelly bemused. "What was that?"

"I am a nice girl," Shelly replied.

"Well, can that nice girl order her food, please? I'm famished," drawled Marian.

The food was delicious. Rose had prawn cocktail to start, followed by a sirloin steak drizzled with peppercorn sauce. Their table was positioned at the very top of the restaurant. It gave them a fantastic view of the rocks and sea and the sun sinking in a blood red sky.

"Anybody fancy a dessert?" asked Marian as she perused the menu. "The ice cream sound delicious."

"Six ice creams it is." Shelly motioned to the hovering waiter. "And another pitcher of Sangria, please."

"Water for me," said Carmella.

"It must be uncomfortable for you in this heat." Rose looked at her with sympathy.

"Yes, my belly is very heavy and my ankles are constantly bloated. Next time, I have a winter baby." Carmella struggled to sit higher in the chair. "Do you want ninos?"

"Pardon?" Rose answered politely.

"Ah, sorry." Carmella clicked her fingers. "Children, Rose, do you want a family?"

"I suppose so," Rose replied, "eventually, at some point."

Carmella threw back her head and laughed. "Do not sound so afraid, hermosa senora. Children is good."

Marian shuddered. "I can't think of anything worse. Stretch marks, piles, leaking boobs, pain – no, thank you! I'm a career woman, and I intend on staying that way."

Rose turned to Shelly. "Do you want children?"

"Yep. Harry wants to wait a few years, but I can feel my biological clock ticking away."

"You're only twenty-eight, Shelly," Rose chuckled.

"I want them young," Shelly said firmly, "and I want at least four."

Marian coughed. "Jeez, rather you than me. I'll be happy playing Aunty Marian."

The waiter returned with their ice-creams. They ate them quickly, before they melted. When it was time to pay, Shelly insisted on footing the bill.

"You can buy my drinks for the rest of the night," she said, when Rose tried to protest.

"Where to now?" Carmella struggled to her feet, one hand supporting her back.

"I thought we could go on a pub crawl," Marian said crisply, as she extracted a piece of paper from her handbag. "I've planned an itinerary for the night and your restaurant is the next port of call."

Carmella rolled her eyes. "My husband will be happy. Now he can keep an eye on me."

"We're only having a few," Marian said hastily, "and then we'll move on." She eyed Carmella nervously. "Are you sure you're up to this?"

"She's been having twinges all day," Isabel divulged.

Marian blanched. "Maybe you should go home, put your feet up."

"I'm not ill," Carmella said. "Movement is good for the baby and I want to celebrate with my friend." Shelly came to stand next to her.

"Hang onto me," she said, holding her arm out, "I'm a first aider."

"Good to know." Carmella gritted her teeth as a wave of pain rocked her body. "They are Braxton Hicks, do not worry. Let's go and see my husband."

Darius was rushing around when they arrived at his restaurant. He stopped with a tray of drinks in his hand to kiss his wife and usher them to a vacant table.

"Are you all right?" he asked Carmella, squatting down beside her.

She took his face in her hands, kissed both cheeks and assured him she was fine.

He brought them complimentary wine and a rose for Carmella.

"The flower man has been in again?" she asked, her voice lifting with mirth. "Every day since I have been pregnant, Darius has given me a flower."

"How sweet," said Rose. Her phone was beeping in her bag. She fished it out and stared at a message from Tom, asking if they were having a good time. A few seconds later, a selfie of the Sinclair brothers flashed onto the screen. Rose zoomed in on the picture, sighing at the sight of his handsome face.

"Give me that." Shelly swiped the phone out of Rose's hand. "Oh, now I know why you are suddenly looking so happy."

"What is this?" Maria asked.

"A picture of my husband-to-be and his brothers. Look!" Shelly passed them the phone.

"They are very handsome men," Maria nodded with approval, "but this one here..." she tapped the phone, "I recognise him."

Shelly slid the phone quickly back across the table, passing it to Rose.

"That's her boyfriend and he lives in Australia, so I doubt it."

Maria nodded her head. "Yes, I've seen him before somewhere, I'm sure of it."

Rose tucked her phone away. "It's funny you say that, because a complete stranger on a boat trip said exactly the same thing."

Shelly laughed. "He must have that familiar look about him. Gosh, it's hot." She fanned her face.

Rose stared at Maria, who was frowning.

"Hey," said Shelly, "anyone want to dance?"

"In here?" Marian replied, casting her eyes around the busy restaurant. "There isn't a dance floor, Shelly."

"We can dance by the sea. Come on, I love this song." Shelly swayed her hips and pulled Rose by the hand. Rose wanted to stop, to stand still and ask Shelly what was really going on with Tom Sinclair, but she didn't want to spoil the evening. Later, she thought firmly, after the wedding, I am going to find out exactly what they're hiding. For now, Rose smiled and allowed Shelly to twirl her round while the other diners watched with amusement.

twenty-nine

An hour later, they were playing pool in a bar on the main strip. It was laid back and quiet inside the pub. The bar attendant sang along to Frank Sinatra as he wiped over tables and a large Labrador padded around, sniffing the floor for scraps. Rose hunkered down to pat him.

"That's two nil to me," said Shelly, to an annoyed looked Marian. "Who wants to play next?"

Isabel and Maria picked up a cue each and the rest of the girls went to sit next to Carmella.

"Gotta say I was shocked when I found out you'd married Darius." Shelly sipped her drink through a straw. Rose noticed she was slurring her words slightly and felt woozy herself. Maybe she should have water next, she thought vaguely.

"A lot of things changed after you left, Shelly. I calmed down a lot without your influence." Carmella smiled. "Darius and I grew close."

"But what happened to what's-his-name?" Shelly clicked her fingers, trying to remember. "The rich guy from Italy, who used to take us out on his speedboat."

"You mean Alfonso?" Carmella sighed. "He married a

German heiress, adding more to his wealth. Last I heard, they were setting up a boating business on Ibiza."

"Wow!" Shelly leant back on her chair. "We've all moved on. So you and Darius are going to be living here permanently?"

"Si." Carmella nodded. "We are happy here. It is a good place to raise children."

"Have you decided yet?" Rose asked Shelly. "Is it going to be Britain or Australia?"

Shelly looked down at the table. "We're going back to Australia, Rose. Britain is great, but my heart belongs to Oz. Harry loves it there, I couldn't take him away, no matter how much I love Twineham."

Rose couldn't help her face from falling. "When will you leave?" she asked quietly.

"Not for a few weeks," she replied. "I wanted to show Harry more of Britain and I wanted to spend more time with you."

"You'll come back to visit again?"

"Of course I will," Shelly leaned across to hug Rose, "and you can come see me too."

"I've already discussed this with Rose," Marian said crisply. "We're going to fly to Australia together. Isn't that right?"

Rose's mind had drifted from the conversation. She was thinking of Tom and her heart felt like it was being crushed. She cursed herself for falling for him. This was supposed to be a no-strings-attached fling like Fin's and Marian's, but now she realised how much she cared for him and that she wanted to spend more time with him – much more. Ten days wasn't enough. It was wholly inadequate.

"We all come!" Carmella suddenly shouted, making Rose jump. "Three cheers for Shelly and her life in Australia as a married woman."

"Hip, hip, hooray!" the woman cheered and raised their glasses, and Rose wiped surreptitiously at her damp eyes, longing for Tom's strong arms to hold her and never let her go.

As darkness fell like a shroud, more people wandered into the pool bar. Marian and Shelly were dancing, throwing their arms and legs around exuberantly. The bar staff were clapping and whistling along to the tune, the chatter was loud and the atmosphere was upbeat and happy. Shelly announced loudly that she wanted to move on, but first she was going to the toilet.

As soon as she was out of earshot, Marian rushed over to Rose, nudging her in the ribs and almost spilling her drink. "We have to stay here," she whispered.

Rose glanced at Carmella, who was discussing baby names with Isabel and Maria.

"Why?" Rose drained her drink. "Isn't it up to Shelly?"

"I've got something organised," Marian winked, "and you do not want to miss this."

"What have you done, Marian?" Rose looked at her suspiciously.

"Nothing bad," Marian drawled, "just trust me, okay? Now, go and get some more Sangria, before she comes back." She pressed a twenty euro note into Rose's sweaty palm.

Rose looked down at the dog who was asleep at her feet. He was drooling over her sandals and some of the slobber had seeped through the material and was tickling her toes. Gently, she shifted him and walked over to the bar. She ordered the Sangria and more water for Carmella and took them back on a tray. As she set the drinks down, she noticed Marian looking repeatedly at her watch.

Then, out of nowhere, a policeman appeared by her side. Handcuffs hung from his low-slung trousers, his blue shirt opened at the top, revealing a considerable amount of chest hair and a truncheon was fastened onto his waistband.

"You're in trouble." His words were coated in a thick Spanish accent.

"Me?" Rose looked up at him with wide eyes.

"You've been a bad girl," he continued, taking off his cap.

Rose gulped. What the hell?

"Not her," Marian hissed, her face red and perspiring as she leant across the table. "Her!" She pointed to Shelly, who was skipping across the room. The fake policeman sauntered over and whispered something in Shelly's ear.

"You got me a stripper!" Shelly shouted. "I'm going to kill you, Marian."

"Please," the man said, "I prefer the term 'entertainment artist'."

The entire bar watched as Shelly was made to sit on a chair while the 'artist' slowly removed his clothing.

"How on earth did you organise this?" Rose had her eyes half covered.

"It wasn't easy," Marian replied, "at such short notice. The reception staff helped. I thought if I told you, you might let it slip."

"Are you sure she's enjoying this?" Rose winced, as she watched Shelly gingerly rubbing baby oil into the stripper's muscular chest.

"Of course she is," Marian said, with a lick of her lips. "He is hot."

Isabel and Maria were giggling as they took photos.

"Please do not tell Darius of this," Carmella swiped her fringe out of her eyes, "it will make him insane with jealousy."

Rose wondered if Fin and Tom had organised a stripper for Harry and felt a stab of jealousy. She gasped as the stripper pulled Shelly into a tight embrace and began a slow, sultry dance with her. She noticed Isabel was now videoing the spectacle on her phone.

"Maybe we shouldn't record this," Rose said warily, "Harry might not like it."

"We keep it to ourselves," Isabel tittered and pressed the zoom button.

"Okay, but please don't put this on social media." Rose had heard horror stories about Fulham Banking's Christmas parties, when people had been hauled before management after being videoed inebriated.

"Will you chill out, Rose!" Marian snapped. "This cost me a lot of money and it's supposed to be fun."

"Okay… fine." Rose sat back and stirred her drink as the clapping and whooping in the bar intensified, and the entertainment artist whipped off his glittery thong and twirled it provocatively on his little finger for all and sundry to see.

"Did you enjoy that, sis?" The girls had left the pool bar and were walking slowly towards the karaoke bar.

"It was embarrassing," replied Shelly, "but thanks for organising it… I suppose."

"Wait a moment." Carmella stopped at a lamppost, puffing and panting.

"Are you all right?" Rose looked at her with concern.

"The baby is kicking. Feel." She pulled Rose's hand flat on her stomach.

"Wow!" Rose could feel Carmella's stomach moving. "Was that a foot?"

"Si." Carmella nodded and motioned for the other women to feel her stomach. "Darius say baby be a footballer."

"Pregnancy is beautiful." Shelly hooked her arm around Carmella. "You are glowing."

"Thank you." Carmella waved her hand. "But now I think I need to sit down."

They picked up their pace and were soon at the entrance to the packed karaoke bar.

"Have you a table for six?" Marian held up her fingers.

A harassed-looking waitress led them inside and handed them drinks menus.

"Oh crikey, look who's here," Marian pulled a face, "on the karaoke."

They all looked to the stage where a bleached-haired woman in a miniscule skirt was belting out Aretha Franklin.

"It's Yorkshire Woman," muttered Marian, "and looks like she's brought all her posse with her."

"Ignore them." Shelly dismissed them with a flick of her hand. "You're with Fin, not her."

Rose sat next to Carmella and watched, cringing as the woman belted the last notes of the song out. She bowed theatrically before stumbling off, careering into their table as she passed by.

"Watch out," mumbled Marian.

The woman gave her a bleary-eyed stare. "Oh, it's you, the rude Southerner."

"Hello again." Marian smiled brightly. "Maybe you should go sit down."

The woman leant forwards, revealing an ample amount of bosom and Rose smelt a whiff of strong alcohol.

"Make me," she slurred.

"Look," Marian said tersely, "we're on my sister's hen night and I don't want any trouble."

"Where's the dishy Australian?" Yorkshire Woman cackled. "He liked me, you know, told me I had a great set of pins, and I would've got lucky if you hadn't stuck your oar in."

"What are pins?" Carmella whispered to Rose.

"Legs," Rose replied, glancing at an angry-looking Marian.

"I doubt that," Marian said derisively, "he's friendly with everyone."

The drunk woman puffed out her chest. "You Southerners are so... arrogant."

"And you're annoying," Marian quipped. "Please leave us alone."

"Fine," the woman swayed, "but not before I do this."

She picked up a pint of beer off a neighbouring table and whoosh, deposited it over Marian's head.

"You... you..." Marian screeched, wiping the rivulets of lager out of her eyes. Rose clasped one hand over her mouth in utter shock at the scene unravelling in front of her. Marian jumped to her feet, picked up a pitcher of Sangria and chucked the contents in Yorkshire Woman's sneering face. Then pandemonium broke loose, as they were suddenly both on the floor, rolling around, pulling at each other's hair, shouting profanities.

"Stop!" Rose tried to intervene but was slapped away. She looked towards the bar for assistance. Two waiters hurried over and pulled the girls apart.

"Any more trouble and you're both out," one of the barmen shouted. "Now, apologise and leave each other alone."

Marian reluctantly muttered "Sorry," then added, "she started it."

Shelly, Isabel and Maria were trying hard to control their mirth, but Rose was aghast. She hated violence and confrontation. Next to her, Carmella had turned extremely pale and had contorted her body into the most peculiar shape.

"I need the toilet," she said to Rose. "Will you come with me?"

"Of course." Rose scraped back her chair, allowing Carmella to cling onto her arm.

Luckily the toilets were empty. Rose went into the end cubicle and heard Carmella shut the middle door.

"I can't believe Marian could act like that," she said, loud enough for Carmella to hear, "over a guy she's only known for five minutes. Where's her self-respect?"

In response, she heard groaning. Quickly, Rose hitched up her underwear, flushed the toilet and exited the cubicle. Intent on washing her hands, she paused outside the locked door.

"Carmella? Are you okay?"

Carmella emitted a sob. "No, everything is not okay."

The door slowly squeaked open. An ashen-faced Carmella stood in a puddle of water.

"Oh, you poor thing," Rose said. "It's okay, it was an accident."

Carmella placed both hands on Rose's shoulder and let out a wail. "No accident. It is not pee, Rose. My waters, they have broken."

thirty

"Are you sure?" whispered Rose. A wave of panic and fear was rising inside her as Carmella winced and then gripped onto her hands.

"Si." Carmella exhaled heavily "I'm having contractions and these are real."

"I'll call an ambulance," Rose squeaked.

"Don't leave me." Carmella's voice was tinged with fear.

"I won't." Rose guided her out of the cubicle. "We'll go back to the table and sit and wait."

"No!" Carmella's face twisted in pain as another contraction shook her body. "Not in front of everyone. I stay here and you with me... please, Rose." She slumped onto the tiled floor, clutching her stomach.

"Okay." Rose thanked God that she had brought her phone in with her. She fished it out of her pocket and dialed Shelly's number.

After seven rings, Shelly answered with a "What?"

Rose quickly explained the situation, telling Shelly to call for an ambulance straight away and to come and help. Then she slid down next to Carmella and rubbed her back.

"I want Darius," Carmella sobbed. "Oh, it hurts! Make it stop, please."

"Hold my hands," Rose instructed.

"I want to push," Carmella shouted. "Owwwwwww!"

The door swung open and a wild-eyed Shelly rushed in.

"Jesus, Carmella," she said. "In the toilets?"

"I think the baby's coming now," Rose said to Shelly. "Go and get some towels and fresh water. And Shelly... ring Darius."

Shelly disappeared with a nod of her head.

"I feel like I'm dying." Carmella's forehead was wet with perspiration. "It hurts so much."

"Ssh," soothed Rose, wiping her face, "you're going to be fine."

"I never have sex again!" Carmella's body shook as a wave of pain gripped her.

"Concentrate on your breathing," Rose instructed calmly, "in and out, big, deep breaths."

"Everything alright in here?" The pub manager stuck his head round the door, blanching when he saw Carmella. "Oh, dear Lord." He made the sign of the cross against his breast bone before disappearing.

"I need to push," Carmella panted.

Shelly was hovering in the doorway. "You have to wait for the paramedics, Carmella."

"She can't." Rose shook her head. "The baby is coming now, Shelly."

"What shall I do?" Shelly swallowed as Carmella let out another wail.

"Support her top half, hold her hands." Rose scrabbled to her feet. "Keep her calm."

Shelly nodded. "I can do that." She sat behind Carmella, smoothing back her damp hair. "Shall we sing a song?"

"What?" Carmella spluttered. "I'm dying here, and you want to sing songs?"

"It will take your mind off the pain," Shelly said brightly, then she launched into a high-pitched rendition of Abba's Dancing Queen.

Through gritted teeth, Carmella joined in and then Rose did, too.

"Friday night and the lights are low," sang Rose. "Push, Carmella, push."

"Looking out for a place to goooooooooo." Carmella's face was turning redder and redder as she sang the words.

"Ow, my hands." Shelly flinched as Carmella dug her long nails into her palms.

"Where they play the right music," Rose knelt between Carmella's legs, "getting in the swing, you come in to look for a king."

Carmella was pushing again and Shelly was still singing. This is surreal, thought Rose.

"I can see something," Rose said to Carmella, with excitement.

"Well, is it a baby?" Carmella leaned heavily against Shelly, taking in deep breaths of air.

"I think it's the head," Rose replied. "Another big push, Carmella. You can do it."

"Okay." Carmella pushed with all her might, letting out the longest and loudest wail Rose had ever heard and then she looked down and there was a baby lying in her hands, blinking up at her.

"Oh, my God!" yelled Rose. "It's a girl, Carmella and she's the most beautiful sight I've ever seen."

"I don't know how to thank you." Darius was standing outside the ambulance, gazing down at his wife and daughter who were laid out on a stretcher.

"Congratulations." Rose stood on tiptoes to kiss him.

He pulled her into a fierce embrace. "You come back to Majorca for free holiday courtesy of me and Carmella."

"Si," said an exhausted-looking Carmella. "Thank you so much, Rose. For everything."

"Your baby is beautiful," Rose said warmly, "and you were brilliant, Carmella and brave."

"I have a daughter!" shouted Darius. Rose thought he looked euphoric and proud. A proud papa.

Carmella clutched their beautiful daughter tightly. "I have thought of a name," she announced. "I like Sofia Rose."

"That is perfect." Darius echoed his agreement.

"Oh, I'm honoured," and with that, Rose burst into tears.

After Darius, Carmella and Sofia had left in the ambulance, the girls decided to call an end to the hen night.

"It's late, I've had enough alcohol," Shelly said with a yawn, "and I'm exhausted after all that excitement."

"It's been a good night," agreed Marian, "but I'm so glad it was you that delivered the baby, Rose. I do not do bodily fluids." She shuddered slightly.

They kissed Isabel and Maria goodbye and walked back to the hotel.

"Thank you for tonight, girls," Shelly said. "I wonder if Harry is okay?"

"Oh, they're probably still partying," Marian said, with a dismissive wave. "Can you slow down, please? My feet are killing me in these heels."

Marian finally quit complaining and took her shoes off when Rose was fumbling with the key slot. The green light flashed, she pushed the door open and Marian barged past, citing that she was desperate for the loo. Rose threw her bag on top of the suitcases, unzipped her dress and was pulling it over her head when she heard a voice saying, "Hello." Rose jumped, pulled her dress back down and peered through the dim light. In the bed, she could make out a figure. It was Tom.

"You scared the hell outta me," she chastised him, sitting down on the bed beside him. "What are you doing here?"

Tom pulled himself into a sitting position. "Harry wanted to come back early. He was missing Shelly. And Fin wanted to spend the night with Marian, so I'm here, if you'll have me?"

Rose grinned. "That's fine with me, but maybe we should check with Marian first."

"What about?" Marian tottered out of the toilet. "Oh. Hi, Tom. Looks like we'll be swapping rooms again then, huh? Is Fin sober?"

"He's okay, considering he's been knocking back the shots all night."

"Then I'll leave you two lovebirds alone." Marian picked up her toiletries bag and left with a wave.

"Did you have a good night?" Tom pulled her against his warm chest.

"We played truth or dare, had a lovely meal, a game of pool and Marian got involved in a cat fight. Yes, I had a great night." Rose kissed his lips. "Oh and I delivered a baby."

"What?" Tom stared at her, bemused.

Rose quickly explained about Carmella.

"So maybe you could train as a midwife?" Tom pulled her dress over her head and removed her underwear.

"Er, no," Rose replied, taking a sharp inhalation of breath. He lifted the duvet and she snuggled next to him. "I mean... not to you. Yes to you."

Tom chuckled as he rolled on top of her, supporting himself with his arms. "I missed you," he murmured, kissing her lips, her neck and breasts. Rose arched her back as desire washed over her.

"I missed you, too. Oh," she sighed, as he nuzzled the curve in her neck.

"You should be kissed and often, and by someone who knows how."

"What?" Rose looked up at him with heavy lids.

"It's a quote from a book. A classic book. Don't you recognise it?"

"Yes, I do, it's from Gone With The Wind by Margaret Mitchell. One of my favourite books." Rose smiled. "Have you read it?"

"Nope. Confession time. I googled 'romantic quotes from books' and that was the first line which popped up." He trailed a teasing finger down her stomach. "I wanted to impress you."

"You already do," gasped Rose as his hand moved lower, "but can we discuss literature later? I want to make love."

"Demanding little vixen, aren't you? We have all night," teased Tom. "Maybe we should talk."

Rose wriggled underneath him and with one swift movement, their positions had changed. "Time to shut up, Mister Sinclair." She moved slowly above him, her body rocking to the sound of the crashing sea as waves of exquisite pleasure encompassed them both, hurling them upwards into the stratosphere.

"How are you feeling?" It was the evening before Shelly's wedding and they were sitting at another seaside restaurant, finishing their main meal.

"Nervous," Shelly replied. "My stomach's somersaulting and I've lost my appetite." She prodded her roast chicken, then pushed the plate away.

"I think Harry's the same." Rose glanced at the eldest Sinclair brother who was pulling at his shirt collar. "So you're sleeping in my room tonight?"

"Of course. I can't sleep with him on our wedding eve, it's bad luck, isn't it?"

Rose laughed. "I never had you down as superstitious, Shelly."

"Call it more traditional." They watched the rolling sea for a few moments, before Shelly sighed. "I wish Dad was here."

"I was thinking the same thing," Marian sniffed, "he would have been so proud."

"Remember when we went camping and he saved those guys stuck up a cliff?" Shelly's eyes had glazed over as she reminisced. "And all those fun runs he did for cancer research."

Marian nodded. "He ran twenty in total. I was there at every finish line."

"He was so brave." Shelly wiped away a tear. "Sorry. I'm feeling really emotional tonight. Harry reminds me of him, you know. I think that's partly why I love him so much."

"Your dad was a lovely man," Rose placed a comforting hand upon her shoulder, "and you're bound to be emotional. It's a big day for you tomorrow."

"Shall we have an early night?" Shelly asked Rose. "Grab some chocolate and crisps. Share a bottle of wine. And you too, Marian."

"Good idea, but what about the guys?" Rose looked longingly at Tom. She was going to miss him tonight.

"They can stay here," Marian replied, "and let Harry enjoy his last night of freedom."

Shelly pulled a face. "You make it sound as if he's undertaking a jail sentence."

"Isn't that what marriage is?" Marian said, with raised eyebrows.

"I used to think that," Shelly said, "until I met Harry and realised I wanted to spend the rest of my life with him. Happily, I might add."

"Marriage is wonderful," Rose said dreamily. "I can't think of anything more special than declaring your everlasting love for another human being."

"Good job you don't work with me, Rose," Marian cut in. "Half of my colleagues are either divorced or having sordid affairs, and as for everlasting love... pfft... I'll save that for my cat."

"Do you mind?" Shelly erupted. "This is one of the most

momentous moments of my life, I don't want it spoilt by your bitterness."

"Sorry." Marian held up her hands. "I won't breathe another negative word. I'm happy for you, sis, sincerely."

Shelly stood up and went over to Harry. She whispered something in his ear and then they were hugging.

"See you tomorrow, wife." He held her face in his hands, kissing her tenderly.

"'Bye, husband." The sight of Shelly crying bought a lump to Rose's throat.

She waved at Tom, blew him a kiss and the three girls made their way to the hotel.

"You two go on up," Rose stopped outside a grocery store, "I'll get the food." The shop was cool; air conditioning hummed as Rose grabbed a basket and walked down the aisles. As she was paying for her purchases, she heard her name being called and spun around.

"Maria?"

"Hi, Rose, I thought it was you. Here," she thrust a ribbon-tied bouquet of colourful flowers into Rose's hand, "they are from Darius and Carmella, as a small token of appreciation."

"Oh, they're lovely," cooed Rose. "Did you want to come up? We're having a girls' night in."

"No." Maria shook her head. "I have to get back, but Isabel and I will see Shelly tomorrow."

"Okay." Rose hugged her. "It will be good to see you both again."

"Gracias, bella dama." Maria moved back slightly. "Rose, I came to inform you of something."

"Oh yes?"

"I said I thought I had seen your boyfriend somewhere." She held Rose's hands. "Now I am convinced."

"Where from, Maria?" Rose's heart began racing quicker.

"Look!" She fished her phone out of her shorts pocket and

typed 'Jack Fallon' into Google. Rose peered at the screen; there were dozens of photographs of a man who was identical to Tom.

"What the...?" Rose scrolled down further. It was Tom, it was definitely him. "But... who is Jack Fallon?"

"Is Tom," Maria said. "I was in Milan when he was there, at the fashion shows. He's famous, Rose. A very famous model. He is big heartthrob in Spain, and Italy too. But why did he not tell you this?"

thirty-one

Why not indeed? Rose tossed and turned for the entire night, her mind consumed with thoughts of Tom. She asked herself over and over why he hadn't told her... why Shelly hadn't told her. She had even looked suspiciously at Marian, wondering if she knew his secret, too. As dawn broke, Rose was wide awake, googling Jack Fallon. He had been a model for years, apparently. She read a brief biography about him. He was Australian, that was true at least. There were pictures of him in London, New York, Paris, Milan. He was a global jet setter, a gorgeous specimen of a man, and he was also a liar.

Rose looked across at Shelly, who was still sleeping. She thumped the pillow and wriggled back underneath the duvet with her romance book. With the help of the light from her phone, she read for an hour, then closed her eyes, praying for sleep to claim her. No such luck; the sun was shining through the blinds, beckoning her outside. With a sigh, Rose sat up, wriggled her feet into flip flops and went to sit on the balcony. The sight of the sea calmed her racing thoughts. Today, she would act ignorant, blissfully unaware of the subterfuge and she would enjoy Shelly's wedding, smile and nod at the happy couple as they took their vows. Then tomorrow, on their way home, she would confront Tom and demand answers from them all.

Marian burst into the room as Shelly was stirring.

"Good morning!" She shouted the words, making Rose look around from her position on the balcony.

Shelly sprang up. "Oh Lord, it's my wedding day!" The sisters embraced before calling for Rose.

"I'm here." Rose pulled back the curtain, fixed a smile upon her face. Shelly rushed to hug her.

"Is the weather good?" she asked.

Rose rolled her eyes.

"Of course it is," Shelly continued joyfully, "we're in Majorca."

"I've ordered us breakfast to be delivered to the room," Marian said crisply. "We can't have you bumping into Harry now, can we?"

"Is he okay?" Shelly gripped her arm. "I bet he's as nervous as hell... I bet he's being sick... it always affects his stomach."

"Harry is fine," Marian replied. "How are you feeling?"

"I'm actually feeling amazing, I had a great night's sleep."

Okay for some, Rose thought sourly. She wanted to yell at Shelly, to demand to know why she'd kept her best friend in the dark, but she kept her mouth in a firm, controlled line as Shelly bounced on the bed with excitement.

There was a rap on the door.

"I'll go." Marian opened it a fraction, sighing with relief at the sight of the waiter.

He brought in a tray of croissants, toast, pains au chocolat and freshly-brewed coffee, then hovered until Marian had taken the hint and tipped him.

"So we'll eat breakfast and shower," Marian had her bossy head on again, "and then we wait."

"Wait? For what?" Shelly placed her hands on her hips. "Tell me you haven't organised another entertainer, Marian?"

"Of course not," scoffed Marian. "I'm talking about hair and make-up. I've organised a woman to do it all for us and she should be here in..." she glanced at her phone, "soon."

"I vote we eat breakfast then." Rose gave out the plates. "Oh, there's damson jam, my favourite."

They sat on the balcony to eat. Marian thumped a bottle of Bucks Fizz on the table and filled three champagne flutes.

"To Shelly and Harry." They clinked glasses in a toast.

"May you have never-ending love," Rose added.

"May you be deliriously happy," Marian continued.

"May you be healthy and blessed." Rose sipped her frothy drink.

"This is perfect," said a grinning Shelly. "I checked the weather app and Britain is in the middle of a summer storm. Coming here was the best decision."

"It's been lovely," Rose agreed, "but I still love a church wedding."

"Maybe you should be hinting to Tom," Marian said, with a smug smile.

"I don't think so," Rose said quietly.

Shelly frowned. "Harry told me that he's never seen Tom so smitten over a woman before. He really likes you, Rose, and I know you feel the same way about him."

Rose turned to look at Marian. "How about you and Fin?"

"Pure lust," said Marian, with a throaty laugh. "I'm under no illusions about flighty Fin. It's been good fun, but we both know it isn't the everlasting kind of relationship. I'll be going back to London soon, back to my workaholic lifestyle and Fin will be in Australia with the surf. We're still going to keep in touch, though. I've told him he can stay at mine if he's ever back in Britain, and he's invited me out to Australia. Although I hate to imagine what his digs are like. Fin is so untidy." Marian shuddered. "I guess you could describe our relationship as being one of friends with benefits."

"Sounds great." Shelly wiped her mouth on a napkin. "I'm glad you're both on the same wavelength."

"I should shower," Rose said, "if it's okay for me to go first?"

"Of course," Shelly answered, following her back into the room. "Rose?"

Rose stopped walking, clenching her hands close to her side. I can't blurt this out, she thought, not today.

"Are you okay?"

"Yes, I'm fine." She turned to smile reassuringly at Shelly. "Just a little bit nervous."

"Me too!" Shelly pulled her into an embrace. "If I forget to tell you later, thank you – for everything, and I love you, Archer."

"Love you too." Rose breathed in deeply. "Happy wedding day."

Marian was struggling with her zip, puffing and panting as she attempted to pull it up.

"Jeez," she complained, "are you sure this is a size twelve?"

"Let me." Rose went to stand behind her and gently tugged on the zip.

"Must be all the food and Sangria." It was Shelly's turn with the beautician and she was sitting in front of the mirror watching blusher being swept across her cheekbones. "Oh cripes, I hope my dress fits me still."

"Well, if it doesn't, we'll have to wear our bikinis." Marian sucked in her stomach.

"There." Rose clipped the clasp at the top of the dress.

"Ah, you both look beautiful." Shelly clapped her hands together with approval.

Rose stared at her reflection in the full length mirror. The dress was beautiful, a sky blue satin number with a sweetheart neckline and a cinched-in waist that swirled down to her ankles. Marian had piled her hair into soft curls, held in place by diamante clips, and the beautician had done a great job. The make-up was fresh and light, just right.

Rose sat on the edge of the bed to put her sandals on and watched the beautician apply lip gloss to a pouting Shelly.

"We should be heading downstairs soon," Marian said, as she paced the room.

"I'm all finished, madam, you look very beautiful."

Marian paid the make-up lady and bustled over to the wardrobe. "I'm so excited to see your dress. Did it take you long to choose it? Knowing my sister, you were probably there all day."

"Actually, it was the first one I picked out and tried on. Isn't that right, Rose?"

"Yep." Rose helped Marian take off the cover.

"That sure is one dreamy dress," Marian sighed. "Come on then, let's get you in it."

Rose stood back as Marian lifted the dress over Shelly's head. It skimmed over her body, fitting perfectly.

"Can you do the back up?" Marian asked. "My hands are sweating."

Rose gently zipped it up then stood back to admire her friend. Tears glistened in her eyes. "You look stunning," she sniffed.

"Absolutely bloody gorgeous." Marian clicked the camera on her phone, then instructed Rose to stand next to her.

After a few more photographs had been taken, Rose doled out the bouquets.

"Are you ready?" she asked Shelly.

"As ready as I'll ever be," quipped Shelly. "What time is it? We're not late, are we?"

Marian glanced at her watch. "We've got ten minutes to get downstairs and on the beach. Fin's just text me, Harry's waiting, sis."

"Then let's go." Shelly clutched her bouquet, smiling softly. "I'm ready to marry the man of my dreams."

thirty-two

The breeze ruffled Rose's hair as she followed Shelly across the beach.

"I can see him." Shelly had the hugest smile on her face. "Oh, he looks so handsome!"

Rose peered past her. Her eyes raked over Fin and Harry, then rested upon Tom. He was talking to Harry, his head bent towards his brother. They all looked dashing in white suits. A crowd had gathered around them. Rose recognised Maria and Isabel but the rest were strangers; holidaymakers there to watch a Mediterranean beach wedding. As they approached, music began playing, a soft, slow number that signified the ceremony was about to start.

Rose squeezed Shelly's hand, silently sending her love.

"Are you ready?" Marian whispered, straightening her sister's veil and skirt.

Shelly nodded and Rose's eyes misted over with tears as she watched her friend head towards her husband-to-be.

Slowly, they walked up a red carpet which was covered with petals. The sun was beating down and the sea was lapping gently in front of them. The guys were standing underneath an arch covered with flowers. Rose could smell the floral fragrance emanating from them. It truly was a simple yet beautiful scene.

Harry turned around and across his face a myriad of emotions flickered: fear, excitement, but most of all love. Shelly quickened her pace, hurried towards him. She clutched his hands and murmured something into his ear. Then the music stopped, the registrar was welcoming everyone to the marriage of Harry and Shelly and the service began.

After they had exchanged vows, they all went down to the water's edge and paddled in the warm sea. Harry swung Shelly up in his arms to the delight of the crowd. The photographer snapped away, taking shots of the happy couple and group pictures of the wedding party.

"You look beautiful." Tom caught hold of her hand, whispering in her ear.

"Thank you." Rose reached up to straighten his awry tie. "You don't look too bad yourself."

"We're going to eat now," said a luminous Shelly. "Everything should be organised."

She called to Fin and Marian, who were kissing in the shallows and they made their way back to the hotel.

The meal was delicious; three courses consisting of a seafood starter, chicken main and a chocolate brownie dessert. The room the hotel had reserved for them was small, but prettily decorated. The hotel manager popped in to see if everything was okay. She had organised flowers in the room and even a small wedding cake.

"You are in luck this evening," she said to Shelly. "Tonight in Sa Coma there is a street carnival."

"That's marvellous!" cried Shelly. "We can't miss that."

After the plates had been taken away, Tom and Harry made speeches, more photographs were taken of the happy couple cutting the cake and then they went outside to sit on the patio in the glorious sunshine. The brothers drank beer out of glass bottles and the ladies drank Margaritas. As Marian and Shelly chatted, Maria came to sit next to Rose.

"Are you okay?" she whispered. "Did you speak to your boyfriend?"

"No. I haven't had chance. Not yet, anyway." Rose swallowed, sliding a surreptitious glance at Tom who was laughing with Fin. Truth was, she was loath to bring it up, reluctant to burst her bubble of happiness. Thankfully, Maria was distracted by the sight of a baby playing in the nearby toddler pool, leaving Rose the opportunity to reminisce over her wonderful night on the beach with Tom.

"Rose..." Shelly's voice brought her back to the present, "Marian and I are going to change into our swimwear. Are you coming?"

"But... your beautiful dress!" protested Rose.

"I've worn it long enough." Shelly wiped at her perspiring forehead. "I need to cool down and it will be fun to go in the pool."

"Okay." Rose stood up and was just going to follow her friend when Tom grabbed her arm and pulled her onto his lap.

"Where d'you think you're going?" He slid one hand along her thigh, while nibbling her ear.

"To cool down, and I think you need to as well!"

Tom laughed. "I could come upstairs with you... rub your sun cream in?"

"That would make me hot and sweaty again. I'm going with Shelly and Marian." Rose elbowed him playfully. "I won't be long."

"Missing you already." He slapped her derrière as she got back up.

"You are such a chauvinist," she said, ruffling his hair. See you in a bit."

Tom coughed. "Are you putting your red bikini on?"

"Might do," she called as she hurried inside.

Shelly and Marian were standing outside the lift, talking to a group of people. As Rose neared. she heard the tail end of the conversation.

"... you look beautiful, dear, many congratulations to you." The woman speaking was elderly; small, with tight grey curls and twinkling blue eyes. She reminded Rose of Granny Faith, Rose felt a pang of homesickness stir deep inside her. Although she loved it here, the old saying, 'home is where the heart is', was true. Rose was missing her family, missing Twineham and its familiarity, peace and tranquillity. It was time to go home, mused Rose, and it was time to ask some awkward questions about the man she was falling in love with.

"Well... it was nice wearing it, but it's time to get comfortable." Shelly was gazing at her wedding dress which had been lovingly placed back on the hanger.

"I'd be still in it if I was the bride," Marian yelled from the bathroom, "especially after the money you've spent on it."

"It's too hot," complained Shelly. "Have you finished in there?"

Marian came out, clipping her bikini top into place. "All yours."

Rose was sitting on the bed, staring down at the red bikini in her hands.

"Can you do my back?" asked Marian, handing her the bottle of sun cream.

"Marian," Rose whispered, throwing the bottle on the bed, "I know Tom's secret."

"What?" Marian turned to stare at her, blank-faced.

Rose cleared her throat. "The other night, I asked Shelly what his secret was. Remember?"

"Oh, that again?" Marian passed her back the cream. "He's not married, is he?"

"No," sighed Rose, "nothing like that. I just wondered if Fin had told you anything about him?"

"Are you kidding?" Marian snorted. "Fin and I don't do much talking when we're together, and he certainly wouldn't divulge any gossip on his brothers. Those three are as thick as thieves."

"Okay." Rose squirted tanning oil onto her palms. It smelt fruity and sweet. "This is a low factor, Marian. Are you sure it will give you enough protection?"

"It's the last day, Rose, and the last chance to work on my tan. Just because you have to use Factor 50 doesn't mean everyone else has to."

Rose nodded. "Don't mention anything to Shelly, please. I'll talk to her tomorrow, when we're alone."

"Sure." Marian shrugged. "Why are you acting so weird about this, Rose? I'm sure there's nothing bad to worry about with regards to Tom. He's lovely and obviously seriously into you, so stop worrying – okay?"

"Ssh." Rose put her finger to her lips as the bathroom door squeaked open. Shelly stood in a miniscule bikini, hands on hips. "Okay, ladies, let's go swim off that wedding cake."

The remainder of the afternoon was largely spent frolicking in the pool. Then, as the sun was slipping southwards in the sky, Tom and Rose went to get ready. Once they were alone, he pulled her onto the bed, discarding her bikini in his haste to kiss her all over.

"I've wanted to be alone with you all day," he murmured. His wandering lips were making Rose tremble.

"You know you can tell me anything, Tom?" She gasped, arching her back and clutching onto the sheets.

He lifted his head. "Conversation is highly overrated and right now I want to make love to you. We can talk later, okay?"

"Okay." Rose sighed with pleasure and all the worrisome thoughts vanished as she surrendered herself to passion.

∼

The streets of Sa Coma were lined with holidaymakers awaiting the carnival. Shelly was sitting on Harry's shoulders. She shouted out that she could see the flotillas coming. Rose peered through the crowd, up on her tiptoes.

"You okay down there, shorty?" asked Tom with a grin.

"I'm five foot four," she exclaimed, "and we can't all be giants like you." She smiled up at him. "How tall are you, anyway?"

"Six foot three." He shrugged. "That's one trait I inherited off Dad. Luckily not much else."

"What's your mum like?" Rose asked, slipping her hand into his.

"Warm, kind, affectionate. You actually remind me of her. Not in the way you look, but your personalities are similar, and she would love you."

"Yeah," drawled Fin, "you're normal, Rose, that's why."

"Were your ex-girlfriends abnormal, then?" Rose squinted in the sunlight.

A muscle flexed in Tom's jaw. "Let's just say they were difficult."

"That's an understatement," Fin burst out. "Think Fatal Attraction and magnify it by ten!"

"Leave it." Harry threw the youngest Sinclair brother a warning look. Tom moved away from Fin, pulling Rose with him.

"Have you had many girlfriends?" she asked despondently. Of course you have, she thought. You're Jack Fallon, international model and possible playboy.

He moved a strand of hair from her forehead. "No one important."

"Sorry," Rose said, "it's nothing to do with me."

"I've never met anyone like you." He gazed down at her. "I love everything about you."

Rose's mouth fell open. "You lo..." She didn't get a chance to finish her sentence.

"Look, you two, the carnival's arrived!" Shelly pulled Rose back towards her.

Rose turned to watch a colourful stream of people dancing past her. Acrobats and dancers twirled to the rhythm of steel drums. Open-backed trucks with cartoon and Disney characters had the children in raptures. A trio of women clad in bright African dress limboed along the road, followed by a group of classical ballet dancers pirouetting on their tiptoes. The crowd cheered as a man blew fire from a baton and behind him, Spanish men strummed guitars, singing joyfully.

As the carnival turned the corner, Tom encircled his arms around Rose. She noticed a group of women turn to stare their way, whispering and pointing at Tom.

"Do you know them?" Rose asked him.

"No," he replied, looking shifty.

They were still staring, then one took out her phone and the flash lit up Tom's face.

"Why are they taking pictures of you?" Rose's lower lip trembled.

"Come on." Tom grabbed her hand, pulling her away.

"Wait!" Rose said breathlessly.

"We have to go," he said firmly.

They weaved through the crowd, walking quickly past the hotel.

Rose glanced over her shoulder. The women were following them, giggling and talking animatedly.

Tom broke into a jog, pulling Rose with him.

"Jack!" They were shouting now, running to catch up.

Tom ran faster. Rose was panting hard, her legs hurting as she tried to keep up with him.

Up a side street they lurched, passing giant bins, squelching over detritus and mud.

"Stop!" she cried, loosening his hand. "I know your secret."

Tom leant against a wall, exhaling heavily.

"Who are you, Jack Fallon?"

thirty-three

Tom held up one hand, "I can explain."

Rose crossed her arms across her chest. "Explain how you lied? You're not an electrician, are you?"

"I was an electrician," Tom insisted, "before I was scouted by a modelling agency."

Rose sniffed. "So what do I call you? Tom or Jack?"

"My name's Tom Sinclair. Jack Fallon's a name my management cooked up. They thought it sounded edgier, more appealing." His laughter sounded hollow.

"So it's true then," Rose whispered, "you're a famous model?"

Tom swallowed. "I'm in a band, too."

"A band?" Rose was incredulous. "But I've never heard of you..."

"We're big in Australia and Asia. Haven't quite made it in Britain and America yet."

"Why did you lie?" Rose implored. "You should have been honest..."

"I wanted to be incognito. I wanted you to like me as Tom Sinclair, not Jack Fallon."

"I don't like being deceived." Rose turned away. "We should go back to the others."

"Rose," he called, "are we okay?"

"I don't know." She shook her head. "I need time to think." As she walked back towards the sea front, she could hear him shouting that he was sorry, but Rose kept on walking.

Rose endured another sleepless night. While Marian snored softly in the bed next to her, thoughts of Tom, a.k.a. Jack, kept her awake. She watched the sun rise through the open door, and then went to make a cup of tea. What did British people do when there was a crisis? she mused. Stick the kettle on, of course! As it bubbled away, she heard Marian stir and turned to glance at her.

"What time is it?" A toned leg peeked from underneath the sheet.

"Almost six," Rose replied quietly. "I'm sorry. Did I wake you?"

"Yes, you did," snapped Marian, "I'll be glad to get back to London for a lie-in. I'm not usually up until seven."

"I couldn't sleep," Rose explained. "I've got stuff on my mind."

"Is that stuff Tom Sinclair by any chance?"

Rose refrained from replying.

Marian made a huffing noise before disappearing into the toilet.

"Do you want a drink?"

"I may as well, being as though I'm up," yelled Marian. The sound of the toilet flushing was a signal for Marian to reappear. Her tousled hair and make-up-smudged face regarded Rose with sympathy.

"What happened between you guys? You seemed so happy."

"You don't know?" Rose looked up with surprise from her tea stirring.

"All I know is that last night you flounced off to bed early and Tom was miserable." Marian shrugged. "Care to enlighten me?"

Rose passed her the tea and sat on the bed, drawing her knees up to her chest.

"Have you heard of Jack Fallon?"

Marian's blank face told Rose she genuinely hadn't.

"Is this a guessing game? Just spit it out, Rose."

"Tom isn't Tom," Rose inhaled deeply, "his name is Jack Fallon and he's famous."

"What?" Marian blinked. "You mean he's, like, an actor?"

"No, Marian, not quite." Rose sipped her tea. "He's a model and plays in a band... in Australia."

"Are you serious?" Marian screeched. "Why haven't I heard of him?" She reached for her phone and googled him. "Crikey, you're right! There's loads of stuff on the internet about him. This is fabulous!"

"No, it's not." Rose's eyes filled with tears. "It changes everything."

"Why?" Marian hopped onto the bed next to Rose. "What's the problem? I would luuurve to be with a famous guy. I picked the wrong brother, huh?"

Through her tears, Rose smiled. "How am I going to compete with supermodels and groupies, Marian? I'm just average Rose from normal Twineham. I work in a call centre, for God's sake. My life is totally mundane whereas Tom has everything..."

Marian reached across to shake Rose's shoulders. "No, he doesn't, sweetheart. From what I've heard off Shelly, before this holiday he was on a real downer. You've been good for him, Rose. So go easy on him, okay?"

"Okay," Rose nodded. "I suppose we should pack."

"What time's our flight?"

"Three o'clock this afternoon."

"We've got plenty of time." Marian drained her drink. "Why don't we relax for a bit, go down to breakfast and then go for one last swim?"

"Sounds like a good plan."

Marian put the empty cups back on the tray and then stretched out on her bed. "Wake me up in an hour and Rose, stop worrying."

The coach picked them up late morning, leaving them plenty of time to wait in departures for the flight home. Shelly and Harry sat next to each other holding hands, Fin and Marian had wandered off to peruse the duty free aisles, leaving Rose and Tom sitting awkwardly opposite each other.

"Are you nervous?" he asked eventually.

"Yes," replied Rose, gazing across at him. He looked tired and she wondered if he'd had trouble sleeping, too.

Harry stood up. "Why don't we go for a wander," he said to Tom.

"Sure." Tom got to his feet and followed his brother.

Once alone, Shelly patted the empty seat next to her. Rose hesitated; she was still angry with her friend's duplicity. They used to tell each other everything, but that was a long time ago.

"Please sit next to me," Shelly said. "We need to talk."

Rose slid her rucksack across the floor and sat next to Shelly.

"First of all I want to apologise," Shelly began. "Nobody set out to deceive you, Rose, and none of us thought you'd become romantically involved with Tom. He was going to tell you once we were back in Britain. I'm sorry I didn't tell you, but he was adamant that he didn't want anyone to know about his career and all this Jack Fallon business."

"Why?" Rose asked. "Why couldn't he have told me, Shelly? We grew close, he should have confided in me."

"He wanted you to like him for being Tom, an ordinary guy. Would you have become involved if you'd known he was famous?"

Rose swallowed. "I'd probably have run a mile. Why did it happen between us, Shelly? He could have anybody."

"You need to speak to him," Shelly placed a comforting arm around Rose's shoulders, "and don't you dare put yourself down, Archer. You're unique, kind, pretty and that's why he likes you. Most other women would be fawning all over Jack Fallon, but you you're different. You love Tom Sinclair, don't you?"

Rose nodded. She couldn't hide her feelings from her best friend. "Was he using me? Just for a holiday fling...?"

Shelly sighed. "All I know is that I've never seen Tom like this with a woman before. Will you be sitting next to him on the flight home?"

Rose shook her head. "I've swopped with Fin and please leave it as that, Shelly. I think Tom and I both need some breathing space. This holiday's been pretty intense."

"I warned you that your life would change, Rose." Shelly smirked. "I did say that it was going to be a summer of madness."

"It's definitely been different from going to Weymouth with Mum and Dad," Rose chuckled, "and I can't wait to see my gran's reaction when I tell her I got cosy with a real life heartthrob."

"She'll probably faint." Shelly laughed heartily at the thought of a flabbergasted Granny Faith, and despite her internal angst Rose joined in, until the tears were rolling down her face at the sheer absurdity of her present situation.

thirty-four

"Rose we're landing." Marian was shaking her arm, pulling her from a dream about Tom. He was standing on a stage, strumming a guitar, playing to thousands of people and she was there in the audience with crowds of other star-struck women, watching him, enraptured.

"What?" Rose mumbled sleepily. Her face was warm, leaning against Marian's shoulder. Someone had draped a blanket around her, the scratchy material tickled her chin.

"Time to put your seatbelt on," Marian continued, pulling off the blanket. Cold air hit Rose's exposed limbs. The rumbling sounds of the engines and the vibrations of the plane shook her wide awake. Her seat... it felt like it was moving!

"What's happening?" She sat bolt upright, clutching the arm rest.

"Just a bit of turbulence," Marian replied. "We're nearly home, Rose, look out of the window.

Rose peered past Marian's shoulder and caught a glimpse of fields and roads, before the plane was enveloped in the white mist of clouds.

"What a surprise that it's raining." Marian's tone was dry. "Welcome back to England."

. . .

After a bumpy landing that had the plane skidding to a halt, the seatbelts signs were turned off and the entire occupants of the plane, including the cabin crew, scrabbled to their feet in the rush to alight. Marian jumped nimbly up, opened the overhead compartment and was subsequently flattened by a falling hand case.

"Are you alright?" Rose helped her to her feet.

Marian turned to scowl at a teenage lad who was sniggering her way. "Just get me back to London!"

The doors opened to wet greyness. Rose moved slowly behind Marian as they exited the plane and filed through the attached tunnel. Once they were inside the airport terminal, the line of passengers dispersed in all directions. Marian strode off in front and Rose had to jog to catch up with her.

"Shouldn't we wait for the others?" she queried.

"They'll catch up," Marian replied briskly. "Let's go get our luggage."

There were already people at the conveyer belt. As it burst to life and cases began tumbling through the flaps, Marian elbowed her way to the front and stood like an Olympic athlete, hands poised and ready. Rose's eyes were wandering, looking for Tom. She soon spotted him, towering above many of the other passengers. Alongside him walked Fin and Harry. They were fine-looking men, thought Rose, and she'd never noticed before how similar Tom and Fin were. They both shared the same height, build and dimples. The notable difference between the brothers was their hair colour. Fin's dirty blonde, tousled look was in sharp contrast to Tom's thick dark hair. And then there was Harry's pale skin and ginger curls, although he, too, was tall and broad. The three of them certainly drew some admiring glances as they strode through the airport.

. . .

A beeping sound emanated from Rose's bag. She fished out her phone and read a message from her mum, asking if she'd landed safely. Rose replied, her fingers flying over her phone quickly.

"Want to share a taxi home with us?" asked Shelly.

"Dad's picking me up," Rose answered, "but thanks."

Shelly stepped towards Rose, pulling her into a hug. "Thanks for being my matron of honour, thanks for coming."

"I should be thanking you." Rose's words were muffled against her friend's hair. "I've had a wonderful time. Will I see you before you leave for Australia?"

"Yes, we're not going back for another week. Harry and I are going to go on a few mini trips, an extended honeymoon."

Rose nodded. "I'll text you then."

"Bye Rose," Marian had pulled the cases off and was holding Rose's out for her.

"Thank you." Rose took the handle and reached across to give Marian a brief hug.

Harry and Fin kissed her cheek, then they all moved away so she was left staring at Tom.

"So this is goodbye," he mumbled, his hands thrust in his pocket.

"Yes," she whispered. "Have a safe flight back to Australia."

"Rose," he pulled her into his arms, "I'm sorry I didn't tell you. I apologise if I've hurt you."

He smelt divine; fresh and musky all rolled into one gorgeous package. Rose wondered how many other women had kissed him at an airport gate.

"It's okay," she said, looking up at him. "Your band must be waiting for you to return."

"Yeah," he pushed a hand through his hair, "it's going to be mad. We're due to start a tour, interviews, photo shoots, band practice till the early hours of the morning... Rose, I'll keep in touch."

Rose's smile slipped. You won't have time for me, she thought, and I'm not going to be left waiting for you to call like some lovesick teenager. She placed her hands on his chest and pushed herself firmly away... Stood up on tiptoes to graze his stubbly cheek with her lips.

"'Bye, Tom." Her gaze roamed over his face, creating an imprint that would hopefully remain in her memory forever. This gorgeous man who had captured her heart in ten days. Rose turned and walked away, her head held high, a smile fixed to her face, while inside she felt as if her heart was breaking.

~

"Whoa, love! Missed me, have you?" Rose catapulted herself into her father's arms, clinging onto him.

"Yes, Dad, I've missed you all."

"You should go away more often, love," Rod chuckled. "Give us your case then and I'll get you home." He picked up Rose's luggage and went to open the car boot. "Your mum's cooked your favourite. Are you hungry?"

"Shepherd's pie?" Rose's stomach rumbled. "Mmm, I haven't eaten since this morning."

"So what was Majorca like?" Rod asked, as he slid into the driving seat. "All night partying? I bet you weren't up until midday."

"It was a quiet resort," Rose replied, "more family-orientated. There were a few bars, but the entertainment was largely hotel-based. Majorca is beautiful, Dad. You and Mum should go." She shifted in her seat as he revved the engine and pulled into the lane of traffic. "Have you even been abroad?"

"Oh aye, we went to Switzerland when we were courting. Got locked out of the hotel for staying out too late. That was over thirty years ago though, mind." Rod switched on the window screen wipers. "You've brought the rain back with you. It's been miserable all the time you've been gone, Rose. What was the weather like over there?"

Rose chatted to him, giving him a brief rundown of the holiday. She omitted to tell him about the romance she had had with Tom, not at all sure if her dad would approve of the knowledge that his only daughter had made love on a public beach...

The motorway was quiet. Rush hour had passed and lights flashed on as the sky darkened.

"So what's been happening here?" Rose asked.

"Your brother's got himself in a spot of bother." Rod scowled. "He's been fooling around with a married woman."

Rose sat up straighter. "But Mrs Mason was separated, Dad."

"I ain't talking about Mrs Mason." Rod gripped the steering wheel. "I mean Gloria Rutherford, y'know, the woman who owns the florist's with her husband."

Crikey, thought Rose, was Marty going around all the female shop workers in the village? First the butcher's wife and now the florist's. Did her brother have a death wish?

"Her husband came round the house. Ranting and raving, he was. Threatened to give Marty a good hiding. Your mum was close to calling the police. But you know your brother's always had the gift of the gab. He could talk himself out of a world war. He turned it around that he was the victim." Rod snorted. "Mr Rutherford broke his heart to us, he was in the kitchen with your mum and Gran for good on an hour. It all came out that Mrs Rutherford's nothing short of a nymphomaniac, and Marty isn't the first young lad she's taken a shine to."

Rose tutted. "What are we going to do with him? He doesn't seem to have any luck with women, does he, Dad?"

Rod sniffed. "I blame your granddaddy. He's passed on his philandering genes to our Marty."

"Maybe he just hasn't met the right woman," Rose suggested. "One day he'll know, then all this fooling around will be behind him."

"I hope so." Rod shook his head and indicated to move into the fast lane. "If the truth be known, I'm worried about the pair of you. There's my own son a womaniser and my daughter who could join a nunnery."

"I'm not so innocent as you think," Rose blustered.

"Does that mean you got lucky in Majorca?" Rod teased.

Rose sighed. "Dad, concentrate on the road!" She winced as a lorry whizzed past them. "Let's just say that I had a holiday experience I won't be forgetting."

Rod let out a whistle. "Sounds promising. Well, I'm sure your mum and granny will be eager to hear all the details. We can have a night in front of the television, and you can tell us all about it."

"Actually," sniffed Rose, "I thought we could all go out for a drink to the new wine bar."

"Eh?" Rod's face crumpled with disbelief. "You mean you won't be rushing off to that church of yours."

"No, not tonight," Rose replied lightly, "let's have a family night out. Let's have a cocktail or two. Let's have fun, Dad."

Rod slapped his thigh. "That's what I like to hear. Count it a family date, love... and Rose, we all missed you. It's good to have you home."

"I know, and I missed you, too." Rose slid down in her seat, checking her phone for messages. But her inbox remained empty and, with a heavy heart, she shook away mental images of Tom Sinclair and thoughts of his strong arms and loving kisses.

thirty-five

When they pulled up in Lavender Close, Rose noticed her mum, gran and brother peering through the window, net curtain tucked behind their heads. Her spirits lifted at the sight of her family and the familiar surroundings. She clambered from the vehicle, opened the iron gate and hurried up the path, leaving her dad to lug the suitcase out. She noticed the lawn had been freshly mown, and there were new flowers in the borders; it was all looking very colourful and pretty. Fran opened the door and stepped out with her arms wide. Rose hugged her tight, inhaling the scent of soap and lily of the valley.

"You look fantastic," Fran said, moving aside so Faith could embrace her.

"Thanks," replied Rose. "Did you miss me, Gran?"

"It was quiet." Faith tweaked her cheeks. "Where's this tan come from? You never turn that colour in Weymouth. You're positively glowing."

"It was hot and sunny every day. We spent a lot of time sunbathing."

"Not topless, I hope," Granny Faith cackled. "Maybe I should go to Majorca, check out the men."

"You're too old," Fran retorted with an eye roll.

"Aye," chipped in Rod, "never mind Majorca, there's a great retirement home down the road you could be visiting."

Faith threw her son-in-law a sharp look and Rose laughed. She had missed this banter, she had missed her family.

"Come on in then, love," Fran said briskly. "I've put the kettle on and there's a nice sponge cake we can share."

As they went into the house, Marty draped one arm across Rose's shoulder. "Welcome home, sis."

"What have you been up to?" she whispered. "Will you never learn, Marty?"

"What can I say?" He grinned. "I'm irresistible to the older lady."

"That isn't the issue," she tutted. "You have to stop fooling around with married women, Marty."

Marty threw himself in an armchair with a scowl. "Never mind me. Were there any Germans there and did they go nude?"

"I met a few," Rose smiled as she remembered the group of lads she and Shelly had spoken to in the sea, "and no, they weren't nude, it was a family resort and they'd probably be arrested if they were."

"Pity." Faith rubbed her whiskery chin. "Sit down then, love and tell us all about it."

After tea, cake and a lengthy chat, Rose went up to her bedroom to unpack.

"You didn't need your suede jeans then?" Fran stood in the doorway, arms crossed.

"No," Rose laughed, "although I think I'll need them here. It's cold." She shivered.

Fran crossed to gaze out the window, "this summer has been a washout so far."

"How was York?" Rose dumped her dirty clothes in a pile.

"Beautiful and interesting," Fran replied. "We had a great time, apart from when your Dad pulled his back trying to carry me into the hotel room. It was a lovely break, though. Who says romance is dead when you've been married for thirty-something years?"

"Ah, that's sweet," Rose said wistfully, "it must have been nice for you to have some alone time."

"It was." Fran sat on the bed and regarded her daughter. "What about you? Did you have alone time with anyone?"

Rose ducked her head and busied herself sorting her toiletries.

"Ros ...?"

Rose paused. Should she fib? No, her mum would see right through her.

"Tom," was all she could manage.

"Ah. Do you want to talk about it?"

Rose shook her head fervently. "It was just a holiday romance and now it's over."

A silence stretched. Rose took her sandals out of the case and placed them in the bottom of her wardrobe.

"Are you sure it's over?"

Rose hung her head. "There's no future for us." She took a deep breath. "I'm going to have a shower and a lie-down if that's all right, Mum."

"Course it is, love." Fran gave Rose's arm a comforting rub. "I'm always here if you want to chat... about anything." She crossed the room and pulled the door softly closed and Rose flopped down on the bed, wrapping herself in the warm softness of the duvet.

Starlight was the name of the new wine bar. It had been converted from a clothing store six months ago into a trendy drinking place complete with fluorescent lighting, thumping music and a beer garden. Rose and her family arrived just after eight. It was full of people, but they managed to grab a vacant window table. Rose draped her cardigan over the back of her chair and sat opposite her mum.

"Fancy a cocktail?" she asked.

"Why not?"

Rose looked at her gran, who nodded enthusiastically.

"Lager for me, Dad." Marty flipped his chair back onto two legs and looked around the bar with interest. "There's a lot of people in here for a week night."

"I've heard it's always busy." Fran perused the drinks menu. After a few minutes discussing cocktails, the women decided on three Bellinis. Rod and Marty went off to order and pay for the drinks. Rose tapped her fingers on the table in time to the music. It was mad to think that Tom played in a band; she still couldn't believe it. She shook her head. No she wasn't going to think about him, not for the next hour at least.

"So you're back at work tomorrow?" Fran's question stopped the imminent daydream from occurring.

Rose blinked. "Yep, back to it." The thought of Fulham Banking made Rose's spirits sink. "Actually, I'm thinking of making a change."

"Oh yeah?" Rod and Marty were back, setting the drinks on the table.

Rose looked at her family then took a deep breath. "I want to go back to college. I want to retrain. I want to change my career."

Granny Faith coughed. "To what, our Rose?"

"I know." Fran observed her daughter. "You've always wanted to work with animals, haven't you?"

"Yep. It's been my dream since I was at school."

"I remember," Fran continued, "all you ever wanted for Christmas was stuffed animals so you could play vets. And all the animal magazines I had to buy. You loved them."

Rod sipped his pint. "How are you going to manage financially?"

"I have savings and I thought I could work part-time. Perhaps I could get a job here, in the evenings."

"You, working in a pub?" Marty looked shocked. "But how would you cope with the leering men, the drunks, the fist fights? Bar work is hard, Rose, and you're s..."

"So what?" snapped Rose, glaring at her brother.

Fran patted her hand. "I think he means sensitive, love."

"Well, I think it's a great idea," crowed Granny Faith. "Weren't we all willing Rose to make changes to her life?"

"I'm sure you could cope with it, love," Rod agreed. "Our Rose is tougher than she looks."

"I'm doing it," Rose said firmly. "No more wasting my life, no more unhappiness."

"Here, here," Fran said. "This calls for a toast." They clinked glasses. "To new adventures and success for our Rose!"

"To a hot romance for my only granddaughter!" Faith winked.

Oh, if only you knew, thought Rose with a sad smile.

"While we're on the subject of romance, is that Jeremy Payne I see over there?"

Rose peered across the room. "Yes, it is. I suppose I should go say hello."

"After the way he treated you?" Marty shook his head. "You're too kind, sis. Want me to beat him up?"

"Don't be so melodramatic," Rose replied, with an eye roll. "I'm going to let Jeremy Payne know that I'm not bothered in the slightest about him and Sabrina. She's welcome to him."

Jeremy had spotted her and was beckoning her over. Rose took her cocktail with her.

"Hello, Rose." He pushed his glasses up and peered at her with beady dark eyes. "I hear you've been on holiday."

"Yes. Majorca."

Jeremy cleared his throat. "We missed you in the folk choir."

Rose was disconcerted that Jeremy had taken hold of her hand. "I missed you..." he added.

"Where's Sabrina?" Rose looked at the people he was standing with; men from the offices he worked at.

"We are no more." Jeremy sighed theatrically. "Sabrina has moved on, to America."

Rose pulled her hand away. "But I thought you were a couple?"

"I realised she wasn't the girl for me." Jeremy shrugged. "I've been foolish, Rose, blind to my true love."

Rose backed away.

"It's you, Rose, it's always been you."

"Oh no." Rose shook her head. "You were right, Jeremy, we are destined to be just friends."

"But Rose, a few weeks ago you were paying me compliments, telling me you wanted to be in a relationship with me!" Jeremy inhaled deeply. "While you were away, I've had chance to think. We are perfect for each other, Rose." He clasped her hands again. "Will you do me the honour of marrying me?"

thirty-six

"Are you serious?" Rose could feel her mouth gaping open in shock.

"Very." Jeremy nodded. "We'd be so good together, Rose, I could make you happy."

Rose inhaled sharply. "Jeremy, I like you, but that's all it is, and you need more than that to base a marriage on."

"Like turns to love. Will you think about it, Rose? Give me an answer in a few days' time?"

Rose glanced at him. He looked sincere enough and pleading emotion was written all over him. Jeremy took her pause for confirmation of his plans. He kissed the side of her cheek and bade her a gallant farewell.

"Goodbye, my love. I await your response. Think carefully, fair maiden." With, that he had gone, leaving Rose gaping after him.

"The nerve of him!" Fran and the others listened as Rose relayed what had just occurred. "So it doesn't work out with Sabrina and you're second choice!"

Marty sniggered. "Did you tell him where to shove his tank top?"

"I tried to let him down gently," Rose scratched her head, "but he didn't seem to be listening."

"You need to make it plain and simple," Faith advised. "A good boot up his arse should do the trick."

"I couldn't do that," Rose said quietly. "What am I going to do?"

"You're not seriously considering his proposal, are you?" Rod looked at his daughter through slanted eyes. "I do not give my blessing to having him as a son-in-law, is that plain and clear enough?"

"Of course I'm not going to say yes." Rose banged her glass down on the table. "I'll explain to him... that liking someone and knowing them for years aren't good enough reasons to marry a person." She swallowed as images of Tom whirled in her mind. "I want love and passion, like... Shelly and Harry and... you and Mum."

"Aye, that's right, our Rose." Granny Faith harrumphed. "Me and your granddaddy married purely for lust. Couldn't keep our hands off each other."

"Mum!" Fran held up her hand. "No more information, please."

Faith flashed a mischievous smile. "I heard you got lucky in Majorca."

"Thanks, Mum." Rose crossed her arms. "Can we talk about something other than my personal life?"

"Have you told Rose about the school reunion?" Marty asked his mum.

Fran's hand shot up to cover her mouth. "I forgot all about that. Yes, Rose, it's this weekend and you and Shelly have been invited. Billy Baxter told me in the supermarket. There's going to be a big celebration at Poole High School. All the teachers will be there. They've even asked your brother to DJ for the evening."

Marty leant back in his chair, a proud smile on his face. "They must have heard about my snazzy skills at Shelly's party."

"A school reunion?" Rose slumped in her seat. "I'm not sure

if I fancy that. I hated secondary school, all the cliques and the bitching."

"That's in the past, love." Fran gave Rose's arm a gentle pat. "Everyone's grown up and moved on. I reckon Shelly would love it. A last celebration before she goes back to Australia."

"Where is she, by the way?" Marty asked.

"Flitting around Ireland, the last I heard." Rose picked at the fluff on her cardigan. "I suppose I should go."

"You definitely should. Buy yourself a new dress," Fran advised. "With your new hair colour and your tan, you'll dazzle everyone. The women will be green with envy."

"Okay," Rose grinned, "I'll go."

Her family cheered and urged Rose to pick up her phone and message Shelly pronto.

The next morning, Rose was up bright and early and in the shower before anyone else had risen. She speed-buttered two slices of bread, popped in some ham and placed it in a Tupperware box together with an apple and a slice of Fran's banana cake.

"You're up early, love." Her mum was watching her from the top of the stairs as she slipped into her comfortable work shoes.

"I've a busy day ahead," Rose replied, with a smile. "I dread to think what state my desk will be in."

Last time she'd been on holiday, Liliana had brought in a temp who had left the reception area a royal mess; unfinished photocopying strewn everywhere, coffee cups piled up, a bulging waste paper basket full of chocolate wrappers and a suspicious sticky residue over the switchboard. It had taken her a morning to clean it all up.

Fran shuffled down the stairs, pulling her dressing gown tight. "Have a nice day, love, and remember we're going dress shopping at lunchtime."

"I'll be there, Mum." Rose picked up her car keys. "See you later." She backed out of the door, struggling into her blazer.

For now, the rain had ceased, the sun was shining and there was a fresh breeze rustling the trees. Rose reversed her car off the drive and headed towards the industrial estate where Fulham Banking was situated.

"Morning, love," Ron greeted her as she keyed in the code and opened the main door. "You're looking well. Did you have a good holiday?"

"I did, thank you." She set her bag down. "How's it been here?"

"Chaos," he replied, leaning on the desk. "They had one of them sales girls here on reception. Useless, she was, cut half of the customers off. Graham came down and gave her a telling-off."

"Oh dear," Rose said. "Well at least she's left the reception tidy."

"I cleared it up for you, love," Ron puffed out his chest, "didn't think it was fair you having to come back to someone else's mess."

"Thank you." Rose smiled at him. "How's Betsy?"

"She's well. Went to knit and natter all on her own, which was a big deal for someone who suffers with crippling anxiety. Will you be going with her this week, love? Only she's started knitting you a jumper and she wanted to check you liked the colour."

"I'll be there," Rose was touched at his words, "and that's lovely of her."

"You're worth it." He took off his hat and smoothed down his hair. "Now, tell me all about your holiday."

As Rose was chatting to him, staff began filtering in. Liliana arrived with a group of the sales girls, giggling and gossiping. She paused by the lift to throw Rose and Ron a look of disdain, a look loaded with disapproval. Rose carried on listening to Ron speaking about his beloved Betsy.

"Well, I suppose I should get off," he said, checking his watch,

"Betsy will have my toast and tea ready. Have a good day now, love and don't work too hard."

"I'll try not to," Rose said, with a laugh. "Give my love to Betsy."

Ron ambled off, twirling his keys and Rose affixed her earpiece and picked up the first phone call of the day.

The morning flew by. There was a steady stream of calls; new customers, disgruntled current ones, colleagues from other offices asking to speak to management. She buzzed Graham's office and was surprised when he answered instead of his secretary.

"How was your holiday, Rose?" he asked amiably.

"It was fantastic, thank you," Rose replied politely. "Erm, I have Maxine from Head Office for you." She connected the call and then set about sorting the mail into neat piles.

Later in the morning, when Rose was on her break, she decided to go and see Graham. His secretary informed her that he was free and told her to go on through to his office. Rose stood in the doorway, feeling awkward. Her heart was hammering as she ruminated over what she was about to tell him.

"Sit down, Rose," he said with a smile, pointing to a chair opposite him.

Rose perched on the squishy leather chair, crossed her legs and took a deep breath.

"What can I do for you?" he asked.

"I'm leaving." There, she had said the two words which had kept her awake last night.

"Leaving?" Graham's face registered his shock. "But why, Rose? You're doing so well here." There was a pause. "It's not the staff, is it? I've noticed the way some of the women talk to you."

"No." Rose shook her head. "I want to go back to college. I want to retrain. Basically, I want to change my career." She explained about the animal care course at the local college. "It's a part-time two year course. I should have done it years ago. I've always wanted to, but I guess I was afraid of change."

"But how will you cope financially?"

"I'm going to get a part-time job, something which will fit around my college hours."

Graham was silent for a moment. He flipped his pen between his fingers. "Stay here, Rose, we can reduce your hours. Fulham Banking can fit around you."

"You mean I could go part-time?" Rose was surprised at his kind offer; as far as she was aware, all of the staff here were full-time.

"Yes. You're a brilliant staff member – hardworking and conscientious. I don't want to lose you. Not yet, anyway."

Rose was so happy she almost bounced on her seat. "That would be wonderful! Thank you so much, Mr Marston."

"Call me Graham," he said.

Rose stood up, smoothing the wrinkles out of her skirt.

"I can imagine you working with animals," Graham said, smiling. "You're kind and caring and you've always been wasted here."

"Oh no," Rose protested. "This is a good company to work for and I'm very grateful for the opportunities I've been given as an employee."

"It's all right, Rose." Graham held up his hand. "I understand how you feel, I had my dreams once, too. Escape while you can is my advice." He laughed, and it was such a lovely infectious sound that Rose found herself joining in.

At the door, Graham caught her attention with the parting words, "Get out there and live, Rose. Get out there and shine."

thirty-seven

"You look stunning." Fran gave her daughter a big thumbs-up sign. "I was right about that dress, it looks perfect on you."

Rose twirled round in her high new wedges and stopped in front of the full-length mirror. Her mum was right. of course; the silver sequin-covered midi dress was beautiful.

"Is the make-up too much?" Rose had been to the local beautician's for the first time ever and the result was dark kohled eyes and scarlet lips, a contrast to her simple understated daytime wear.

"Absolutely not!" Fran bustled over. "You look vampy and extremely sexy."

"Thanks." Rose grinned and stared again in the mirror.

"What time is Shelly coming for you?"

"Seven," Rose replied. "I'm early as usual."

"You're punctual," Fran corrected gently. "Come and show your gran, love, she's beside herself with excitement. Anybody would think that it's her going to her school reunion."

Rose tottered down the stairs, following Fran. "Crikey," Rod said, his spoon of ice cream wavered in the air, "is that really you, our Rose?"

"Doesn't she look lovely?" Fran knocked his feet off the coffee table and sank down next to him.

"You look smashing." Granny Faith flashed her a gummy smile. "I bet half of your class mates won't recognise you."

Marty sauntered in, glancing up from his phone. "Whit-woo. Is that really my sister?"

Rose turned to face him. "Shouldn't you be at the school?"

"I'm going," he replied, picking up his box of equipment. "Don't forget to buy me a bottle or two of beer." He squashed his cap on backwards, a move which created a twist in Rose's stomach. Tom, where are you? she wondered. Last night, she'd broken her self-imposed abstinence from him and messaged him. She hadn't received a reply, and now she was bitterly regretting asking how he was, telling him she missed him and topping it all off with three kisses. He obviously didn't care, she thought miserably. What was the saying? No response is a response.

Rose paced the lounge, growing angry with herself. No more pining after Tom Sinclair, she told herself – or should she address him as Jack Fallon from now on?

"You're going to wear that carpet out." Rod patted the empty seat next to him. "Sit down, then I can be a rose between two thorns."

"You should be so lucky," Fran snorted. "Put the news on, love, see what's happening in the world."

As they all were searching for the remote, Marty poked his head round the door.

"You've got a visitor," he said to Rose.

Rose brightened. "Shelly?"

"Nope," he pointed his thumb backwards, "it's tank top guy. I told him to wait in the garden."

There was a sudden knock on the window. Jeremy's face was squashed against the glass as he tried to peer through the net curtains.

"Jeez," Rod shook his head, "has the man no self-respect? You've told him no already, haven't you, Rose?"

"Not exactly." Rose flinched. "I've been avoiding him."

Granny Faith waved her stick in the air. "Want me to give him a clout?"

"No," sighed Rose, "I'll speak to him." She went to the front door, telling herself to be brave and straightforward.

Jeremy was standing beside the hydrangea bush. When he saw Rose, he picked a flower and handed it to her.

"My word," he gushed, "you look beautiful."

"Thank you." Rose drew him off the lawn and away from the house. "I'm sorry I haven't replied to your messages."

Jeremy pushed his spectacles up his nose. "I was starting to worry, Rose. I thought you might be ill."

Yes, thought Rose, I'm suffering from unrequited love. She looked down at the flower in her hands and Jeremy's large, moccasin-clad feet.

"Will you give me my answer... please?"

Without warning, he dropped to his knees, clutching her free hand. "Allow me to tell you how ardently I love thee." Rose gasped at his reference to Pride and Prejudice. This is all wrong, she thought. It's Tom I want to hear this from and certainly not Jeremy Payne. Rose pulled her hand away.

"Jeremy, thank you for your proposal, I'm very flattered and you are a fine man," she gulped as she saw the glimmer of hope in his eyes, "but I can't accept. I'm sorry but the answer is no."

"No?" Rose watched the redness spread from his neck into his cheeks. "But you said yourself that I'm a fine man. I'm a catch, Rose... any woman would be lucky to have me."

Rose bit her lip. "I love someone else." Truly, madly, deeply, her internal voice added.

"Love?" Jeremy sneered. "Little, picky, frigid Rose Archer is actually in love?"

Anger bubbled inside Rose at his cruel words. No more kindness, she vowed; not towards him at least. "And even if I wasn't in love with someone else, you are the last man who I would ever contemplate sharing the rest of my life with."

For a long moment they surveyed each other, both equally furious.

"Okay." Jeremy backed away from her. "But there will be no more folk choir. From this moment, I QUIT!"

Rose folded her arms and gave him the strongest glare she could muster. "I'm sure we'll manage without you."

"You... you..." Jeremy blustered, searching for a suitably scathing comeback.

Then Rose heard movement behind her. "You heard my daughter, she said no! Now get off my property before I throw you off." Rose turned to look gratefully at her dad, who had a menacing look on his face and fists clenched tightly by his side.

Jeremy backed further away. "I'm going. Goodbye forever, Rose Archer."

Behind her, Granny Faith hollered, "Good bloody riddance!" Jeremy Payne practically sprinted off the drive and that was the last time Rose ever saw him.

It was so good to see Shelly again. Rose held her tight, kissed her hair and gushed over her gold jumpsuit.

"You're not looking too bad yourself, Archer."

"How are you, Rose?" Harry stepped forward to embrace her.

"I'm good," replied Rose. "How is Fin?"

"Oh, he's all right," Harry smirked, "currently staying with Marian in London."

"And Tom?"

Harry coughed. "He's there, too. Haven't heard much from him, but I think he's okay."

Rose looked down at her feet. "Great."

"So," Shelly began brightly, "I can't believe we're going to a school reunion. Are there many going?"

"Apparently so," Rose replied. "We should set off, we're already half an hour late."

She hollered goodbye down the hallway, then pulled the front door closed.

Rose clambered into the back of their hire car and they set off to Poole High School.

"Did you have a nice time in Ireland?"

"We did." Shelly twisted in her seat to face her. "I'm worn out, though. Too much travelling, I think." She gave Rose a brief recap of their mini break.

"When will you be leaving for Australia?" Rose enquired.

"Next Monday. Then it'll be back to the grindstone, back to normality."

"Will you come back?" Rose's voice wobbled slightly.

"Of course!" Shelly patted her friend's hand. "We're already planning a trip for next year. The big question is, am I ever going to get my best friend to Australia, hmm?"

Rose twisted her fingers in her lap. "I think Marian's already organising it."

"Is that a yes?" Shelly grinned with excitement.

"It's a possible maybe. I'm starting the animal care course in September." Rose took a deep breath. "I've notified them at work that I want to leave."

"Rose... that's brilliant!" Shelly nudged her husband. "Isn't that great, Harry? At last you're following your dreams!"

"Good on you, Rose," piped up Harry. He was squinting through the windscreen. "Is this your old school?"

They all turned to look at the dull grey building in front of them.

"That's Poole High," confirmed Shelly.

"It looks more like a prison," Harry muttered, as he turned into the car park.

"It felt like one," drawled Shelly. "Oh Lordy, is that Mr Jenkins?"

Rose looked at the grey-haired man, limping across the tarmac. "Yes. He looks different."

"He looks haggard," Shelly said drily. "He was our head

teacher, a power-crazy megalomaniac. Rumour was that half of the staff left because of his bullying. Don't tell me he's still in charge?"

"No, it's someone new," Rose said, as she unclipped her seatbelt, "a super head from Scotland. He's turned the school around from unsatisfactory to outstanding."

"How do you know all this?" Shelly asked.

"The vicar's friends with him." Rose picked up her handbag and exited the car. "Mr French knows everything that goes on in the community and he relays it back to the folk choir. We hear all the gossip."

"I never would have thought the folk choir could be so exciting." Shelly laughed. "So are you ready to do this, Archer?"

"Let's do this." Rose took a deep breath, linked arms with Shelly and stepped towards the entrance.

"You're looking good, Rose." Billy Baxter eyed her up and down. "Fancy a drink?"

"Yes, please." Rose followed him to the makeshift bar.

"Does Shelly want one, too?"

"I think she's busy." She pointed to the dance floor, where her friend was smooching with Harry.

It had felt strange to Rose, walking through her old school, passing the classrooms where she had once sat as a teenager. The place had been redecorated. The dull grey walls and furnishings had been replaced by vibrant blues and greens. The graffiti on the walls had been scrubbed away, staff photographs and school accolades had taken its place and the old, cheap vinyl floor covering had been replaced with smart carpets. It smelt fresh and new, and the old, shabby gymnasium looked amazing. It had been made over for the evening with balloons and banners and lights that dipped and beamed.

Marty was up on the stage in his element, playing an eclectic selection of music which had the dance floor heaving with staff and ex-students. There must be hundreds here, Rose surmised, as she waved at a few of the women she recognised.

"Have you been to the toilets?" Billy asked, handing her a flute of cheap wine. "They have gold taps now. I remember flooding them with Dean Round, and Andrew Parsons getting the blame." Billy chuckled. "The good old days, eh?"

"Is Andrew here?" An image of a thin, bespectacled boy popped into Rose's mind.

"No. He was sent an invite but he declined, and can't say I blame him, us guys were horrible to him, but it seems like he's had the last laugh. He's a business tycoon now, Rose, owns properties in New York, London and Tenerife. Last I heard, he was dating a supermodel."

Rose flinched and her thoughts wandered to Tom. As she was wondering if he was okay, she was vaguely aware of Billy's continuous chatter.

"Is that a yes?"

"Sorry?" Rose shook away the mental image of an evening of passion on a Majorcan beach.

Billy was staring at her expectantly. "Will you dance with me, Rose?"

"Oh, I..." Rose was about to refuse when Billy grabbed hold of her hand and propelled her onto the dance floor. Thankfully, Marty had increased the tempo and Rose found herself being flung about to the pop beat of the B52s.

"You're a good little mover, Rose Archer." Billy twirled her around and around. "I always liked you."

Rose laughed. "I remember you liked Shelly."

"Did I?" Billy smirked. "There's thousands of Shellys in this world, but you're the different one, Rose. You were always unique, even back in primary school, always got your nose in a book, like a Disney character." He pulled her closer. "You remind me of Belle from..."

"Beauty and the Beast?" Rose finished for him. "That's my favourite Disney film, actually."

"There you go then." Billy stared down into her eyes. "I've known you a long time, Rose and I've always admired you. Will you come on a date with me?"

"I... erm..." Rose floundered. Billy Baxter was a nice guy and he was good-looking. What better way to get over Tom Sinclair than by flinging herself at another man? Do it, an inner voice urged; live on the wild side for a change, enjoy life.

Rose smiled and had just opened her mouth to say yes when a ripple of excitement spread around the room. One of the teachers was holding back the edge of the huge curtains and lights were beaming into the gymnasium. People were surging towards the window to look outside. Marty abruptly cut the music and a roaring sound encompassed the hall.

"Bloody hell," shouted the PE teacher, "there's a helicopter landed on the school field!" Rose looked for Shelly and noticed her staring back at her with the hugest grin on her face.

"What's going on?" Rose stood in the middle of the dance floor, as if in a hypnotic trance. Her feet refused to move. Then Shelly was beside her, shaking her arm, pointing to the double doors of the gymnasium. There, bathed in the light, stood the handsomest man she had ever seen. His name was Tom Sinclair.

He walked into the room and there were audible gasps. This was the effect he had on others and Rose felt her knees shaking as she gazed at him. He was dressed in a suit, with a dazzling white shirt open at the neck to reveal wisps of dark hair – hair that Rose had laced her fingers through in the throes of passion.

"Is that really Tom?" she whispered.

"It's Tom," Shelly confirmed.

"But... why is he here?" Rose's voice shook as he smiled her way.

"You'll find out." Shelly hugged her. "Just listen to him, Rose, okay?"

"Okay." Rose nodded fervently, licking her suddenly dry lips.

Tom crossed the floor to where she was standing, lifted her hand and kissed it tenderly.

"I've got something I want to tell you," he said huskily, staring at her with his gorgeous green eyes.

"Do you... do you want to go somewhere more private?" She was aware that everyone was staring at them.

"Nope. I want everyone to hear this. Don't move." He bounded away from her and jumped up onto the stage. Rose watched him whisper something to Marty, who duly passed him the microphone.

Tom pushed a hand through his tousled hair as the main light rested directly on him. Rose stood still like a statue, terrified yet exhilarated at the same time. Is this really happening? she asked herself. The hall was deathly silent as Tom gazed straight at her and began speaking.

"I didn't come to this school." His voice sounded shaky and Rose was overcome with love for him. "You can probably tell from my accent that I don't even come from England. I came here reluctantly on holiday. But since I've been here, I've met this girl. This wonderful person who is beautiful and kind and sweet and funny and caring. Her name is Rose Archer," All eyes turned to look at her, "and in the few short weeks I've known her, I've fallen for her." There was a murmur from the women in the room, a chorus of aaahs.

Tom paused to take a breath and inside her chest, Rose's heart was hammering. "She's everything I've always wanted, everything I've been looking for. I came here tonight to tell her I'm hers... if she'll have me." Rose gasped. "I love her, you see. I've loved her from the moment I saw her."

Tears slipped from Rose's eyes as people started clapping and wolf-whistling.

"So, Rose Archer… what's it going to be? Do you feel the same?"

"Quiet!" shouted Mr Jenkins, the formidable ex-head teacher. "Let Rose speak."

Rose wiped away the tears, walked slowly towards the stage, held out her hands and shouted, "The answer is YES! Yes to love, yes to happiness and yes to you!"

∽

The music was back on, the dance floor was full again and Rose was in his arms, squashed against his torso as they revolved slowly.

Shelly and Harry came over to congratulate them.

"Did you know this was going to happen?" Rose looked at her friends with suspicious eyes.

"I might have had an inkling." Shelly laughed. "You two make a great couple. I'm so excited and happy for you both."

"Leave them alone," Harry pulled her away, "I think they've got some catching-up to do, and in the meantime, wifey, you can buy me a beer."

They wandered off, bickering light-heartedly.

"I guess that's a no then, Rose," Billy Baxter said to her, wryly.

"Sorry," Rose called as he shimmied past, on the lookout for more single women.

"Who was that?" Tom quizzed. "Should I be jealous?"

"Not in the slightest." Rose stood on her tiptoes and kissed his lips softly. "I love you, nobody else. But Tom, where have you been all week?"

Tom looked suddenly pleased with himself. "In London, searching for properties. I've bought a flat, Rose and the band are relocating here for the next twelve months. We're concentrating on building a UK following."

"That's terrific!" Rose beamed. "So does that mean you won't be going back to Australia with the others?"

"Nope," he pressed her hands against his heart, "I'm all yours. So what are you doing now, Rose Archer?"

Rose cocked her head to one side. "What do you mean?"

Tom laughed. "Come with me?"

She followed him off the dance floor, pausing to kiss Marty and old school friends who wanted to wish them well.

They walked through the maze of Poole High's corridors and out onto the field, towards the helicopter which suddenly burst into life; engine thrumming and the blades rotating.

Rose swallowed. "You want me to get in that?"

Tom nodded. "I'll look after you. Do you trust me?"

"Yes." Rose watched as he opened the door and held out his hand.

"Then come with me, Rose. Come and see my world."

THE END

about the author

Julia Sutton lives in Wolverhampton, England with her husband, two children, an energetic Border Collie and two frisky chinchillas. She has had a variety of jobs ranging from secretarial work to working in primary schools as a teaching assistant. When she is not busy writing, Julia loves walking, drawing, cooking, travelling and watching films. She enjoys connecting with others on social media.

To learn more about Julia Sutton and discover more Next Chapter authors, visit our website at www.nextchapter.pub.

Cocktails, Wedding Bells and Summer Madness
ISBN: 978-4-82412-707-5

Published by
Next Chapter
1-60-20 Minami-Otsuka
170-0005 Toshima-Ku, Tokyo
+818035793528

18th February 2022

9 784824 127075